PLAYBOY BILLIONAIRE

THE CAROLINA SERIES BOOK THREE

JILL DOWNEY

Playboy Billionaire

The Carolina Series
Book 3

by
Jill Downey

Cover Design Copyright © 2020 Maria @ Steamy Designs
Editor April Bennett @ theeditingsoprano.com

DEDICATION

To my first and forever love...mom!

1

---

*P*enelope Winters pressed her legs against Raven's flanks, urging the mare into a rolling canter. Her long blond hair, windblown and tumbling around her shoulders, was in vivid contrast with the horse's jet black coat.

The tension that had been her constant companion of late began to ease its grip. There would be no paparazzi lurking behind bushes or popping out of nowhere. This was her safe zone, no hidden agendas, just her and Raven in the endless wild beauty of Montana's Big Sky Country.

She hand galloped most of the way back home, riding the final mile at a walk to cool down. Her ranch manager Walt Hardy was there to greet her.

"You've got company," he said, his brow creased in a frown. He held her reins while she jumped down.

Her nose wrinkled. "Who?"

He snorted, "Your manager, Ms. Monroe."

"Constance?" she said, eyes widening in surprise.

"Yepper."

"Oh no!"

"That's precisely what I thought," he grumbled.

"Did she bring luggage?"

"Yep. Barked orders at Josie and me. I unloaded a suitcase that looked like it could hold pert near a month's worth of clothing. She's all settled in one of the guest cabins."

"Shit."

"That woman had a determined glint in her eye."

Penelope rolled her eyes. "When doesn't she? We'll see who's the most determined. Wish me luck."

A slow smile spread across his weathered face, the deep laugh lines around his eyes crinkling. "Always. Let me know if ya need me to escort her off the ranch."

Penelope laughed. "As much as I hate to spoil your fun, I'm sure it won't come to that. She really does want what's best for my career. That *is* her job after all."

"I s'pose. If ya ask me, her priority is to herself."

Penny squeezed his arm, "You're just protective and I truly appreciate it. Will you take care of untacking my girl?" She hugged Raven's neck, brushing her cheek across the soft coat.

"Sure enough."

"Thanks, Walt."

He touched the tip of his cowboy hat, "Good luck. I'll be around if ya need me."

"I know I can always count on you."

Penelope quickly ran her hands through her tangled hair then smoothed it down before tucking it behind both ears. Taking a deep calming breath, she strode purposefully toward the house. Her boots clomped loudly on the wooden porch, announcing her arrival before the screen door banged shut behind her.

Josie came from the kitchen wiping her hands down the front of her flour covered apron, with Penelope's dog Archie at her heels. "I'm sure you've heard."

"Yes, and I'm sorry you got barked at." She leaned down and picked up her pug, who greeted her as if she'd been gone for weeks.

Josie nodded her head in the direction of the guest house. "She's settling in. She said she had to make a few calls."

Penelope grinned, "Let's hope it takes her awhile."

"That woman is pushy."

"That's one way to describe her."

They both turned as the screen door opened and Constance entered.

"My ears were burning."

Penelope and Josie exchanged a glance, then Penelope said, "What brings you all the way out here to the middle of nowhere?"

"After your last phone call, I thought it would be prudent to come talk some sense into you. Always better in person."

Josie held up a hand, "I don't mean to interrupt but I have pies in the oven. Ms. Monroe, refresh my memory, do you have any dietary restrictions I should know about?"

"I'm lactose intolerant and gluten-free. Other than that, the sky's the limit."

Josie shot a worried look at Penelope. "I had

planned on chicken pot pie for supper, but I suppose I could pull out a couple of steaks to throw on the grill."

"Splendid!" Constance interjected, not giving Penelope time to respond.

"That will work. Just take out one steak; I'll still eat the pot pie. Thanks Josie." She placed Archie back on the ground and he immediately began sniffing around Constance's feet.

"I'll put a salad together along with a baked potato for Constance."

"Don't forget the wine darling," Constance directed. "A nice Cabernet would be lovely. Please and thank you." She smiled guilefully, glaring down at Archie. "Homely little thing, isn't he?"

Penelope glanced down, smiling affectionately at her pug. "Shh, don't you dare let him hear you, he's very sensitive."

Constance rolled her eyes. "You and that dog."

After Josie disappeared around the corner, Penelope grasped Constance's arm and tugged her outside onto the porch. "You will not order Josie or Walt around like they're hired help."

"But darling, they *are* hired help."

Penelope mentally counted to ten then blew out a breath. "They're like my family. I'm lucky to have them, not the other way around."

Constance waved her hand dismissively, "Whatever. I will try. Do I have to get your permission to even speak?"

Penelope glared, "I'm going to take a walk. I'll come find you in a bit and we can have that talk you felt was so important you had to fly all the way to

Montana. Make yourself at home but stay out of trouble."

She bit back a laugh, "Darling, I'd be hard put to even *find* trouble in this God forsaken place."

"Knowing you, I seriously doubt that." She pivoted and left her standing on the porch.

*T*ypical of August, it was a delightful seventy degrees and sunny. She'd been clinging to this place for the past six weeks. It was the only thing that had made the grueling publicity tour for her latest film bearable. She needed to quiet the thoughts that were currently cycling in an endless loop of pain and regret. Here, she could hear herself think. She impatiently brushed away her tears. Two years ago today, her mom had lost her battle with cancer.

Her mom would have been the one comforting and encouraging her while she endured the embarrassment of having her private pain splashed across the front pages of the tabloids. It was hard enough coping with the ugly breakup and betrayal, then to have your life dissected by people who had no clue of what had really happened...it was cruel. She felt as vulnerable as she'd been when she'd left home for the first time with only her hopes dreams and a suitcase. Constance was the last person she'd expected or wanted to see.

*P*enelope massaged her neck, feeling a dull headache coming on. She and Constance had finished dinner and were continuing their discussion on the front porch. They had barely sat down before Constance pounced.

"You're being incredibly obstinate Penelope."

Gritting her teeth, Penelope said, "I don't know how else I can say it to get you to understand. *I do not want to do this film!* Obviously, it will be beyond awkward to work with Noah after our breakup and secondly, I need a break. For real. I barely had time to grieve my mama before the last film started production. I've just finished the promotional tour. I can't do it. You *have* to get me out of it!"

"Impossible."

Penelope crossed her arms over her chest, lips tight. "Nothing is impossible."

"Said the girl with her head in the clouds who knows nothing about contract law!"

"That's what lawyers are for." Archie decided at that moment to jump up against Penelope's leg, demanding attention. Picking him up, she smiled as the dog covered her neck and face with kisses.

"Yes, and your lawyers agree with me. It would be sheer recklessness to back out only three weeks before you start filming. You would be blacklisted, no one would want to hire you in the future...too big a risk. You would lose a boatload of money; and more than likely you'd be sued by the movie studio. I'm afraid you have no choice."

Penelope buried her face in Archie's fur, holding him close, "I can't! You don't understand. I'm suffering. I'm burnt out. I'm grieving, I hate my co-star. It's going to bomb at the box office. How can I put in a decent performance? I'm not all here. My heart just isn't in it."

"Yada yada yada. Suck it up buttercup. You cannot let Noah Davis ruin your career...Or any man for that matter. The public is rabid to see you and Noah reunited. Surely it's not beneath you to use that to your advantage."

"Wow, you're sure missing the empathy chip. This is my real life, Constance. I'm not just tabloid fodder."

"I'm your manager. I have to keep your eye on the prize even when you won't...which by the way is your career. You're hot right now. You must seize the moment. Whether you like it or not, you and Noah rode the wave to superstardom together. Your destinies are forever linked. Think of Miley and Liam, darling."

"Yeah and look how well that worked for them."

"This is your future. Acting careers are made and broken with the snap of a finger. Your mom wouldn't want you to continue to grieve. The show must go on as they say. And for God's sake, don't throw it all away over a man." Constance patted Penelope's arm, as she pressed her point. "It's a great script. All the Hollywood A-listers would give their right arm to have the lead."

"They can have it."

"Have you read the script again?"

Penelope nodded, "Yeah...it *is* great."

"This could be the next *Fifty Shades,* darling. Trust me, once you begin, you'll lose yourself in the character just like you always do. That's what makes you great."

She chewed on her bottom lip, "I suppose..."

She beamed at Penelope like a proud parent. "Good girl! Now that we have that settled."

"You win...as always. Now I'm going to bed."

"I'll be leaving first thing in the morning. You've

made the right decision. I know I may seem heartless, but its tough love. You'll thank me later."

"I hope so." Penelope put Archie down and he happily followed her as she headed for bed. The minute she escaped to her room she deflated like a punctured balloon. She threw herself on top of the king-sized bed, buried her face in her pillow and sobbed. Archie rooted his snub nose in Penelope's thick mane of hair, attempting to comfort her. Fourteen pounds of wiggling energy had her smiling through her tears.

"I guess we'll be going to North Carolina whether we like it or not." Archie looked at her with worry in his intelligent eyes, sensing all was not right in his mistress's world. She kissed him on his cute little mug and tucked him against her as she burrowed into her pillow, her eyes already heavy.

The following afternoon, after seeing Constance off, she decided to take another quick ride. This time, she chose to ride Breeze. She could certainly use the attention and exercise. She bridled the chestnut mare then hopped on bareback. They rode for some time, her seat warm from the direct contact against the mare's back. Their bodies moved like one, sensing and in sync with one another. When she reached the mountain-framed meadow she hopped down. She stroked Breeze under her thick chestnut mane. Her gaze took in the breathtaking grandeur of the mountains and wild grassy view. It never got old.

Taking a deep breath, she exhaled slowly. "It's beautiful isn't girl?" The mare nickered softly and rubbed her large head against Penelope's chest.

The air was crisp and fresh, permeated by the scent of sagebrush, prominent after last night's rainstorm. When she wasn't in LA or on location filming somewhere, this Montana ranch was her sanctuary, the place she ran to anytime she felt overwhelmed. Here she felt connected to the bigger picture and it comforted her.

She walked Breeze to the stream's edge for a drink. The spirited four-year-old Morgan pawed at the water playfully before dipping her head down to drink. The water rippled over the rocks and stones, soothing Penelope's frayed nerves.

She could almost forget about the next project, only three weeks away. Almost. Constance had dashed her tiny remaining hope that she could get out of it. Unless a miracle happened, she was due on set in a seaside town in North Carolina the last week of August.

She pulled out her peanut butter and jelly sandwich and thermos of tea from her backpack, then plopped down on a rock to eat her lunch. Breeze nudged her impatiently and Penelope pulled out the apple slices she'd packed. The horse's lips felt like velvet across her palm as they searched for the treat.

The mare nudged her for more. "You're getting spoiled. I'm nothing more than your vending machine here." She dug the last two slices out and Breeze quickly finished them off. As Penelope took the last bite of her sandwich, she imagined what it would be like to have a full year off from the bright lights. Hunkered down here in her fortress. This is what she needed most. Time alone, time to heal. She sighed, *If only…*

2

_____

Griffin Bennett peered covertly at the cards he'd just been dealt and blew out his breath in disgust. His hand was so bad, it wasn't even worth a bluff. He waited his turn so he could fold. Glancing down at his watch he was surprised to see that it was only one a.m. He'd give lady luck another hour to make it up to him. She was fickle and hadn't given him any breaks at the table tonight...understatement...he was having an ice-cold streak....down seventy grand, and he'd only bankrolled one hundred thousand.

On a whim, he'd made a spontaneous decision to fly into Vegas earlier this evening in the family's corporate jet. His intentions had been to leave first thing tomorrow morning, however, unless his luck changed directions, he would extend his stay another night to try to recoup his losses.

The gorgeous cocktail waitress was flirting outrageously, making it abundantly clear that she'd be available for some after-hour socializing if he was interested. She'd been ogling him since he joined in the high-stakes poker game. Nothing he wasn't used to. He was not only used to it, but he took it for granted. Women loved him. He'd always had his pick of beautiful women vying for his attention. He could have anyone, anytime he wanted.

He winked at the waitress and nodded his head, signaling he was ready for another bourbon on the rocks. Her eyes gleamed with interest, like a cat eying the canary. She exuded confidence and he was fairly certain that she usually captured her prey.

As she served his drink, she made sure to give him an eyeful of her cleavage. She was so close Griffin could smell her perfume, an exotic musky scent, applied a bit too heavily for his taste but what the hell. He could live with it.

She whispered, "I'm off at two."

"I'll keep that in mind."

The dealer dealt the next hand and Griffin turned his attention back to the game, his blood rushing with adrenaline when he glimpsed his cards. He schooled his expression to stay neutral after seeing his hand. *Finally!* He'd been dealt a pair of aces. *Hallelujah!*

The familiar sounds of chips being stacked and cards being shuffled faded into the background as he concentrated. He loved the rush of gambling. It was almost the same high he experienced skiing down a black diamond slope or jumping out of an airplane.

He'd be the first to admit that he was a thrill seeker. He had no fear and loved adventure.

Since moving back to his hometown in North Carolina last year, things had been on the sedate side, and he thought he'd been adjusting to the slower pace. Sitting in the electrified energy of the casino, he realized that he'd been feeling restless lately.

"I'll raise you," Griffin said.

The two players still left in the game decided to fold. Griffins eyes sparkled as the pile of chips were placed in front of him. After a few more winning hands, he was almost back to where he'd started.

"You're going to pull a hit and run?" one of the players asked as Griffin picked up his chips.

"Hardly—I'm breaking even, barely," Griffin replied good-naturedly. He didn't consider it rude to quit since he hadn't really won anything. He tipped the dealer and servers generously and headed to the bar for one more drink before retiring.

It was half past two and Griffin was surprised to see the cocktail waitress waiting for him at the bar. He'd forgotten all about her. He veered quickly toward the elevator before she had a chance to see him, then rode it up to his suite.

He walked outside onto the terrace overlooking a spectacular view of the Vegas strip. The lights glittered like colorful jewels in the night sky. A city that never sleeps. He thought of the beautiful bombshell he'd just left sitting at the bar and shook his head in disgust. *What the hell is wrong with me?*

Must be losing it. He felt a twinge of regret. He

could be lying in bed with a warm luscious body next to him right now...*dammit*. He went back inside and stripped off his clothes, crawling naked under the sheets he was asleep soon after his head touched the pillow.

3

―――――

Penelope took off her silk eye mask and moved her seat to the upright position in preparation for landing. The flight attendant was picking up empty glasses and trash from her colleagues' trays. The film company had chartered a private jet for the actors and a few of the production crew that weren't already on location. She'd cut short her Montana retreat to catch the flight from LA.

She had dozed for much of the five-hour flight. She peeked in at Archie, who lay contentedly snoring in his soft crate. He was quite the savvy traveler, having been toted around since he was a puppy.

She unzipped the top of the carrier and scratched him behind his ears. "Hey Archie, we're here." He looked at her groggily. Noah Davis took that moment to grab the seat on the other side of Archie and buckled himself in.

"How's my little buddy?" he asked, reaching down to pet him.

Penelope rolled her eyes. "Like you care."

His dark eyes pierced her. "I do. Is this how it's going to be? If so, we're in for a very long shoot."

"That goes without saying, I'm afraid."

"Really Penny? I'd think with your experience you could show a little professionalism."

"Oh, I intend to, but we're not working at the moment...unless I missed something?" She arched one brow.

His lips twisted. "You're such a bitch."

"Nice, now we've already progressed to name calling," she hissed.

"I'll play nice if you do. Rumor mill has it that the studio wants to make us an item in the public eye. Good for PR."

"Over my dead body."

He laughed dryly, "Let's hope it doesn't come to that."

"Who did you hear that from anyway?"

"My manager. He said the public is still grieving the loss of their favorite couple, Winoah." He mimed quotation marks as he referenced the moniker the tabloids had christened them with.

Her mouth tightened as she glared at him. "How sweet. Constance already reminded me of that as well."

Noah's eyes softened for a moment with something that looked a lot like regret. "We were good once, Penelope."

She unbuckled her seat belt and stood as the pilot and attendant waited by the exit for the passengers to disembark. "That was then, this is now." Putting on her sunglasses, she grabbed the dog carrier and walked swiftly to the exit.

The sun warmed her skin as she stepped onto the tarmac. A large SUV with tinted glass waited to whisk her and Noah to their temporary private seaside homes. She wasn't pleased that they were going to be next-door neighbors, and after hearing about the studio's desire to use their relationship as bait, she wondered if it was an intentional setup.

The driver opened the door for Penelope and before sliding in she asked, "Will it take long to get there?"

He smiled shyly, looking a little starstruck. "No ma'am, about twenty minutes."

She ducked into the cool Mercedes. "Thanks." Unzipping the carrier, she took Archie out. His whole body wiggled as he enthusiastically checked out his surroundings. Noah sulked as Penelope did her best to pretend that he wasn't there.

"Since we're going to be neighbors, I guess you won't be able to avoid me."

Silence.

Noah's voice softened and he said, "Penelope, the baby wasn't mine."

Her lips twisted. "Isn't the point that it could have been, and it took a paternity test to find out?"

"Baby, you know damn well we weren't getting along. It's on me, but it's not like we weren't having troubles already."

"Yeah and sleeping around *always* improves on any existing problems. Why didn't I think of it first? You're brilliant Noah. Bonus, you got to fuck her whenever you wanted in between takes. God, how blind and stupid could I have been? Right under my nose the whole time."

"We can talk about that later, but right now I want to find a way to work together peacefully."

"On set it will be fine. Off set, skip it. There's nothing to talk about."

"Good thing our script calls for a contentious relationship. We won't have to do much acting," he said dryly.

"There are a few scenes I hope to get cut."

He stroked his chin squinting, "Hmm let me guess. The rough sex scenes?"

"You've always had a keen eye for the obvious."

"Lighten up, for fuck's sake. You won't get them to change the script this late, even if you *are* Penelope Winters. You've already agreed to the terms; the sex scenes were spelled out, signed, sealed, delivered."

"Don't sound so happy about it."

"Who wouldn't be excited about the prospect of a naked Penelope Winters in bed next to them? Every man's fantasy. And it's still mine. Plus, I've been working out overtime to get my body in shape for the nude scenes," he said, patting his six-pack abs. "The world is waiting to see us naked in bed together."

"Pathetic."

"Don't ruin the film with petty grievances. We both need this to be a success. Let's work together to see that it is."

They pulled into the drive of an oceanfront home that looked big enough to accommodate a basketball team. She fastened Archie's leash and was startled when Noah grabbed her arm, pulling her off balance. He gripped her chin tightly and his mouth came down on hers. Penelope was so taken aback that she didn't move for several seconds as he kissed her. She quickly recovered and tried to pull away just as the driver opened her door.

"Here we are. This is your place Ms. Winters. Mr. Davis is the next house to the right."

Her face heated with humiliation.

"Just a little dress rehearsal," Noah whispered, grinning rakishly.

"Go to hell," she said, through gritted teeth.

"You're so beautiful when you're spitting venom."

"Don't *ever* do that again."

"Lighten up."

"Let go of my arm."

"No problem," he said, releasing her.

Archie jumped out first and relieved himself on the first shrub they came to. The real estate agent stood at the front door, "Hi, I'm Nadine with Surfside Realty."

Penelope had always loved a southern drawl and was immediately charmed as Nadine effusively fawned over Archie. She showed Penelope how to gain access inside with the code on the front door lock. Once inside, Penelope bent down and removed Archie's leash. He immediately began to explore, making himself at home.

Nadine smiled apologetically and said, "I'm sorry, but would you be offended if I asked for your autograph for my daughter? She worships you."

Inwardly groaning, Penelope plastered a smile on

her face and said, "I don't mind. Do you have something to write on?"

She had come prepared, excitedly pulling out a copy of *People Magazine* with her and Noah on the cover. "Yes. If you could just say *To Sarah, my number one fan, Love Penelope Winters* that would be great!"

Penelope quickly jotted down the message and her autograph. The faster she finished, the sooner she'd be alone. "Here you go."

The realtor seemed in no hurry to take off. "Um, not to be nosy or anything, but we were devastated that y'all broke up. It almost felt personal. Is there any chance...?" She let her voice trail off as she saw Penelope's eyes begin to glitter dangerously.

Forcing herself to keep her cool, Penelope said, "Speaking of Noah, don't you have to let him into his house as well?"

"My heavens no!" She held her palms to her cheeks. "I'd never keep anyone waiting like that. My colleague is taking care of him. I'm sorry if I spoke out of turn... where *are* my manners, it's just that you're so nice in person...I suppose we all think we know you...and it might seem weird to you, but I really feel like I do...I meant no harm. I hope there aren't any hard feelings?"

Penelope softened; unfortunately it came with the territory. "It's fine. I'm just exhausted from traveling. Maybe I can meet your daughter sometime while we're here filming. Do you have a business card?"

Her cheeks turned a bright pink. "Really? Oh my God! My daughter will be over the moon! Thank you so much Penelope...oh...I mean...Ms. Winters...oh I'm so embarrassed. See what I mean?"

By this time Penelope had let go of her irritation. She patted Nadine's arm. "Penelope is fine. And thanks for the welcome."

"There are instructions and phone numbers for just about anything you'll need on the kitchen counter. I hope this will feel like home while you're here. Here's my card with my cell number on it."

Penelope took the card and stuck it in her pocket. "I'm sure I'll be more than comfortable here. It's absolutely lovely. I mean, just look at the view." She subtly herded Nadine toward the front door.

Penelope leaned back against the door, closing her eyes for a moment. *Finally. Alone.* She walked over to an entire wall of glass doors leading out to the deck and opened them all. The sound of waves crashing to the shore worked their magic.

Maybe this wouldn't be so bad. She loved the ocean. She and Noah had similar work ethics. Always on time, considerate of behind-the-scenes workers and other actors, no diva behaviors, it was going to be fine.

It's not like she hadn't done nude scenes before now. They were always challenging, but she felt they added artistry and authenticity. She was committed to the film now that the time was at hand. With several days to decompress before filming started, she planned to take full advantage of the pool and the beach. It could be so much worse. In that moment, she made a promise to herself to make the best of it.

4

*G*riffin buckled himself in as the pilot announced they were finally cleared for take-off. The whisper of discontent he'd felt the night before lingered like a hangover. He felt jittery and unsettled. Normally, he didn't let his emotions get in the way of enjoying all that was out there for the taking. He liked skimming the surface...life was what you made it, may as well make it fun.

Taxiing down the runway, the turbo jet roared to life as the plane's nose tilted up and lifted into the air. He felt the familiar sensation of sinking as the flaps retracted, then the powerful engine sound as the plane accelerated.

After they reached cruising altitude the flight attendant approached. "Can I get you anything Mr. Bennett?" Natalie asked.

"How about a neck massage?"

Her mouth curved into a smile. "I was thinking

more in terms of snacks and the beverage of your choice."

Flashing his killer grin, he said, "See how you are? In that case I'll have a Bloody Mary. Belvedere, extra spicy, extra strong, extra olives and a couple slices of celery. Breakfast of the champions." His eyes boldly wandered across her face.

"I'm good with spicy, Mr. Bennett."

"Good to know." He opened his laptop to check e-mails. There was the usual mix of political requests for donations and newsletters from the charities he supported, a few personal notes from friends in faraway places, and some information about the upcoming pro-am golf tournament he'd entered for charity. He felt passionate about his philanthropy and this was a way to give back and do something he loved at the same time. Plus, he was a damn good golfer; he'd been in the pro-circuit for a short time.

"Here you go." Natalie set his drink down into a cup holder built into the table beside him.

"Thanks."

"The pilot says we have perfect weather conditions, and it will be a smooth flight."

"Great. I'll be able to catch up on my beauty sleep." He winked, then returned his attention to the laptop, effectively dismissing her.

He smiled as he read the roster of celebrities lined up for the tournament. A couple of reality TV stars from the Carolina series and a big-name film celebrity that would be a huge draw. It was only two weeks away and he felt excited for the challenge. He had to hit the links and get in some serious golfing between now and then or face humiliating himself.

Satisfied that there was nothing urgent to attend to, he closed his laptop and put it aside. Downing the last of his drink, he sank his teeth into a fat green olive, enjoying the kick of alcohol from the marinated fruit. He leaned his seat back, closed his eyes and was asleep within minutes. He didn't wake up until the pilot announced that they were coming in for landing.

The pilot and flight attendant waited for him by the open door of the plane. He grabbed his overnight bag from under the seat and made his way to the exit.

"Hope you enjoyed your flight Mr. Bennett," the pilot said.

"Slept like a baby. Smooth landing. Thanks." He held out his hand and the pilot grasped it for a warm shake.

Natalie smiled, and said, "I'll see you next trip."

"Yeah, thanks a lot, Natalie. Next time."

Griffin took a deep breath as he descended the metal stairs onto the sweltering tarmac. August in North Carolina. The air was thick, and he felt like he was breathing through a wet wool blanket. The forecast called for hot humid conditions for the rest of the week, with highs in the low nineties.

Why the hell wasn't he in Turks and Caicos right now? Low humidity, gentle easterly trade winds, usual high in the mid-eighties, great snorkeling and diving... if it wasn't for the upcoming tournament, he'd be on a plane tomorrow. It had been far too long since he'd visited the islands.

. . .

*W*hen he got to his car, he turned his cell phone back on and saw that Brianna had been text bombing him since last night. She'd already called four times today. He blew out a breath as he raked his hand through his unruly hair. Thumbing through her texts, he tamped down his irritation. The downside of dating someone so young. Drama. Insecurity. Possessiveness. Jealousy.

Brianna, a fashion model based in New York City, had been home visiting her parents about a month ago and they'd attended the same art gala fundraiser. Her parents happened to be friends of his father's and they'd been there to make the introductions.

He'd made the mistake of asking her out and now found himself entangled. This romance would be short lived. He blew out a breath. Already bored, he just had to find the right time to cut the cord. He should have known better than to date a twenty-one-year-old. She was too clingy and already making commitment noises. He didn't do commitment. He knew she'd bust his balls about the Vegas trip, as if she had every right to do so.

They had a date planned for tomorrow night and he'd made dinner reservations at the Yacht Club. He hoped she be over her snit by then. He was tired from his late jaunt and had zero tolerance for drama.

She picked up on the first ring.

"Hey," Griffin said.

"Why haven't you returned any of my texts or phone calls?"

"Because I had my phone turned off so I could enjoy myself without distractions."

"How *unselfish* of you. How do you think that makes me feel?"

"I told you where I was going and that I wouldn't be available. What was so urgent that it required four phone calls all before noon?"

She sighed dramatically into the phone. "I wanted you to be the first person I shared my news with." *Silence.*

"And?"

"I got it!" She squealed with excitement. "My face is going to be plastered on magazines all over the world!"

"Congratulations baby! The new face of Dior. So now our dinner date will be a celebration. I'm really happy for you Brianna. I'm not surprised; you're stunning."

"You can show me how happy you are tomorrow night. I can't wait to see you. I've missed you so much. Did you miss me?"

"It's been less than twenty-four hours." *Silence.* "I'll pick you up at seven."

"Don't even think of picking me up on the Ducati. I don't want my hair messed up."

"I'd planned on taking the Audi anyway."

"Good."

Fighting annoyance, Griffin said, "I've got to go. See you tomorrow." The last thing he wanted to do was go out with Brianna. He pinched the bridge of his nose. *What the fuck is wrong with me? Brianna is young, beautiful and great in bed.*

His muscles were coiled, ready to spring with a restless energy. He couldn't put his finger on it. What was bothering him? *Let it go! This will pass.* He wasn't used to overthinking everything. He generally avoided intro-spection, since it never led him anywhere that he wanted to go anyway. This unfamiliar self-analysis stopped him in his tracks. Maybe it had something to do with his looming thirtieth birthday. A week from now, he'd be kissing his twenties goodbye.

~

The following evening, Griffin pulled into Brianna's drive and beeped the horn. She ran to the car and had barely shut the door before throwing her arms around him and kissing him full on the lips. He peeled her arms from around his neck then backed out of the drive. She flipped her hair back over her shoulder before fastening her seat belt.

"That wasn't the greeting I was expecting," she said, pouting.

Griffin didn't go for the bait.

"How was Vegas?" she asked coolly.

"Broke even."

"Were you a good boy?"

His lips twisted. "Almost saintly."

"Griffin, why are you being so mean to me?"

He glanced over and seeing her glassy eyes, felt a tug of remorse. He grabbed her hand and held it. "I'm tired. And how have you been keeping yourself enter-tained in my absence?"

"Catching up on the local gossip for starters. Have you heard?"

"Probably not," Griffin said dryly.

"They're making another movie here. Big name director and you'll never guess who's starring in it."

"Let's see, Brad Pitt?"

"Just as big but think younger and hotter."

"I give, who?"

"Penelope Winters and Noah Davis."

"No shit?" His heart squeezed slightly at the mention of Penelope Winters. He'd had a big-time crush on her since he'd watched her in the film *Forever Yours*.

"I swear. I heard it from a reliable source. Some of the production crew and location scouts have already been spotted around the island."

"That will be a welcome boost for the local businesses."

"I know right?" She said, as she checked her makeup in the sun-visor mirror.

Glancing over at her, Griffin said, "You look beautiful."

"You always say that."

"Because it's true."

"Then why won't you put a ring on it?" she said, sticking out her tongue.

He laughed at her. "We've been dating exactly one month. That's if you count the night we met. I told you from the beginning that I don't do long term, I'm not even sure I believe in love."

"I'm a romantic, what can I say. Besides you say that now, but you can change."

"Look Brianna, this isn't on you, it's on me. It's nothing you're doing wrong. I'm just jaded. I've never lied to you and I'm not going to start now. You're young, you're sweet, you're beautiful, and you're too young to settle down anyway. You've got your whole life ahead of you...and by the sounds of things, you're off to a great start on a successful career."

She rolled her eyes. "Oh, and you're sooo old. Besides who are you to tell me I'm too young? My parents were already married by my age."

"Those were different times. There's a world of difference between twenty-one and thirty...trust me."

"I don't care. I know what I want, and I want you."

"And tonight, you've got me. I'm all yours."

*T*hey pulled up in front of the club and the valet approached. "Hey Samuel. How's it going?"

"Fine Mr. Bennett."

Brianna's eyes sparkled inquisitively as she asked, "Samuel, have you seen or heard anything about the movie that's being filmed here on the island?"

His eyes darted left then right before he lowered his voice and said conspiratorially, "They're here! Right now."

Brianna squealed, barely containing her excitement, "Who is?"

"Noah Davis, Penelope Winters, that director Stewart somebody, and the head of the local chamber of commerce."

"No way." Brianna clapped her hands in excitement. "I hope I get to meet them. Noah Davis is so hot."

"What about Penelope Winters? She's a babe," Samuel said.

Griffin grinned, "Good taste my friend." He clapped Samuel on the back and handed him a fifty. "Careful with my baby."

"You know it sir."

*T*he maître d' greeted Griffin. "Good evening sir. Your table is ready. Would you care to be seated immediately or will you be having drinks in the lounge first?"

He arched a brow at Brianna. "You?"

Her eyes rabidly searched the lounge, hoping to catch a glimpse of Hollywood royalty. Her eyes suddenly widened, and she hissed, "There they are, over in the corner."

Griffin rolled his eyes, "And? They have a right to their privacy Brianna."

"Let's sit here in the lounge and have a drink before we get seated."

"Whatever you say." Turning back to the maître d' he said, "I guess we'll have a drink in the lounge first."

"Very good, Mr. Bennett."

He grasped Brianna's arm and steered her toward the bar. "You do know you're staring, right?"

"They're used to it."

"Nobody else here is gawking."

She stuck her tongue out at him. "Party pooper."

Griffin ordered their drinks then allowed himself a discreet glance at the celebrities' booth. The head of the chamber of commerce, Patrick Gregory, was waving at him trying to catch his attention. *Great.* Brianna was going to lose her shit.

"Do you know him?"

"Business connections."

She elbowed him in the ribs, "What are you waiting for? He's calling us over."

Griffin reluctantly led Brianna over to the table.

"Griffin! Great to see you!" Patrick pumped his hand enthusiastically. "I'd like to introduce you to some very special people!"

Griffin shook hands with Noah and Stewart as the introductions were made. Penelope was sitting on the far side of the booth, he nodded hello. Brianna tugged on his belt. Sliding his arm around her waist he pulled her forward.

"This is Brianna Wescott," Griffin said. "Patrick I'm sure you know her parents, Donna and John Wescott."

"Yes, of course! They're big sponsors of the Heritage Festival. Nice to meet you Brianna."

She gushed, "It is so thrilling to meet you all!"

Griffin happened to lock eyes with Penelope, and his nerve endings tingled as if a bolt of electricity had shocked him. Vaguely aware that Patrick was still talking, he forced himself to focus on the conversation.

"We were lucky enough to persuade the producers to film right here. They've rented the entire Butler House as their headquarters. They'll be here for the next several months."

"Quite the feather in your cap, Patrick. Congratulations. Great boost for the local economy."

"We're thrilled of course." He turned toward his guests, "Griffin Bennett comes from one of our most prominent families. Bennett Enterprise is responsible for many of the developments in this great state as well as locally."

"When did you arrive?" Griffin directed his question at Penelope.

She ignored him and let Stewart squirm uncomfortably, trying to cover the gaffe.

"I've been here scouting locations for about a week. Penelope and Noah just arrived yesterday."

"A pleasure to meet you all. I hope you enjoy your time here on the island," Griffin said coolly, trying to ignore the magnetic pull toward Penelope.

"I'm sure we will. Nice to meet you," Stewart said.

Noah had been sitting back lazily, observing them as if he were bored with the whole exchange. Penelope had folded her arms across her chest and her eyes were downcast.

Griffin nodded and grabbed Brianna's hand, leading her away. "Let's grab our table."

She smiled and said enthusiastically, "I am such a huge fan of both of yours...Winoah," she said giggling.

Penelope rolled her eyes and Noah snorted with laughter, "Thanks, Brianna, we *both* really appreciate it."

Griffin highly doubted that by the expression on Ms. Winters' face. He signaled to the maître d' that they were ready to be seated. As soon as they sat down, he ordered another stiff one. The only good thing about the evening...Brianna was so narcissistic that she didn't even notice he wasn't listening to her. As long as she had a warm body to talk *at,* she was happy. He just had to murmur here and there...make a little noise, and she was content. And he wondered why he was bored?

5

"Chug—chug—chug," the small but rowdy group chanted.

"What are we, twelve?" Griffin said, laughing as he tipped back the birthday shot of bourbon, grimacing as it burned its way down his throat.

"It's not every day a person turns thirty!" His older sister Faye said, ruffling his hair affectionately. She owned the establishment they were currently celebrating in and had just taken a break to join them while her fiancé Jesse Carlisle tended bar.

The place was packed, unusual for a Thursday night. Since Faye had hired a cook, her business was really picking up. Nothing fancy, great bar food, southern style. Fried everything. From oysters to hushpuppies to collard greens and green tomatoes...if you were looking to eat healthy, you'd probably want to bypass the Pelican. But it was damn good.

Jesse yelled over, "Food's up."

Griffin and Faye's nephew, Tyler, walked by on his way to the kitchen with a tray loaded with empty beer bottles. "I'll get it Faye. Sit down and celebrate with your brother for a few minutes."

Faye smiled her thanks then leaned in close to Griffin's ear. "You'll never guess who's been hanging out here."

"Wanna bet? I've already met them."

"No way! The people from the film? The big stars haven't been in yet but the director and some of the crew have. They love it here. The director said he may want to rent the place out for a private party. They may even shoot a scene here. I just have to name my price."

"Good for you, sis."

"You aren't acting very excited. I thought you were a big fan of Penelope Winters."

"Was, is the operative word…If you like having your balls frozen off, she's the girl of my dreams. After meeting her, I'd say unfortunately, the fantasy is much better than the reality."

Faye shook her head chuckling, "What am I going to do with you?"

Jesse helped Ty serve the two large trays of food, rearranging napkin holders and ketchup bottles to make room.

"What's your little brother up to now?" Jesse asked, as he leaned down to brush his lips across Faye's cheek. She smiled up at him, her eyes sparkling with affection.

"Licking his wounds after meeting his fantasy woman Penelope Winters and discovering she's immune to his charm," she said, laughing. "I told him about the private party and filming here."

"You'd better keep that on the down low or you're going to have swarms of gawkers hanging out disrupting everyone's plans."

"I know, I'm trying but it's just too juicy not to share. You'll keep it to yourself right Griff?"

"Yeah but what about the rest of these guys?" he asked, looking around at the half dozen friends sitting at his table. With the music blaring and all the conversations going on at once, nobody had picked up on their discussion.

"I think we're safe," Faye said.

The front door opened, and a group of people walked in. Faye hissed excitedly in Griffin's ear, "It's them!"

Seeing the new arrivals, Jesse said, "I'd better get back behind the bar. Babe I might need your help. When does Addison get back from her break?" He lightly caressed her bare arm.

"There she is now," Faye said.

"Just in time."

"I'll be there in a minute," Faye said.

Griffin studied the new arrivals. It was hard to describe the energy surrounding the film crew. They stood out without even trying. They practically screamed big-city hipsters, and yet they were all dressed casually and seemed relaxed and out for a good time. He didn't recognize any of them except the director, and Penelope Winters was most certainly not amongst the group. He felt let down and was surprised. He quickly tamped down his disappointment.

The door opened again, and his breath caught as she entered, deep in conversation with Noah. *Fuck me.*

She was mesmerizing. Her long, ridiculously thick blond hair was piled on top of her head with loose tendrils escaping from the clasp. She wore a soft, rust-colored, free-flowing mini dress that moved as she walked. The narrow straps of her dress were tied at the shoulder, and he imagined pulling on the laces.

His eyes continued their assessment, admiring her long shapely legs all the way down to the brown flip-flops on her feet. He pulled his gaze away before he embarrassed himself. His friends were also transfixed, and Faye had to check them.

"Um guys, they are my guests, do you think you could put your tongues back in your mouths?"

They all laughed sheepishly, then grumbled, but did manage to tear their gazes away.

After greeting them at the door, Addison grabbed menus and led them toward the waterfront outdoor seating area. This time of year, the entire wall was open, linking the indoor and outdoor space. As the group passed by their table, Jake, one of Griffin's more loud and obnoxious friends, stood to insure he had everyone's attention.

"I'd like to make a toast to my best friend Griffin, who holds the current title of man least likely to settle down. To high winds and mermaids! Happy thirtieth, my friend!" The whole bar participated in the cheers and joined in to sing happy birthday.

Penelope arched a brow as she passed by his table, the only acknowledgement that she remembered meeting him. After seating the group, Addison approached Griffin and leaned down to say, "Stewart

Abrams, the film director, would like to buy you a drink for your birthday. What'll it be?"

Griffin's eyes widened in surprise, "The director, hey? I'll have a bourbon on the rocks. Tell Stewart thanks." When she returned with his drink, he looked outside at the film crew's table and caught the eye of the director and raised his glass, giving a slight nod of his head. Stewart Abrams raised his own glass and nodded back.

A short time later Addison returned. "The director would like you to join his group for a drink."

"What?"

"You have been summoned. Maybe they're sick of their own company."

Griffin stood and confidently strolled over to their table.

Stewart Abrams immediately stood up and said, "Great to see you again. Griffin, right? Please, have a seat." He gestured to the space on the bench between Penelope Winters and himself. Griffin swallowed. Stewart introduced him to the group and after greeting him, they jumped back into their animated discussion, Noah being the most vocal.

Griffin was acutely aware of Penelope's leg touching his in the close quarters.

"Thanks for the drink," Griffin said.

"Least I could do. It's your birthday. I overheard your friend say it's the big thirty."

"That's right."

Griffin turned toward Penelope and was caught off guard by the hostility in her emerald green eyes. His brow furrowed, "Did you get out on the wrong side of the bed this morning?"

"Excuse me?"

"I said..."

"I heard what you said," she said, curtly.

"Well?"

"Well what?"

"Is it the bed or are you always this ill-natured?"

"You're being a little presumptuous, aren't you?"

"Are there different rules for you then?"

She sputtered, "Who do you think you are?"

"I could say the same."

Her eyes practically spit at him. "Of all the brazen...arrogant..."

Stewart interrupted, "Penelope..."

Griffin watched the anger dance across her face before she turned her back to him. Stewart shrugged his shoulders and gave him an embarrassed grin.

"Listen, the reason I called you over...and trust me, I know I'm coming out of left field here, but I've got something I'd like you to consider."

Griffin's brow furrowed, "What's that?"

"We have an emergency that's come up. One of our actors had to drop out of the film today due to a family emergency. I'm sitting over here watching you and I'm suddenly hit with this crazy idea."

"You can't be suggesting what I think you are."

"Seriously, you'd be perfect. I'd like you to do a test screening. Read for the part. I know it sounds insane, but I've got a hunch. You've got something that sets you apart. A star quality if you will. I've been in this business long enough to know it when I see it."

Griffin shook his head, "Not interested...not even remotely. What the hell, I've never acted a day in my life."

Penelope, overhearing the exchange, turned back to them and said, "Are you kidding right now, Stew? It's bad enough I have to put up with you know who! No way! If he's in, I'm out."

"Penelope, calm down. Look at him. He'd be perfect."

She looked him up and down with disdain. "No."

Griffin felt his blood boil, so he returned the favor and slowly raked his eyes over her...from her face...to her chest...allowing his gaze to linger insolently there, before returning to stare mockingly into her narrowed eyes.

Stewart held up his hand toward Penelope, "You don't have the final say. I do. Now as I was saying, I figured it'd be a hard sell, but it's just a test screening. If you do well, we'll have you do a read through with the other actors. See what the chemistry is like."

Despite himself, Griffin was intrigued. It certainly would be an antidote for the boredom he'd been feeling lately.

"Like how many lines are we talking?"

Penelope stood up abruptly. "I'm leaving. I've heard enough."

Stewart said, "Get Ben to drive you home."

She glared at him then motioned to a younger guy across from her that she was ready to leave, and he shot up to do her bidding like she was the Queen of England.

She stormed out of the bar without a backward glance.

"I don't think the reigning diva will agree to work with me."

"Let me worry about that. Let's see how you do first, then, we'll go from there." He slapped Griffin on the back as if it was already a done deal. "Monday, meet me at the Butler House around noon. Your friend mentioned to you that we've rented the whole place out for the duration. Eighteenth century. It's magnificent! Are you familiar with it?"

"Yes."

"It's basically become our studio. Dressing rooms, showers, meeting room, we set up a theater room for the dailies. We'll even shoot some of the scenes there."

"What should I expect on Monday?"

"We'll do a read through. Real easy and casual. You should be recovered from your birthday celebrations by then."

"I don't know what to say except that I think you're nuts, but what the hell, I'm always up for an adventure."

"I knew it! I have a good feeling about this."

"I wouldn't get your hopes up. Between my lack of acting chops and your diva, it doesn't seem very promising. I'd better get back to my party." Griffin stood up, adrenaline surging through his body.

"Great! See you Monday." He shook Griffin's hand heartily.

Griffin returned to his friends a bit shell shocked. They were all over him, drilling him about what had transpired between him and the famous director.

When he filled them in, they all guffawed except his friend Jake who said, "I can totally see it dude. You're going to be a star!"

"Shut the fuck up," Griffin said, deflecting the comment.

"You just wait. It could happen. Why not?"

Griffin pinched the bridge of his nose, "I don't believe I agreed to this, it's the last thing I want to do."

"It's just who you are dude. You've never said no to a challenge before, why start now?"

"Let's change the subject. And this goes no further than this table. Got that?"

They all shook their heads in agreement. "Let's get this party started!" Griffin said. And they ordered another round.

6

*G*riffin drummed his fingers on the arm rest as he waited in the foyer for the director's summons. Unbelievably, he'd passed the first challenge and had nailed the read-through. The next step was to read the script with other actors. He had been given an hour to study the scene he'd be auditioning with. He shook his head. *Auditioning...surreal man.*

A young man approached, ear buds dangling and clipboard in hand. "Mr. Bennett?"

At Griffin's nod he said, "Follow me."

Griffin stood. *What am I so nervous about? I don't even want the part.*

They entered a large and grand formal dining room that had a massive table with a half dozen scripts scattered around. "Have a seat. Do you need anything to drink? A bottle of water?"

"Yeah that'd be good, thanks," Griffin said, clearing his throat nervously before taking a seat.

Stewart Abrams arrived first and eagerly pumped his hand in greeting. "How ya feeling? You nailed that first read through, Griffin. You're a natural. Don't let your nerves get the better of you."

Griffin grinned, "I don't know why I let myself get talked into this."

"Who could resist?"

The door opened and Noah Davis entered. As confident as Griffin was in his own skin, he had to admit to himself that it was a little intimidating to be auditioning in front of an actor of his caliber. He'd been hoping to have some unknowns sitting in as fill-ins. This made it all too real. That could only mean that Penelope wasn't too far behind.

Noah nodded his head toward Griffin and said, "So you're the next big star, hey?"

Griffin bit back a laugh, "Hardly."

Noah narrowed his eyes as he studied Griffin, "I have to agree with Stew, he could be on to something. You've got the look at least."

The door opened again and suddenly it felt as though the air had been sucked from the room as Penelope Winters entered. Griffin's heart pounded. Holy shit was she ever beautiful. Too bad it was only skin deep.

She managed to make even a simple black tee shirt and jeans look sexy. Griffin scrambled to find his bearings. Catching himself staring, he forcibly looked away.

The director fawned solicitously over his star, pulling out her chair with an overenthusiastic welcome. She had yet to even glance his way and he wondered, not for the first time, if this wasn't the biggest mistake he'd ever made. His hackles rose.

"Okay, so he nailed the read-through. Now we're going to see how it goes with you guys," the director said.

Penelope looked at him and Griffin felt his chest tighten. Her green eyes skewered him. *Whoa, talk about feeling like an unwelcome party crasher.*

Exactly what he'd expected from her. He was doing them the damn favor to even consider auditioning and she was behaving like some imperial princess. He didn't need this shit.

Griffin's eyes narrowed as he inclined his head, "Ms. Winters," he said coolly. She ignored him.

Two more people entered and were introduced as producers. They greeted everyone, then took their seats.

Stewart clapped his hands together and said, "Okay we're all here. Let's get started. Let's have Noah and Penelope start by reading through their scene that starts on page fifty. That will give Griffin a taste for it and segue nicely into his first scene with Penny."

Griffin caught the look exchanged between the two stars and was surprised by the tension between them. He was obviously behind on the latest Hollywood gossip. They certainly weren't acting like a couple in love.

He leaned back in his chair and watched intently as they slipped into character. It was spellbinding. There was undeniable chemistry between them and like the flick of a switch they had morphed into their characters. Griffin raked his hands through his hair then he interlaced his fingers behind his head. No pressure here. His foot tapped restlessly against the floor.

Just as he was considering his escape plan, Penelope looked up and caught his eye. The corners of her lips tilted up contemptuously, like she was fully aware that he was about to bolt. He took a deep calming breath and willed his muscles to relax. *Fuck her.*

"That was great you two! No surprise there. Now let's turn to page eighty, one of Penelope and Griffin's scenes. Remember Griffin, your affair is new, and you've just had mind-blowing sex. You're getting cold feet but completely under her spell," Stewart instructed.

He watched as Penelope studied her lines. She glanced up from the script and caught him staring, her eyes flashed with irritation as she said, "You've got the first line."

"Who me? Oh, sorry." Clearing his throat, he began, *"Looking at you makes it hard to breathe. We just made love and I'm aroused all over again. I crave you."*

Penelope smiled seductively at Griffin, her gaze roving over his body, *"Then what are you waiting for?"*

Griffin sucked in a sharp breath, then read the next line, his hands shook slightly as he gripped the pages of his script, *"We're getting careless. If your husband discovers our affair, he'll make your life a living hell."*

"Quit worrying darling. He's busy campaigning and way too self-centered to concern himself with me."

"I may be getting paranoid, but I swear I was being followed the other day."

"You're definitely getting paranoid. Now bring that impressive body over here and make love to me again and

that's an order. This time let's take it real slow," Penelope read.

Griffin swallowed hard. Her voice was so smooth, like velvet and sexy...slightly husky...he felt like he was being stroked with her words. Running his hand through his hair, he read the next line, *"We've got to be more careful. I can't risk it for either of us. Your husband has everything at stake. His election is on the line and God only knows what he's capable of doing to defend it."*

She flashed him a dazzling smile, *"Whatever you say. Now could you please come play with me?"*

"Damn you, you're a temptress, you know that, right? I don't think I could quit you even if I wanted to. No matter how hard I try or what I tell myself...you've cast some kind of spell over me. I dream about you...you're all I can think about." He swallowed hard reading ahead to the blocking for this scene.

It was going to be torture. He'd be in bed, making love to Penelope Winters—or rather Sydney O'Connor, the character—a very dangerous mistake to forget that important detail. And now the scene called for him to be on top of her, devouring her. He wasn't sure he'd be able to keep it straight...what was real and what was acting. When she looked at him with those sultry eyes, he didn't feel much like it was acting...he hoped he didn't get the part.

Looking pleased with herself, she said, *"You make me feel like the most beautiful woman in the world."*

He groaned inwardly, *"You should feel like that Sydney, because you are. Your body is so lush." Scene fades as the camera cuts,* with him on top of her making passionate love.

Dead silence. Griffin was beginning to wonder if he'd bombed when Stewart stood up and began to clap, his eyes gleaming with excitement. After another moment the two producers joined him, "I knew it! You two are off the charts sexy!" the director said.

Griffin glanced around the table noticing that Noah's lips were tight, and his face appeared pinched. Penelope kept her gaze lowered but her cheeks looked slightly pink. The producers were grinning from ear to ear.

"On to phase three as far as I'm concerned," Stewart said.

Both producers nodded their heads in agreement, one adding, "That was sizzling hot. You two were combustible."

Noah chimed in, "Yeah but he is a complete novice. No offense Griffin, but this is one of the leading roles. We can't afford to have this film tank."

"You're right and that's precisely why we need Griffin. It all makes sense. He is stunning, sex appeal up the wazoo, chemistry between him and Pen is undeniable, an unknown brings something special to the table. A blank slate if you will. No baggage attached. We'll do a real scene tomorrow and if it's even half of what I'm expecting, Griffin is the next Bryan Kent."

Noah said, "Penelope we haven't heard a peep from you. What do you think?"

Her eyes flickered with some hidden emotion. "I have my own concerns with casting Griffin. It's going to be more work. He'll be learning on the fly. It's a lot to ask of him and of Noah and me."

"They're right you know," Griffin said. "Look I'll be the first to admit I'm in way over my head here."

"Nonsense. You read beautifully. I think you were made for this part. We need someone that can hold his own and be believable opposite such star power. You're it. I have an instinct for these things," Stewart said.

"I'm just not interested. I'm sorry I wasted your time." Griffin stood up to leave.

"I know this must be intimidating as hell, but we're desperate. We're already behind on shooting. Production got pushed back when the actor backed out. You can name your price."

Griffin bit back a laugh. "It isn't about the money, trust me on that."

Noah sat with his arms crossed over his chest, while Penelope worriedly bit her bottom lip. Penelope spoke again, "I've changed my mind. I trust Stew. He's brilliant and he's never steered me wrong. I say we give it a try."

Griffin's eyes widened in shock. Was this the same woman who only minutes before had insulted him? "Why the change of heart?"

She shrugged one shoulder nonchalantly, "Stew's right. We must put the film above our personal feelings. I don't have to like my co-stars," her eyes strayed to Noah, "I just have to be a professional and do my job."

He sputtered, "You're unbelievable. Two introductions and you've already decided you don't like me."

"I have my reservations yes, but again, I bow to Stew's wisdom."

"Gee thanks for the hearty endorsement," Griffin said, his tone dripping with sarcasm. She looked away.

"Well I've put my two cents in, but I'll respect your

decision Stew." Noah grinned, then said, "May as well give it a shot Griffin. If you like adventure, this will be the ride of your life."

That jogged Griffin's memory of why he'd even considered it in the first place. Boredom. Well hell, he'd sure got his adrenaline fix today. Despite major misgivings he heard himself say, "I guess I'm willing to go the next step. If you believe in me at least I can give it a try. If by some miracle this happens, I'd have to find a substitute golfer for a charity event I'm scheduled to participate in. If I can't find one, I won't accept the part."

Stewart grinned, "Then I'd advise to start looking for a replacement now. After the run through tomorrow you can meet with our lawyers to go over the contract," Stew said, beaming.

"My brother Kyle Bennett is a local attorney; we can meet at his office."

"Perfect. If there are no objections, everyone here tomorrow, ten a.m."

Penelope turned on her heel and left without saying goodbye and Noah cornered one of the producers for a chat. Griffin stood there at a loss until the assistant entered the room with a full script in his hand. He handed it to Griffin.

"Study your little heart out," he said, eyeing Griffin appreciatively.

"Thanks. I'll definitely be doing that. Don't want to humiliate myself."

Stewart turned to Griffin and said, "Start memorizing your next scene with Penelope, the one that comes after what you read today. I think it starts on page ninety-five. Don't sweat it, just do your best. We'll all be here to help you."

Griffin raised one eyebrow, "You sure about that?"

The director grinned, "Yes. Despite themselves they're ultimately team players and nothing but professional. No worries." He clapped Griffin heartily on the back and left the room whistling.

What could possibly go wrong?

7

*P*enelope tucked her hair up in the ball cap and slipped on her sunglasses, hoping it was enough disguise to protect her anonymity as she pedaled her bike to the beach house. Her forehead creased thinking about her new potential co-star...*Griffin Bennett.* He was gorgeous, she'd give him that at least. His unruly mop of brown hair and his intensely blue eyes were compelling. Tall, lean and muscular, killer smile, perfect white teeth.

So why was she less than thrilled? He was irritating and for the life of her, she couldn't figure out why she was so triggered by him. He only had to open his mouth and she felt annoyed.

She refused to give notice to the tingling she felt between her legs when she thought about his piercing eyes. She'd caught him staring at her more than once today and her fluttering pulse was entirely unwelcome. She was tired of men objectifying her. He could keep his wandering eyes to himself. If she were honest though, she'd have to admit that his interest had seemed appreciative yes, but not leering or creepy.

He was a bit too cocky for his own good. *Who* is that confident? He waltzed in like he'd been reading scripts his whole life. He might say he was in over his head, but his attitude belied his words. Men. They were so damn entitled. They never had to worry about power... they were born into it. She frowned. *I've become a certified cynic. But with good reason. They'll use you and abuse you if you give them an inch!*

A chill went down her spine when she flashed back to her early days in Hollywood. That had been the end of her innocence. A few foolish choices had cost her dearly. But she kept those secrets and memories locked away. She'd finally put to rest her worry that one day her past would resurface to haunt her. If it was going to be uncovered, it already would have been.

She locked her bike to the rack beneath the car port and went straight inside to don her swimsuit. She put on a white bikini and floppy pink hat, grabbed Archie, a towel and headed outside to the pool.

Her phone pinged with a text from her make-up artist Dolly.

Penelope: Can't wait for you to get here. So much to tell you. Noah is still an ass and the new co-star is going to make some waves I'm sure. I'll tell you all about it when you get here.

Dolly: So excited! See you Friday. Can't wait to hear all of the juicy deets.

Penelope smiled and set her phone aside. Dolly was the only one she trusted with her hair and her confessions. They'd worked together for over three years and Penelope didn't know what she'd do without her. Dolly had been a rock after her mom had died and that had solidified their friendship. At Penelope's insistence, they'd be roommates during filming. The house was huge, and she needed a friend.

She threw her hat on the lounger and dove into the pool. The cool water felt like silk against her skin and soothed her tense muscles. She ducked under and touched the bottom before springing back to the surface. Rubbing her eyes, she turned onto her back and floated, the sun warming her exposed skin. She let her whole body relax, suspended like a jelly fish. With her ears submerged she heard her own breath as if through a tunnel.

A muffled voice startled her out of her reverie. She kicked her legs and feet to tread water as she glared at Noah, who stood towering in his swim trunks, dipping his big toe into the water.

"Hey beautiful. Mind if I join you?"

"Do I have a choice?" she said irritably.

"Nope," he said, jumping in with a big splash.

He emerged and shook out his hair, slicking it back from his movie-star-handsome face. A face that used to make her weak-kneed every time she looked at him. No longer. He had successfully extinguished that flame.

"What did ya think?"

"About?"

"Our new co-star?"

She shrugged. "He has something."

"He seems to have a little crush on our headliner."

"I hadn't noticed."

"Whatever you say. He's a bit sure of himself."

Contrarily even though she'd been thinking the same thing, she defended Griffin, "He's just confident. Good thing too. Can you imagine how you'd feel? Can you picture yourself auditioning for an orchestra without any training? I was quite impressed."

"Oh really? You sure hid it well. You seemed pretty pissy to me."

She flushed, "I did not."

He grinned rakishly. "Are you hot for him, too?"

"No!"

"Good. There's still hope then."

"That ship has sailed." She dove under the water and swam to the opposite end of the pool.

He popped up beside her. His eyes burning with desire, regret, pain…"I miss us. I love you Penelope."

"Please, don't start Noah. It will never be us again. It's time for you to move on. I have."

"You're so shut down. Thirty-two is way too young to give up on love."

"Who said I've given up?"

"I can see it in your eyes. It breaks me that I did that to you." He grabbed her arm and pulled her to him. She felt his erection pressing into her belly. Her breasts smashed against him as he hugged her tightly to his chest. She struggled, pushing him away, as ancient memories of another life and time gripped her heart in a vice, almost paralyzing her.

"Noah, stop! Please. We've got to work together,

don't blow it. I would like to find our way back to friendship. But this isn't going to get us there."

"God, I fucked everything up so bad. You're killing me."

Her chest rose and fell with ragged breaths, "It is what it is. I have forgiven you Noah. You're human. I realize that I needed more from you than you had to give. I want to be the only one. I want a mate...someone who needs nothing more, and I need to know that I'm enough."

"I can be that now...you *are* the only one. I screwed up. I'll never do it again. Besides, at this point in your life and career, would you ever really be able to tell who loves you for you...or if they're only hungry for your fame and fortune? We knew each other before we were famous. We rode the star together."

"I'll have to take my chances, won't I? I'd never be able to trust you again Noah. I wasn't enough for you then and nothing has changed." She knew that he loved her, he just didn't love her as much as he loved himself.

He climbed out of the pool. "I'll see you in the morning."

"Bye Noah."

With her calm mood completely disrupted, she got out and decided to make a slushy frozen Margarita. She called to Archie who had found a comfortable spot in the shade and went inside.

8

Griffin sat at the bar regaling his sister Faye and her fiancé Jesse with his latest dramatic chapter.

"Only you Griff. I swear," Faye said, rolling her eyes.

He held up both hands. "I wasn't looking for it. You can hardly blame me."

"Wanna bet? I completely blame you. You could have said no from the git-go." Griffin looked so flabbergasted that Faye sputtered with laughter. "See, that's exactly how you find yourself in the middle of everything. Your adventurist side is going to be your downfall one of these days. So, tell me, has your opinion changed? What's she like?"

"Cold."

"I don't believe it. She seemed kind of shy the other night."

He bit back a sarcastic laugh, "Shy? Try stuck-up snob."

"Did you know that her mom died in the last couple of years? The tabloids said she was devastated. I'm sure she's still grieving."

Griffin rubbed his chin, "I didn't know that about her mom, but she came right out and said she didn't like me."

"Ha! Penelope Winters is resistant to your charms," Faye said.

"You can say that again. Her royal highness, Ms. Penelope Winters, is barely even civil to me."

"My little brother may have finally met his match."

"Very funny. Maybe she's met hers," Griffin said.

"Damn dude, I envy your swag," Jesse said. "I guess it comes from women throwing themselves at your feet. By the way what ever happened to Brianna? Haven't seen her around lately."

"Too young and too clingy. I had to cut her loose. She's back in New York. I've taken myself out of the dating pool for now. If I land the part, I'll be too caught up in filming anyway." Griffin changed the subject. "Faye I was wondering if you'd help me practice my lines?"

Faye looked at Jesse, "We're pretty slow, do you mind babe?"

"Go. It's not every day you get to brush elbows with a future movie star."

Faye and Griffin went into her office and closed the door. "I'm going to try without the script. I've been studying my lines all day. You'll just read Penelope's lines and correct me if I'm wrong," Griffin said.

Faye bounced on her tiptoes excitedly. "This is so

surreal! My little brother playing opposite Noah Davis and Penelope Winters."

Looking slightly dazed Griffin said, "Fucking weird."

"What page?"

"We'll start on eighty."

Faye read Penelope's part and Griffin remembered almost every one of his lines and stayed in character throughout the entire scene. Faye only had to prompt him once. "Oh my God! S-t-e-a-m-y!"

"Yeah I've noticed," he said, dryly.

"Griffin," she squealed, "You are fabulous! I am so impressed. Who knew? I mean it."

"Really? You think I did alright? Was I believable?"

Faye looked tenderly at her little brother. As confident as he appeared, she knew he carried the same scars from their fucked up childhood as she, he just hid them better. "You rocked it. Honestly, I'm shocked right now."

He smirked and the vulnerable moment was gone like a puff of smoke. "I hope I can retain it all."

"You'll do fine. Go home and get some rest. No more beer tonight. You have to be sharp tomorrow."

"Yes ma'am."

"I'll bet your southern accent will be a plus for all the swooning fans out there. Noah Davis has nothing on you."

"Um, do ya think you might be a little biased?"

She pinched her fingers together. "Just a teeny tiny bit."

"Thanks for the read-through. I'll stop in after the screen test."

"Break a leg."

"See ya Faye. Night Jesse." He put on his helmet as he left the bar and hopped onto his Ducati. He fired it up and peeled out of the parking lot.

He loved the power and thrill of his bike almost as much as he loved piloting his plane. The faster...the higher...the bigger...the better. He'd skied the highest mountains and jumped out of airplanes, but he had to admit, this acting shit had him more terrified than anything he'd ever done before.

Going full throttle, he hit the straightaway to blow off some of the nervous energy. He couldn't as easily eradicate the image of Penelope's full breasts, straining against the black cotton of her tee shirt and the faint outline of her nipples. The nude scenes were going to be interesting to say the least. Surely, they had ways to orchestrate the scenes for maximum comfort. His gut clenched. He felt edgy and more alive than he had in a very long time.

9

Penelope had to admit that she was impressed with Griffin's performances so far. He always came prepared, knew his lines, and was picking up his marks very quickly. The blocking could be difficult for new actors...kind of like walking and chewing gum as the saying goes. But he was catching on extraordinarily fast. Her worries about him slowing down the filming were dissipating. Maybe she'd been wrong about him.

She toyed with a lock of hair as she waited for Stew to finish his discussion with Griffin. They were standing off in the corner quietly talking something over. Already a week into filming, today they'd shoot their first intimate scene together. No nudity yet, just an intense making out session. She had lain awake for several hours last night worrying about it. What the hell was wrong with her?

Gorgeous arrogant men were a dime a dozen in

Hollywood. Why was Griffin getting under her skin? But he was. He was so damn sure of himself for one thing. It made her want to take him down a peg or two. At least he'd been keeping things professional. He wasn't trying to ingratiate himself off camera. She told herself that she was relieved, but a nagging voice in the back of her mind called her a liar.

Stew and Griffin approached. "All set?" Stewart asked.

Penelope nodded. Her gaze roved over Griffin's naked torso, lean and muscular with a dusting of soft dark hair covering his chest. The film was a romantic thriller. Penelope's character was married to a United States Senator up for reelection. Noah Davis played her husband and Griffin was playing her contractor-turned-lover after being hired to remodel their million-dollar home.

"Remember Griff, she's the aggressor here, at this point you're still trying to resist but losing the battle," Stewart reminded him.

He nodded then stood on his mark. Penelope saw him take a deep breath and had a fleeting twinge of compassion. "Three...two...one...action," Stewart called.

Penelope slipped into her character, abruptly morphing into Sydney O'Connor as easily as putting on a mask. She exaggerated the sway of her curvy hips, the short silk robe leaving little to the imagination as she walked toward Griffin. *No not Griffin, Bryan.*

. . .

"*Y*ou're back...and it appears that we're alone."
Bryan's eyes narrowed as she approached,
his body stiffened warily.

"Alone, Ms. O'Connor?"

She chuckled seductively, "When did we go all formal again? Ms. O'Connor?" Sydney playfully skimmed her hands over his toned hard belly and felt him shudder beneath her fingertips. "I sent them away."

Eyes widening, he visibly gulped, "You did what? They work for me."

"They're gone. I sent them on a wild goose chase. Ultimately, they're working for me, but let's not waste time arguing the point." Glancing at her watch, she said, "We should have at least an hour to play."

Bryan took a step back and she took a step forward. He swallowed hard then his gaze took a slow journey from her face to her breasts, lingering before returning to pin her with his intense electric blue eyes. He looked hungry for her. "Tell me why this is a good idea," he said on a groan.

"Because you're a very naughty boy Bryan, and you want this as badly as I do," she said. "I've noticed your eyes following me." She smoothed the palms of her hands up his chest then wrapped her arms around his neck, pulling him down for a kiss. Her skin heated through the silk fabric. Her nipples hardened as they pressed against him.

He kissed her tentatively at first but as the heat ignited, he opened his mouth and covered hers. Running his hands down her back, he cupped her bottom and pulled her hips against him. Her fingers clenched tightly, gripping his hair as she moaned against his lips. He ground his pelvis against *hers.* She stiffened for a moment as she felt him grow hard.

He broke away and put his hands on her shoulders, holding her away from his body. "No Sydney. We can't do this. It's a slippery slope. Your husband is a fucking Senator for God's sake!"

"I don't care. I'm lonely. All he cares about is his reelection. He's had countless affairs. I'm sure of it."

"Then divorce him, but you're not going to use me like I'm some boy toy."

"Is that what you think?" Her eyes welled with tears. "You must think I'm some kind of slut. I've never done anything like this before. I've been the perfect politician's wife. Seen but not heard. His needs always coming before my own. But for the first time, I'm doing something I want. I need you Bryan."

"Jesus Syd, don't cry," Bryan pulled her back into his arms and buried his nose in her hair. "You smell so good."

"I can't do this anymore. I feel trapped, like I'm living someone else's life. I don't even know who I am anymore. I don't want this life." She began to sob.

"Baby. Shh. It's going to be okay. Shh." He held her in his arms brushing her hair back from her brow. He rained kisses all over her face, licking her salty tears then tracing the outline of her mouth with his tongue. She shuddered and felt a warmth between her thighs...for real! Yikes. This was feeling a little too authentic. Snap out of it, girl.

She slid her arms around his waist. "Please just hold me."

His body suddenly tensed, "I heard a car door. I thought you said they'd be gone for an hour." He disentangled himself and stepped away. She felt lonely and missed the warmth of his arms around her. Wait a minute. Who? Sydney or Penelope?

"*C*ut," Stewart called. "Fantastic! You both nailed it. Let's take five before the next scene."

Griffin stared into her eyes, his burning with intensity. Her breath caught in her throat. Looking embarrassed, he said, "Sorry about...you know."

"It happens. Even to the seasoned actors. I won't hold it against you."

"That was certainly interesting," he said, then raking his hands through his hair, he blew out a breath.

Dolly swooped in just then to powder Penelope's nose and Griffin walked off the set and disappeared outside. Dolly whispered, "What the hell! That was gorgeous super-hot sexy. I felt like a voyeur watching. It almost made me blush!"

Penelope felt her cheeks grow warm. "Thanks."

"He doesn't know it yet, but his life is never going to be the same after this film is released! My God! He is scrumptious."

Penelope laughed. "Down girl."

"How are you not swooning?"

"I told you, I'm off men...maybe permanently."

"I give you another week until you're completely under his spell."

"Gee, I thought you were my friend. Thanks for the vote of confidence."

"I'm rooting for you, can't you see? You two would be perfect for each other," she said, her eyes twinkling.

"Places everyone," Stew said.

Griffin returned to stand in front of Penelope, his eyes veiled.

She looked up at him from under her lashes and felt that annoying heat dance across her cheeks. He smiled at her and winked. As if he knew. That did it. Her irritation canceled out the embarrassment and she glared.

"There she is..." he whispered.

"Three...two...one...action."

Noah entered the set and it was game on.

10

Griffin breathed a sigh of relief when Stew called it a wrap for the day. He was a bundle of nerves and if he didn't get away from Penelope soon, he could potentially embarrass them both. After the first scene, he had managed to contain his desire for her, but it was taking its toll. His neck muscles felt as tight as guitar strings and his stomach was in knots. He grabbed his water and was walking off the set when she called to him. He turned and watched her approach.

"Hey, I've invited the cast and crew over for a catered cookout this Saturday. Can you make it?"

He bit back a laugh, "What? I thought you didn't like me."

Her body stiffened, "You know what? Do whatever you want. I was trying to be nice. I didn't want to leave anyone out." She pivoted and stomped off.

"Penelope," he called out, but she ignored him and kept walking.

He stood there scratching his head. What a bitch. That woman was as prickly as a cactus. He couldn't seem to find the right approach with her. He was continually off balance. She was moody, aloof, and frustrating. He'd tried charm, which had gone over like a lead balloon, he'd tried cool, she didn't even notice, he'd tried funny, she had no sense of humor...now he had offended her over a simple off the cuff comment.

Whatever. He could usually read women, but he was failing miserably with Penelope. She was complicated. Never one to shy away from a good challenge, it took sheer force of will not to get sucked into finding out what made her tick. She was almost irresistible. Almost. He had to fight it; this was one challenge he'd have to pass on. She'd made that perfectly clear.

Dolly touched his back as she passed him on her way out. "Hey, great job. Honestly, you'd never know you weren't a seasoned actor. You're keeping up just fine with the headliners."

He grinned at her, "You sure about that?"

"Cross my heart." She nodded her head toward her friend Penelope. "I'm not trying to be disloyal here, but I just wanted to say, don't take it personally."

He comically widened his eyes and put his hand to his chest. "Who, *moi*?"

"She can be a bit intense but she's just defending a very vulnerable heart."

Griffin looked skeptical, "If you say so. I don't know what I did to piss her off, but she sure as hell knows how to hold a grudge."

"That's just it. You didn't do anything. It's really not about you, I swear."

"She hates men then…is that it?"

"Pretty much. With good reason, I might add."

"Dolly, thanks. I could use a friend here on set."

She grinned. "I think you're pretty awesome. Give her a little time. It takes her a while to warm up to people, once she lets you in, she'll melt your heart."

"I won't hold my breath."

She laughed. "Yeah, don't. That would be downright dangerous."

The corners of his eyes crinkled as he gave her a full-on thousand watt smile. She put a hand to her throat. "Fire alert! Damn Griff, you're going to give me a heart attack."

He slung his arm across Dolly's shoulders and gave her a brotherly hug. He happened to raise his eyes and caught Penelope watching them. She sent him daggers, then turned her back to him before continuing her conversation with their director. *Geesh can I catch a fucking break with her?*

"Thanks for the pep talk Dolly. See you tomorrow."

"Yes, and I hope to see you at the cast party this weekend. It'd be a great way to get to know everyone a little better. We have a great pool and view of the ocean. We're having The Hennessey Restaurant cater it and a chef on premises. It will be a hoot, I promise. This is a wild group when they're not on the clock. You can bring a date if you want to."

"I'll have to think about it, thanks."

"Welcome."

He smiled and felt a little lighter than he had before

their talk. It was nice to know someone had his back. He felt awkward, like the new kid in school...an outsider most of the time. Everyone was cordial but he still hadn't made any friends...until now. The olive branch Dolly had offered was a welcome surprise.

~

"*W*hat was that all about?" Penelope asked.

Dolly remained pokerfaced. "What was what about?"

Penelope's eyes narrowed, "Yeah right. You know exactly what I'm talking about. Your cozy little conference with Griffin over in the corner."

"I wanted to compliment him on his performance. You know you could be a little nicer to him. He's new... doesn't have any friends on the set. It's got to be hard."

"He's a big boy."

"Penelope quit being such a hard-ass. I think he's struggling a little."

"Doubtful. He knows he's got the world by the balls. He had the nerve to tease me about my embarrassment right before we shot the last scene."

"He's being playful. Do you even remember what that's like?"

Penelope tilted her head and looked heavenward like she was pondering the question. "Vaguely."

"You're too much. It's obvious you have your mind made up about him but I, for one, plan on giving him a chance. I think he's lonely."

"Wolf in sheep's clothing. Be careful."

"You're such a cynic."

Penelope sighed, "It's been a rough day. I started this film on a deficit and it doesn't take much to throw me off."

"Especially when it comes in the form of a six-foot blue-eyed Adonis! He'd throw me off too."

"Don't be ridiculous."

"I know you. Don't worry, it will remain our little secret. I want you to think about it from his perspective. You are every guy's fantasy; you're a huge star and he has to fall in love with you every time you do a scene together. You're an actress and used to turning it off and on, but he's had zero experience with that."

"He's a guy, he has experience with that, trust me."

Dolly laughed, shaking her head, she said, "We can argue about this later, I am smart enough to know when to quit."

"Good. Let's go home. I'm exhausted."

"Pizza sound good?"

"Divine."

Dolly pulled out her cell, "I'll phone it in now. The Pinot Grigio is calling."

"Yes, let's get the hell out of here."

"Wine, pizza, pool."

"And no men." Penelope couldn't resist one last poke at her friend. Dolly might worry about her love life, or rather the lack thereof, but Penelope was burnt out on men. She'd been betrayed by men at every turn, beginning with her father's abandonment then continuing with her first lover and finally by Noah.

She had a sudden flash of shame as an image of her dirty little secret escaped from where she'd buried it.

She hugged herself, running her hands up and down the cool skin of her arms. *Breathe.* Put that right back in the ancient history archive...where it belongs. Her body might be betraying her on set, but her mind was very clear about where Griffin Bennett fit into her personal life. Nowhere.

11

*G*riffin squeezed his motorcycle between two cars and pulled right up to the massive car port. He waited for his date to climb off before dismounting. She handed him her helmet and after securing it to his bike, he grabbed her hand, slipping it through his crooked elbow.

"I'm just reminding you, what happens in Vegas stays in Vegas," Griffin said, for the third time.

"I promise," Isabella said, rolling her eyes.

"No photographs and no autographs."

"Griffin we've been friends our whole lives, I'm not stupid. Why are you so nervous? You usually don't care about what anyone thinks."

"I respect their privacy."

She flipped her hair back and smoothed down her sun dress. "Do I look alright?"

Griffin's gaze, hidden behind dark glasses, admired

her classic beauty and elegance. "You look amazing. I really appreciate you doing this."

"Why wouldn't I? I hope I can stay cool and nonchalant. You know, as if I see movie stars every day. Ain't no big thing." She giggled.

Griffin was glad he'd made the last-minute decision to ask his old friend Isabella to tag along. Her fiancé, who was also one of his best friends, happened to be out of town on a business trip. She'd fit right in and he knew she'd have his back.

The front door was unlocked, and they let themselves in and followed the music blaring from outside. Dolly greeted them from the back deck, "Come on out and join the party!"

"Hi Dolly, this is Isabella."

Isabella smiled brightly and Dolly smiled back all the while sizing up Griffin's date. She had immediately noticed the huge diamond sparkling on her ring finger. You could see the wheels turning as she tried to figure out their relationship.

"Glad you could make it. I hope you wore your suits, if not it's clothing optional." She laughed at Isabella's shocked expression. "Just kidding. Us Hollywood folk have to keep up with our free-spirited reputations."

"Fortunately, we came prepared," Griffin said. He pulled his cargo shorts down at the waist giving her a glimpse of his swim trunks and unintentionally, a peak at his tanned and toned abs.

He really liked Dolly. She was the exact opposite of Penelope. Warm, open and friendly. No guessing where you stood with her.

"Fabulous. We've got about anything you might want to drink, and the grill master is barbecuing baby back ribs, chicken, and pork. There are servers carrying appetizer trays around and trays of mimosas, champagne, wine, and a bartender set up outside, coolers full of beer...like I said, whatever your heart or stomach desires. I don't think I've forgotten anything. Oh, and the DJ takes requests."

"Sounds like you've thought of everything," Griffin said.

"We aim to please. If you don't mind fending for yourselves, I'm going to go check and see how the chef is coming along with the sides."

"We'll be fine. Come on Izzy," Griffin said, taking ahold of her hand.

Stewart spotted them and rushed over, greeting Griffin like a long-lost friend. "Hey buddy! Who's your gorgeous date?"

"Isabella meet the director, Stewart Abrams, Stew meet Isabella."

"Izzy is fine," she said, holding out her hand.

"We're so impressed with Griffin's performance, it's like he's been acting his entire life."

"I'm sure. I haven't heard of one thing that he's tried and hasn't mastered. Multipotentiality. He's certainly had nothing but positive things to say about how helpful everyone has been. Seems as if you've taken him under your wing."

"We try. Please mingle...swim...drink...I'll catch up with you later," He was already moving off to greet one of the production crew.

"He seems nice," Izzy said.

"Yeah, I like him."

"Wonder where the big stars are hiding?"

"I think I spot Noah over by the hot tub."

She sighed, "Oh my God. Pinch me. I'm really not dreaming, am I?"

"No, it's for real."

"He's so sexy. I hope I can keep my tongue from hanging out."

Griffin laughed, "Don't embarrass me."

He scanned the patio, not even realizing that he was searching for anyone until his gaze landed on *her*. Penelope. A Goddess. She wore a colorful sarong wrap, tied low around the swell of her hips, and a bikini top that she filled out to perfection. Her voluptuous breasts were practically spilling out. He sucked in a sharp breath.

"Griff what's wrong?" Izzy followed his gaze and lighted upon Penelope. "Wow! She shines like she has literally been sprinkled with stardust! How the hell do you remember your lines working opposite that?"

He watched Penelope disappear into a screened gazebo, then said, "What did you just ask me?"

"Oh Griffin, you have it bad."

"FYI, I've had a crush on her since the first film I saw her in, but the reality doesn't live up to the fantasy. She's as cold as the ice cubes in the drink I'm about to order. Speaking of...I'll go grab our drinks, what would you like?"

"I think I'll have a glass of white wine please."

"I'm going for a bourbon on the rocks. I'll be right back."

Griffin might be the outsider here, but years of

experience had taught him the way around a party. He'd been jet-setting since he'd been in diapers. On his way to the bar, he ran into a few behind-the-scenes workers and stopped to chat. Everyone was loose and informal, and Griffin found himself relaxing.

As he waited for the drinks, he overheard one of the crew say, "She's actually in a relatively good mood today." Griffin didn't need to guess who they were referring to. He was relieved to hear that it wasn't just him.

As he turned to deliver the glass of wine to Izzy, he practically bumped into Penelope. His body heated, immediately responding. Every other person at the party faded into the background.

She raised a skeptical eyebrow. "A two fisted drinker?'

Confused for a moment, he suddenly got it and said, "Um no, this is for my friend over there." He nodded toward Isabella.

The ocean breeze blew tendrils of Penelope's platinum hair across her cheek and she tucked it behind one ear. Her eyes were the color of jade today and now they sparkled with curiosity. "Your date?"

"Yeah I suppose you could say that."

He knew he was crazy to think that he saw a hint of disappointment dance across her face before it quickly disappeared. She licked her bottom lip sending desire rippling through him. "Why don't you introduce me?" she said.

He cleared his throat, "Sure, follow me."

"Izzy, this is the one and only Penelope Winters. Penelope, meet Isabella Martin."

The two women sized each other up. "I've seen every one of your films! I'm a huge fan."

Penelope smiled, her voice naturally husky and inviting, "Thank you. Which one was your favorite?"

"*Surrender,* for sure! The ending was a total surprise."

"That was one of my favorites. Have you been taken care of?"

"Yes, we're all set. I'm salivating for the ribs, they smell divine."

"I've been told that Chef Irvine makes a mean barbeque. I hope it tastes as good as it smells."

"I just sampled a shrimp appetizer, and it was scrumptious," Izzy said.

"I'm going to take a dip in the pool, either of you care to join me?" Penelope looked at Griffin with a challenging glint in her eyes.

"I'll pass for now, but Griffin feel free to get in. I'm fine to mingle."

"I'll wait for you," he said to Isabella.

"I'm fine really. Go."

Penelope slowly untied her sarong and slipped it off, which had Griffin confused. Was she even aware that she made it look like she was doing a strip tease? She looked at Griffin from beneath her long lashes and held it out to him. "Could you hang on to this for me?" He nodded and slung the wrap over his shoulder.

She walked away, arms swinging loosely as her hips swayed seductively. The skimpy bikini bottoms barely covered her luscious ass. Her long blond hair fell thick around her shoulders. Whether intentional or not, it had the desired effect and Griffin admitted to himself that he craved her. She was a drug he had to have. He'd never experienced anything like it. He wanted to bury his face between her thighs and make love to her all night long.

"Oh snap! The ice maiden seems to have melted," Izzy joked.

"Must be the alcohol."

"Griffin, what are you waiting for? You're nuts if you didn't get that blatant invitation."

"I brought you here and you don't know anyone. I'm not going to abandon you."

Ben Donavan, one of the set coordinators approached, and they got into an animated conversation about car racing and classic cars. When Griffin described his own collection, Ben raised his brows. "I guess that takes you out of the poor starving actor category."

Isabella choked on her wine. "Hardly. He comes from a very prominent real estate development empire. The Bennetts are pretty high up on the food chain in the south." Griffin nudged Izzy with his elbow.

"What made you decide to agree to doing the film, since it wasn't for money?"

Izzy answered for him, "He's a thrill seeker...risk-taker...whatever you want to call it. Right Griff?"

His attention had strayed to the pool, and she said, "Earth to Griff."

"What?"

"Ben asked you why you had auditioned for the film. I told him you were an adrenalin junkie."

He grinned. "No lie, one hundred percent junkie. Hey, will you hold this? I'm going to take a dip after all."

She smiled at him and held out her hand. "Gimme."

He handed the sarong to Izzy, then unzipped his cargo shorts and stripped them off before tugging his black tee shirt over his head. He tossed them to the side in a pile.

"What about your watch?"

"Waterproof. You sure you don't want to get in?"

"I'll pass. Ben will keep me company." She held out her palm. "Sunglasses."

"Yes, Mom. Glad I brought you." He grinned at her. "I'll be back."

He walked confidently to the edge of the pool and dove in.

12

*P*enelope tried to tell herself she didn't care that Griffin had a girlfriend, but she wasn't very convincing. It could have been just her and Griffin at the party as far as her body was concerned. She was aware of him *every single second*...where he stood, who he was talking to, when he smiled, when he laughed, even when she wasn't looking at him her body seemed to sense him.

She caught him undressing out of the corner of her eye and her nerves tingled in anticipation. He was so tanned and muscular. His abs flat and ripped. He looked relaxed; his shoulders moved freely as he walked confidently toward the pool. The dusting of dark hair formed a tantalizing trail into his swimsuit. She couldn't deny that he was a very sexy man indeed and he was waking up her libido big time. She was neither happy nor prepared for that.

She watched him dive in and come up for air, shaking his thick hair out like a dog. He rubbed his eyes then glanced up, catching her staring. He flashed a dazzling white smile before going back underwater, then popping up right beside her.

"Hey, great party," he said. He looked deeply into her eyes and her body tingled.

"The producers are footing the bill." She was dying to brush away the stray lock of hair that dripped water across his forehead. She bit her bottom lip. His eyes darkened as he stared at her mouth. She felt her center heat with desire.

Griffin reached out and traced her lips with his finger. "You're so beautiful."

She blinked, startled that he'd touched her.

The corners of his eyes crinkled as he studied her. "Don't look so surprised. I'm not immune."

Her lashes fluttered, "Is that so? I'd have never guessed."

"Really? Have you ever met a man who was unaffected by you? And what was that show you put on a few minutes ago? Why the turn around? I thought you didn't like me?"

"I don't like or dislike you, I'm indifferent. I don't know you."

"Hmm, indifferent huh? Would you like to...know me?"

"I suppose it's inevitable isn't it?"

He glanced over her shoulder and she turned as Noah swam over. He nodded. "Griffin."

"Hey Noah."

"Penelope, can I get you a drink? Rumor has it the barbeque is done," Noah asked.

"I'll have another vodka and tonic when I get out of the water. Twist of lime."

"Babe, don't you think I know what you drink?" he slung his arm across her shoulders proprietarily.

"Has the acting bug bit you in the ass yet?" Noah asked Griffin.

"The jury is still out."

"I think you're killing it. Just don't go getting confused between fantasy and reality...it's not easy playing opposite a babe like this."

Griffin's eyes narrowed and he said, "I guess you'd know. Got any pointers about that?"

Noah laughed. "Good comeback. No, the lines can get blurred sometimes, can't they Penny?"

She shrugged out of his embrace. "I'm getting out."

Griffin's eyes glittered as they met hers. "Nice talk."

"I'll save you a rib," she laughed. "Your girlfriend seems nice."

"She is."

She dove underwater and swam to the shallow end. Her bikini bottom had ridden up her crack and she hooked her finger to tug it down. Her breath caught when Griffin snuck up behind her and said softly, "Need any help?"

Her cheeks grew hot. "No thanks. I doubt your girl-friend would appreciate you groping my ass." Then she climbed up the pool stairs and onto the patio.

She had never been this turned on by someone. *Griffin Bennett.* Noah was right. She couldn't afford to blur the lines. She'd have to be very careful. They needed chemistry for the scenes to come alive and to be believable, however she had to remember that they were actors. In real life she was far from interested in pursuing a relationship with the gorgeous playboy.

13

*P*enelope leaned back in her chair watching the outtakes from last week's shoot. Now four weeks into filming it was undeniable. She and Griffin were H-o-t! They lit up the screen. No reason for false modesty. You either had it or you didn't. They had it. And then some. Noah was not happy about Griffin stealing the scenes. Right about now, he'd switch parts with Griffin in a heartbeat, even if that meant giving up the leading role. He was making that perfectly clear in this meeting.

Noah scowled, arms crossed over his chest, "Look, I may be the actor with the most screen time, but Mr. Fifty Shades is sitting right next to me. I think I got screwed."

"Your part is complicated and dynamic and you're nailing it," Stewart said.

"Yeah Noah, I'm playing a glorified cabana boy,

Sydney's boy toy. Doesn't take nearly the acting chops that your part requires," Griffin added.

"What are you worried about?" Stew asked

"Truthfully? That my career as a leading man is over."

"At forty, you're far too young to be worrying about that."

Penelope threw up her hands, "For Pete's sake! Imagine being a woman in Hollywood! You have a couple dozen more years at least. My shelf life is rapidly approaching."

"I'm quite a bit older than you are," Noah said.

"Still, you know how it is. I'm thirty-two, which is like fifty in terms of available scripts for women. I think you're worrying over nothing. Most actors would kill to be a part of this film, let alone nab the leading role. Your character is complex, and remember, the better Griffin is, the better the film is, the better we are."

"I know all of that. I'm glad he's killing it, it's just that I don't want to come off as the old man."

Penelope kept a poker face as much as it pained her too. She wanted to laugh. His ego was enormous, and they all had to baby him like he was a twelve-year-old boy. *Men!*

"Noah, think Oscar! You're that good. Leading man verses supporting role? You're due for another nod and I think this is the vehicle to take you there," Penelope said firmly.

"I agree," Stew chimed in.

They could see Noah's jaw soften and she and Griffin exchanged a look. Her lips twitched. The corner of his mouth tugged up and he winked. Her stomach flip-flopped. An unexpected shot of pleasure coursed through her at the intimacy of the moment.

"Griffin, Penelope, we're on schedule to shoot your first sex scene toward the end of the week. Are we clear about the contract? Any questions or objections? Have you both read ahead to the blocking?"

Griffin cleared his throat, "Yes sir."

"Yes," Penelope said. "No one but Griffin and I and the two camera operators allowed on set."

Stewart smiled, "Aren't you forgetting someone?"

She laughed, "Oh yeah, you."

"Griffin, I'm sure you're a bit nervous, but Penelope is a seasoned professional and she's had experience with nude scenes. She'll coach you through it. It helps that it's a closed set. We'll make sure everyone is as comfortable as possible."

"I just hope my ass is buff enough for the part," he joked, and everyone laughed, breaking the tension.

"Nobody will be looking at you anyway," Noah said.

Griffin stretched his arms overhead, chuckling. "One hundred percent true."

"Today we finish the fight scene between Noah and Penelope, then if that goes smoothly, we'll try to film the beach scene with you and Griff," he said, looking at Penelope.

She nodded and stood grabbing her script. "I'm going to my dressing room to have Dolly start on my makeup."

"Be on set at half past," Stew said glancing at his watch. "That gives you forty-five minutes."

"Done."

"When should I check back in?" Griffin asked.

"I'm going to say around two. If we're way behind, I'll have someone text you."

Griffin saluted everyone and left, and Penelope felt deflated when he walked out. Not good. Not good at all. She glanced up and caught Noah watching her and her face got hot. His eyes strayed to her breasts and lingered before bringing his attention back to what Stew was saying. She abruptly pushed her chair back and stomped out of the room.

$\sim$

*G*riffin jumped onto his motorcycle and decided to head home. He thought he'd hop on his board to catch an hour of windsurfing. A quick sail was just what he needed to blow off steam. Perfect weather and he had several hours to play before he was due back on set. Plenty of time.

He'd started to feel antsy after he and Penelope had exchanged that intimate moment during the meeting. It had taken him by surprise when she'd looked at him like they were both in on some private joke.

Was she actually softening toward him? And when the hell had that happened? There had been a definite thaw since the party, but today seemed to be next-level. Scared the shit out of him. He'd always been the one in control of his emotions. Never go too deep...when things get serious...time to bail.

Somehow, he doubted that he'd be able to put this genie back in the bottle once it was released. He'd read through their sex scene about thirty times. He'd also read their individual contracts, and the scene required them both to be nude except for a small cloth bag tied around his dick. No body doubles. Him and Penelope in bed...together...buck naked. He scrubbed his face with his hands. *Jesus take the wheel*, he thought dryly.

He changed into his trunks and headed out to the garage. He'd caught the sailboarding bug in his teens and since moving back, the ocean was his back yard and he took full advantage. Pretty damn convenient.

In no time he was out on the water sailing. Keeping close to the beach, he stayed in the lower levels of water. The conditions were perfect, and he sailed cross-wind with good power. Bending his legs like a spring, he popped the board out of the water. His muscles strained as he deftly powered the sail. It was the best workout there was.

There were a few others out on their boards, but today he kept to himself. He craved the solitude after the intimacy of the movie set. After an hour on the water his quads and arms trembled with fatigue, his cue to head back to shore. He hauled his equipment back to the garage and went in to shower off the sea salt.

As he lathered his chest and arms, he remembered Penelope touching him and the intoxicating scent of her. He had three days to get his shit together before their first erotic scene. He'd read that some actors used alcohol to loosen up before a scene like this. He smiled, maybe a bottle of whiskey on set was a good idea. Just in case.

14

*P*enelope watched as Griffin paced the room, waiting for the crew to finish setting up their bedroom scene. She had managed to eat several bites of toast for breakfast, but her stomach was so full of butterflies that she'd barely gotten that down. She envied Griffin his confidence in broadcasting his nervousness. She was the opposite and kept it all bottled up inside.

"Everybody, clear the set." Stew looked over at Penelope as Dolly put the last finishing touches to her makeup and left the room. "Are you ready Pen?" She nodded. "Griff?"

"Ready as I'll ever be," he said.

"Places," Stewart called.

Griffin took a deep breath and concentrated on channeling his character Bryan. He faced Penelope and she smiled.

"You've got this," she reassured him.

He grimaced, "No promises."

"Action," Stewart announced.

*B*ryan tenderly stroked Sydney's face, running the pad of his thumb over her kiss swollen lips. *"I can't fight it any longer. You win."*

"He'll be out of town the entire weekend. We have the place all to ourselves."

"I don't even care anymore. I have to have you."

"I'm yours. Take me Bryan," she said breathlessly.

His large, tanned hands stroked her, caressing her shoulders then sliding down her back. He groped her bottom and squeezed, pulling her tightly against his pelvis. She slipped her arms around his neck and pulled his head down for a torrid kiss. He cupped the back of her head as he plundered her mouth. Lifting his head, his eyes smoldering with lust, he peeled her shirt slowly up her torso. She raised her arms overhead so he could pull it off.

She took his breath away. A magnificent creature. Almost too beautiful to be real. His finger slid under her bra strap and he pulled it down over her shoulder and softly kissed her there. He could feel her chest rise and fall as her breath quickened. He picked her up and carried her to the bed. Ripping off his tee shirt and pants, the camera zoomed in on his muscular back and buttocks.

He unzipped her pants and slid them down the long length of her thighs, leaving her bare except for her lacy bra and panties. Trailing kisses over her torso and belly, he nuzzled her through the silk when he reached her apex. He licked his way back up to her ripe cleavage and buried his head between her breasts. Reaching under her, he unfas-

tened her bra and her breasts spilled out. He swallowed. Five seconds of exposure before he shielded her from the camera with his body.

She gripped the sheet in her balled-up fists and arched her back, crying out, "Bryan, please now."

Positioning himself over her, his full buttocks on display, he faked entering her and began to thrust. His back and arm muscles bulged as he held himself over her. Pinning her arms over her head with one hand, she moaned and bit her lip, her eyes tightly closed. "Look at me," he commanded.

She looked up at him through her lashes. "Tell me you're mine," he said, his voice hoarse.

"Yes, Bryan. I'm all yours."

He groaned as they both feigned orgasms.

"Cut!"

Griffin whispered, "I'm so sorry."

"I told you it's okay." She didn't meet his eyes.

Griffin wrapped the sheet around her before he rolled off the bed. With his back to the crew he slipped on his jeans. "I need a minute." He walked off the set and went into another room and dropped to the floor and began doing pushups.

Dolly came back on set and handed Penelope her a robe. "Let me touch up your lips. Pen, you're shivering. Are you okay?"

Trying to stop her teeth from chattering, she said, "That was intense."

"I'm sure. Not every actor can pull it off."

"I found myself becoming aroused. I swear it was like the cameras weren't even there."

"What about him?"

"Same." Her lips turned up. "Poor Griffin can't hide it like I can; fortunately, I don't have the tell."

"No wonder he's in the other room doing pushups," Dolly whispered, grinning.

Penelope suddenly got the case of the giggles and couldn't stop. Picturing Griffin doing pushups was beyond funny to her. She held her belly, breathless, as she said, "Oh I needed that."

"Get a grip, he's walking towards us."

Griffin came right up to them. Looking at Penelope with a penetrating gaze, he said, "Can I have a minute?"

"Sure." He grabbed her hand and pulled her along behind him.

"Let's go outside," he said.

He didn't release her hand until they found a spot away from everyone else.

Griffin reached toward her and tucked a strand of hair behind her ear. "I'm really sorry about what happened in there. I mean no disrespect. I know I should be able to contain it, but with you it appears I don't have any control."

"The important thing is that you're taking responsibility for it. You're human. We women are lucky that we don't wear our arousal on the outside like you guys do," she said, looking up at him through her lashes.

"Are you saying that the scene was hard for you too?"

"If it's any consolation, yes."

He grasped her chin and tilted her face up. "Were you aroused Penelope Winters?"

She met his gaze boldly this time. "Yes."

His face creased with a smile, "Thank God! You don't know how relieved I am to hear you say that. I'm so fucking confused right now. This acting shit is hard. I want to be in character but then I'm not sure where Bryan ends and I begin. How do you do it?"

"Some scenes are harder than others. True chemistry isn't faked. We just need to harness it and use it to make our characters come alive. Then put it back in the box when the director calls cut."

"I'm not sure I can do that."

"You're already doing it Griffin, don't you see? We're having a logical discussion about it. We're both fully aware of what's happening between us on set and not expecting it to spill over into our personal lives."

"You sound so sure, but I've got to be honest with you, I'm not leaving it on the set. I think about you all the time. I want to know you. I want to spend time with you off the set."

"That's a terrible idea Griffin. Trust me. Lots of actors fall into that trap. They start relationships when filming...it's only natural, you spend long hours together, you're on the same team working on a common goal, you develop relationships because it's so damn intimate."

"Why not us?"

"What about your girlfriend?"

He looked at her, puzzled. "What girlfriend?"

"Isabella, I think that was her name. You brought her to the party."

"She's just a friend. She's engaged to my best friend. He was out of town, so she agreed to be my plus one."

Penelope chewed on her bottom lip, "I see. Well, anyway, as I was saying, when filming stops, all the reasons why it seemed like a good idea disappear. Then what? Do we really have anything in common? Throw in the utter craziness of fame, paparazzi invading your lives, crazed fans, no privacy at all...We can't let our thinking get clouded by the circumstances."

"Is that your final answer?" Penelope looked away from the disappointment she saw in his eyes.

"Yes, but we can be friends."

"Tell that to my heart," he said. "I'm not feeling the friend vibe Penelope. I want to take you out on a date. Just you and me. No crew, no set, no camera. I'm a pilot...I've got my own plane. I can whisk us the hell out of here. No one will find us. Please think about it. Would you at least do that for me?"

She sighed, "I'll think about it. Full disclosure, I don't have a very high opinion of men at the moment. You might want to take that into consideration."

He laughed heartily. "Shocking."

She punched his arm playfully. "We'd better get back to the set. This next scene should be easier since we've had a go at it."

"Yeah, you naked is so boring now."

It was all Penelope could do not to throw herself into his arms and kiss those sexy lips. Unfortunately, that was exactly what she'd be doing in a few minutes. She could hardly wait for this day to be over and yet contrarily...part of her never wanted it to end.

15

---

*T*he set was cleared of extras again for the last shoot of the day, and Penelope and Griffin crawled back into bed together, naked again. This time there was something different about him... Penelope could tell he felt surer of where he stood. He seemed bolder and more confident.

When he smiled into her eyes there was an intimacy and warmth that hadn't been there before their talk. Her pulse quickened and she felt dampness between her legs.

"Action."

"I love you Syd. You've got to leave your husband. This is no life for you...for us."

"That's never been on the table. I told you that up front, Bryan. This is all it can ever be."

"That's bullshit!" he said angrily. "Are you denying that you don't feel the same?"

"It doesn't matter what I feel. There's too much at stake. When you're serving in the Senate, your life is no longer your own. It's a service bigger than our pathetic little lives."

"Boy has he ever got you brainwashed."

"I knew what I was getting into when I married him."

"Did you? You were just a kid; how could you have known? Listen to me, we'll move away, out of the limelight. I'll take care of you."

"Bryan!" she said sharply. "Stop...just stop."

He held her face between his palms and covered her lips with his, roughly pushing his tongue inside her mouth while she struggled to get out from under him. She tried turning her head away only to have him grip her face harder.

"No!" She tore at his hands and thrashed underneath him, kicking out wildly.

"Isn't this what you want? A fuckbuddy? Well you've got him." He shoved her legs apart and thrust wildly. With one last shove she managed to push him off her and she scrambled out of bed, pulling the sheet with her. Lips trembling and eyes shimmering with tears, she turned her back to him.

He punched the pillow and swore, then stood up and wrapped his arms around her from behind. He cupped her breasts through the sheets holding her. Her legs were weak and unsteady. He nibbled her neck and murmured, "Babe, I'm sorry I got angry. We'll do it your way. I'll take anything I can get."

She turned in his arms to face him, rubbing her cheek against the soft hair on his chest. The scene called for one last kiss. She pulled his head down then slipped her arms around his waist holding him tightly.

This time Penelope was expecting a response from Griffin and when it didn't happen, she felt let down. *OMG girl! You'd better get your shit together. You're making a film...This isn't real life.*

"Cut. It's a wrap for today. Great job you two. We'll meet to go over the dailies tomorrow morning. Be at the hotel by nine."

Griffin held the arms of Penelope's robe so she could slip it on.

"We'll be there," he said.

They were given a couple of minutes to dress before the rest of the crew trickled in to tear down. Griffin turned his back so she could put her clothes on.

"Need a ride?" Griffin asked over his shoulder.

"I usually ride with Dolly or Stew, but she probably already left since it was our last scene...that'd be great."

They walked out together, and he handed her his helmet. "Where's yours?" she asked.

He mounted the bike, "No helmet laws here; jump on."

She got on behind him and put her arms around his taut waist. He covered her hand with his for a brief moment before starting the bike. He pulled onto the scenic road that ran parallel to the ocean and went full throttle. She hung on, thrilled with the speed. She gripped him tightly with her thighs as he rounded a sharp curve.

He yelled over the noise of the bike and wind rushing around them, "You can keep doing that."

She laughed feeling free for the first time since

she'd left Montana. "I'll keep that in mind." She couldn't resist flattening her palms against his toned belly and resting them just below his navel. Her whole body tingled.

When they got to her place, he walked her to the door. Holding the bare soft flesh of her upper arms he gently pulled her against his chest then ran his palms down her back resting them on her hips. Her face pressed into his chest and she breathed in the manly scent of him...musky...spicy...earthy. Her body softening, she allowed herself one fleeting moment of surrender before mentally shaking herself out of it.

With his chin resting against the top of her head, he said, "The lines are definitely blurred for me. I want you Penelope, Bryan gets to have you and I don't. Lucky Bryan."

"I don't know what to say to make it all clearer for you, because frankly in some ways, it's easier to do these scenes with someone you're not attracted to in real life."

He chuckled. "There is that."

"It will all work out. You'll see. Quit worrying...oh and thanks for the ride Griff."

His eyes burned with desire, "Penelope..."

"Griffin, please don't complicate things. I'll see you tomorrow."

"One kiss. Please. I need to feel the real thing, us, Griffin and Penelope, not Bryan and Sydney." Before she could protest, he swooped down and covered her mouth with his. She stiffened at first, then her lips parted to receive him. Feeling his hardness pressing into her belly was by now, oddly familiar and definitely pleasurable. She let the sensation of his tongue probing her mouth carry her away until she found the willpower to pull away. He reluctantly released her, his breathing ragged and eyes scorching her skin with their intensity.

Without a word she turned and bolted into the house. Locking the door behind her, she leaned back against it. Had it only been five weeks since she'd arrived here? It seemed like months ago. She touched her mouth with her fingertips, taking in a shaky breath. What had she gotten herself into? She should have kept up her guard. It wasn't too late. Tomorrow was a new day

Tomorrow...she suddenly remembered that she had another sex scene, only this time it was with Noah. She dreaded it. He wasn't too happy with the friendship developing between her and Griffin. He'd been sulking around the set like a child. Too bad. She hoped he'd be able to contain his jealousy.

It was inappropriate and annoying. So far, he'd kept things professional, but she could see his control beginning to slip. She'd worry about that when and if they got there. Meanwhile she'd put some distance between Griffin and her. That settled, she grabbed a bottle of wine from the fridge and two glasses and went to find Dolly.

~

riffin pulled away with steel in his pants. He had a feeling he was going to have a hard-on for the next two months. He was restless as hell. Tired but wired. Normally he'd call some random girl and wine and dine them. But that was the last thing he wanted tonight. All he could see were a pair of large bottomless pools of green, and plump lush lips.

He was glad they didn't have any more scenes together until next week. At least he thought he was glad...fuck, he didn't know up from down right now. If someone had told him a month ago that he'd be lying naked in bed with Penelope Winters, he would have had them committed. He'd had some wild adventures in his life, but this was definitely the craziest.

He'd only have to stick around tomorrow until they'd reviewed today's shoot, unless they had to redo something, then he'd be a free agent until Monday. A whole weekend off. Maybe he could convince Penelope to take him up on his offer.

Like he was on auto pilot, his bike headed in the direction of his sister's bar. A Faye fix was exactly what he needed right now. She always knew what to say to bring him back to earth. A couple of beers to drink a hard day off, then home. He didn't go looking for this trouble but here he was.

16

*G*riffin slouched in his seat with his arms crossed as he watched the daily outtakes of their love scenes from the previous day. The raw unedited footage was good. Watching himself make love to Penelope onscreen was weird. He had to admit, they were convincing. Who was he kidding? Very little acting going on there. The heat was not feigned.

He glanced from the corner of his eye at Penelope, who sat next to him. Other than her balled up fists, she showed no outward sign of emotion. She appeared to be disengaged.

Stew sat sandwiched between her and the assistant director. Also watching was the director of photography, as well as first and second camera assistants. The script supervisor and her assistant were there as well. A few of the support crew had joined them out of curiosity. Dolly along with the rest of 'The Glam Squad' were in attendance.

Since the hotel had virtually become their studio, it served as their conference room, theater, the actors dressing rooms, cafeteria, and production headquarters. He was continually amazed by how many people were involved behind the scenes. From sound to special effects, visual effects, craft services and caterers, not to mention location managers and assistants, it was an impressive operation. He was excited to be a part of it all. There was a natural camaraderie from the common goal of producing a great film.

Griffin shifted slightly, leaning into Penelope's shoulder. He wanted to see what kind of reaction he'd get. She stiffened and put space between them. He smiled inwardly. Not as detached as she'd have him believe. *Good.* Emboldened, he stretched his arms overhead then casually draped one arm along the back of her chair.

Leaning in, he whispered, "Have you thought about my proposition?"

"No," she said, looking straight ahead.

His breath stirred her hair as he murmured, "Liar." He saw a smile tugging at the corners of her lips.

Noah sat in the row behind them and leaned forward to whisper, "Nice job you two. It'll be a hard act to follow, but I'm looking forward to the challenge this afternoon."

Griffin saw Penelope's fists tighten and he turned his head to glare at Noah. "You could at least attempt to be classy."

"Fuck you," he hissed. "You think you're some hot shot now because you're the director's new darling?"

Griffin shook his head in disgust and turned his attention back to the screen. They were reviewing the part where Bryan becomes angry with Sydney. Griffin thought they'd put out a good performance. Overall, once he'd adjusted to seeing himself, he could say somewhat objectively that they'd captured their characters.

When the video ended, everyone erupted in applause. "That pretty much sums it up. We have a huge hit on our hands folks," Stew said, beaming.

Griffin said, "Hear that Pen? Not just a hit...but a huge hit."

Ignoring him, Penelope stood and turned toward Stew. "I'm going to my dressing room. Page me when you're ready to start shooting."

"Don't you want to join us at the buffet?"

"I'm not hungry, thanks."

"You've got to eat."

"I'll eat an energy bar back in my room."

"See you in about an hour then," Stewart said.

She left without another word to Griffin. Noah chuckled, "Don't take it personally. She can be one cold bitch."

"Don't ever call her that again or I'll wipe that smirk right off your face," Griffin said, steel in his voice.

Noah laughed. "You're a fool if you think you have a shot at that. Dream on."

"With you as her last lover, I'm not surprised she's turned off by men," Griffin said over his shoulder as he left the room.

~

*P*enelope practically ran to her dressing room. She closed the door behind her and sat in the chair facing her vanity. Between her dread of the upcoming scene with Noah and her aching response to Griffin, she was a ball of nerves. She ripped the wrapper from her energy bar with unsteady hands. She hoped the skipped breakfast was partially to blame for her shakiness.

There was a tap at the door and before she could respond, Jack, the script supervisor's assistant walked in. He held out a bottle of water. "Here, the director said to keep hydrated."

She reached back for it, looking at him from the mirror's reflection. "Thanks Jack."

He stood behind her and placed his hands on her shoulders. "You're so tense," he began kneading. "You could use a massage."

"I'm fine." She tried shrugging him off.

"I'm sure those nude scenes are intense. Griffin is my new hero. I don't know how he can keep his cool." He continued massaging her shoulders.

Penelope grew increasingly uncomfortable with him touching her. "Please, I'm sorry but I need to be alone to study my lines before the next scene."

He suddenly leaned forward and slid one hand down the front of her chest to grope her breast. Her breath hissed and she stood abruptly. Whirling around, she slapped him hard across the face. The crack rang out and left an angry red mark.

He covered his cheek with his palm as his eyes

darkened with rage. "You've been flirting with me for days and now you want to act all virtuous?"

"Flirting with you? Where did you ever get that idea? Get out now! You have two seconds, or I start screaming at the top of my lungs."

His eyes glittered. "Maybe you changed your mind about me when you got a little action from your costar, but you won't convince me that you weren't leading me on. By the way, I'll deny that this ever happened if you decide to report me."

Voice trembling with anger, she pointed to the door. "Get out!"

He left, slamming the door behind him. She collapsed into her chair and buried her face in her hands. She felt like she was going to throw up. Were all men incapable of thinking apart from their dicks?

She racked her brain trying to recall anything she might have said or done to make Jack believe she was interested or leading him on. She knew that there wasn't. He'd conjured up what he wanted to believe to fit his narrative. This wasn't the first time a male had projected his fantasies onto her. She wasn't sure how she should handle it.

She jerked when she heard another knock at the door. She didn't want anyone to see her like this. "Who is it?"

"It's me, Griffin."

Her chest ached, "I'm busy right now. Can we talk later?"

He must have heard something in her voice, because he said, "Are you alright?"

"Yes, I'm fine. Please, go."

"I need to ask you a quick question, I promise I'll leave after that."

She got up and cracked the door, "What?"

Griffin studied her face, his eyes flashed with concern. "Have you been crying?"

She sniffled. "I'm fine. Just one of those days."

"Let me in."

"No."

"Penelope, please. Don't make me stand out here in the hall."

She reluctantly stepped back and let him in. His eyes narrowed, "What happened?"

"Nothing you need to concern yourself with."

"Sorry, it doesn't work like that."

"What did you have to tell me that couldn't wait?"

His brow furrowed as he studied her face. "I'm leaving and I wanted a chance to convince you to get out of Dodge for a day. This weekend. With me. No strings, no agenda. I'll be the perfect gentleman."

"Can you just hold me?" He looked so surprised that she couldn't help but smile. He pulled her against him, and she melted into his tight embrace.

"What's wrong? Why were you crying?" he asked, while stroking her hair. "Can you talk about it?"

"I can't, not yet."

"Did I do something to hurt you?"

"I...no...I'm okay," her breath hitched.

"Whatever it is, I'm available anytime you want to talk about it."

"I'm sorry," she said, wiping her nose on her sleeve.

Griffin grabbed a tissue, keeping one arm wrapped

around her. "Here, blow." He held the tissue to her nose.

She blew into the handkerchief like a child, then chuckled at the absurdity of it all. "I feel like a big baby."

"You're allowed to express emotions off the set too," he said quietly.

"If I confide in you, you have to promise you won't tell anyone and you won't take matters into your own hands."

"I have a feeling that I'm not going to like whatever it is you're about to say."

"Promise me."

He looked heavenward. "Okay I promise."

"One of the assistants barged in and was sexually inappropriate with me."

His blue eyes darkened as he said through gritted teeth, "Did he touch you?"

She nodded her head. "He said I'd been leading him on, but I swear to you there is no way."

He tilted her chin up to gaze into her eyes, "You don't have to convince me. I've seen your interactions with the crew, and you're nothing but professional."

"What do you think I should do?"

"Tell Stew," he said without hesitation.

"He'll be fired."

"As he should be."

"Will you go with me?"

"Yes."

"Should I tell him now?"

"Yes. That dude should be thrown off the premises immediately. It was Jack, wasn't it?"

Her eyes widened. "How did you know?"

"I've seen him ogling you."

"What is wrong with me? Why didn't I see it?"

"You weren't looking. So now you're going to blame yourself because a guy's brain is in his dick?"

She wrinkled her nose, her lips turning up at the corners. "I guess not."

"If you're ready, we'll go find Stew."

She took a deep breath and forced a smile. "Let's get this over with."

Griffin grabbed her hand and held on tight as they went to find the director.

17

*I*t took a lot to get Stewart Abrams riled up, but his face turned scarlet as he listened to Penelope relay the incident in her dressing room.

"That son of a bitch. He won't work in this industry again."

"I'm sorry."

"You're sorry? I'm sorry. You should be able to feel safe with your own fucking team. I'll take care of this immediately. We'll postpone filming your scenes until Monday. Take the weekend to relax and put this behind you."

"Stewart, thank you for believing me without question."

"Anyone with a brain could figure that out. Don't let it get to you, kid."

"I'll try not to."

He looked at Griffin. "Can you take her home?"

"Absolutely."

He clapped Griffin on the back, "Thanks for convincing her to come to me immediately. It was the right call."

"Have a good weekend and thanks for taking care of this," Griffin said.

They left him barking into his phone at his script supervisor to get her assistant Jack and report to his office immediately.

"I like Stew," Griffin said.

"He's been like a father to me. This is the third film I've done with him."

"Want to grab a bite to eat? If you have a hat and sunglasses we can try for incognito."

"We could get carryout and eat back at my place."

"Sold."

When he opened the car door to the Audi R8 Vio Spyder, she gaped at him.

"Is this your car?"

"Yeah, do you like it?"

"It's a two hundred thousand-dollar car!"

"A car enthusiast, huh?"

"Somewhat. It's the car Christian Grey drove in *Fifty Shades*."

"I had it first," he said grinning wolfishly, revealing perfect white teeth.

"But how?"

"How what?"

"I'm sorry, I'm being rude."

"Go ahead, ask me anything."

"How does one afford such a car? I mean what do you do when you're not shooting a movie? I know that chamber guy said you came from a prominent family but..."

"I was born into it. Old money. Then my dad capitalized on his good fortune and catapulted the Bennett portfolio into the stratosphere. He built the company into what it is today. I can't take any credit for it. The company plans and develops billion-dollar properties. Think shopping complexes, stadiums...designer complexes."

"You're full of surprises. Why did you even agree to be in the film?"

"Truth? Boredom...adventure...something new... honestly, I didn't think I'd get the part...but here we are."

She buckled herself in as he peeled out of the parking lot, going from zero to forty in a millisecond. Her pulse raced with the sensation from the raw power of the vehicle.

"What suits your fancy?" he asked.

"Pizza."

He raised a brow. "Seriously?"

"Yes."

"I know just the place, and we won't need to carry out."

He pressed a talk button on the steering wheel and said, "Call Faye."

Faye's voice came through the car speakers, "The Pelican."

"Hey sis. Are you busy?"

"Just Jesse, Ty and me."

"Can you put a 'be back in an hour' sign on your door? I'm bringing Penelope."

"Sure. We've been slow since we opened anyway."

"Could you throw a pizza in the oven?" He glanced over at Penelope. "Pepperoni okay with you?" She nodded yes.

"Pepperoni, please."

"Now?"

"Yeah we're on our way, see ya in five."

"They don't have to go to all that trouble," Penelope said.

"Are you kidding me? My sister is probably flipping out as we speak."

"I really liked her place."

"Yeah they've put a ton of work into it. When my sister bought it last year, it was an old dilapidated building. At one time, it was the favorite dive bar of the locals. Faye and Jesse, her fiancé, have brought it back to life."

The large brightly-colored Pelican on the roof of the bar was an inviting touch. He pulled right up to the entrance and hustled her inside, locking the door behind them. She remembered the tall willowy blond from the night she'd been in. Faye hugged Griffin then turned to greet her.

"So glad to get to properly meet you," Faye said.

"Me too."

"I'm sorry if I'm a little star struck. I've loved all of your films. Not to sound too cliché, but I'm a huge fan."

A gorgeous guy with a mop of coppery brown hair and eyes the most unusual whisky color she'd ever seen, came out from the back room drying his hands on a bar towel.

"This is Jesse, my fiancé," Faye said shyly, reaching for his hand. "I'm still not used to calling him that."

"Hi, I'm Penelope," she said.

"I can't wait to write in my diary tonight," Jesse said, flashing a wide friendly smile.

"I'm sorry Griffin sprung this on you both."

"Don't be. We're thrilled to have you. I feel a little embarrassed serving you a frozen pizza, but my chef doesn't come in until five," Faye said, flustered.

Penelope laughed. "I don't mind. I eat frozen pizza all the time."

"Yo!" They all turned as Faye and Griffin's nephew Ty came in. He was lugging a keg of draft beer to switch out, bare-chested, his ripped body and tribal ink displayed in all its glory.

"Hey Ty," Griffin said. "I've got someone you might like to meet."

He loped over and stopped like he'd been hit with a stun gun. "No fucking way!"

"Ty, meet Penelope Winters."

"Dude, this isn't happening."

"This is our nephew Tyler."

Penelope took off her sunglasses and smiled into his eyes. "Wow, Ty. Have you thought about a career in film or modeling?"

He straightened and puffed out his chest a little, "That's what my girlfriend Addison is always telling me."

"If you'd be interested in a walk-on part with no lines, I know we need some extras. That goes for all three of you."

"That would be sick! What about my girl?"

"Sure, it would just be a bar scene or a crowd, but it would give you a taste."

"Hell yeah...that is if my boss will let me off." He raised his eyebrows at Faye.

"Like I can ever say no to you." She rolled her eyes and looked at Penelope. "He has me wrapped around his little finger."

"That's what aunts are for, right Ty?" Penelope said, winking at him.

He clutched his heart dramatically and took several steps back. "Is this really happening?"

"You're a clown, you know that?" Jesse playfully pushed Ty as he walked toward the kitchen. "I'm going to make sure the pizza isn't burnt. Get that keg switched out, Ty."

"Can I get a selfie with you before you leave?" Tyler asked her.

"Yes. Only if you share it with me. By the way I love your ink!"

"Thanks," he beamed.

Faye said, "Where are my manners? What would you like to drink? Griffin you want to sit outside on the deck?"

"Yes. Perfect."

"Go on out, I'll get your drinks."

"I'll have a Heineken," his hand rested in the curve of Penelope's back, just below her waist. "What would you like?"

Her cheeks grew warm and her skin burned where he touched her. It felt so natural...*warning...warning*...little alarm bells started going off in her head.

She cleared her throat and slipped her sunglasses back on.

"I'll have a vodka and tonic please...with a twist of lime."

"Go sit, you two, I'll be right out with those."

Griffin led her to the deck adjacent to the marina and they sat at a table big enough for all of them. Penelope looked around, "This is really nice. I didn't get to fully appreciate it the first time."

"Yeah, my favorite drinking hole."

"You're so lucky to have family."

"You don't?"

"Nope. My mom passed two years ago, and my dad has never been in the picture. No siblings."

"I'm sorry." He covered her hand that rested on top of the table and unconsciously stroked it with his thumb.

She lifted one shoulder in a shrug, "I am too. I miss her."

"We were raised by nannies and boarding schools, but my brother and sister were always there for me. My parents not so much. How'd your mom die..." Seeing her pained expression he quickly said, "You don't have to talk about it if you don't want to."

"It's okay, it's probably good for me to talk about it. I tend to bottle everything up. She died of breast cancer. She was only fifty-four."

"That really sucks."

Faye set their drinks and plates down and plopped in a chair next to Penelope. "How do you like our little seaside town?"

"I honestly haven't explored much. It becomes a bit of a management problem at times."

"That would be so hard. The loss of freedom."

"It is. Nobody can prepare you for it."

"Did you always want to be an actor?"

"Yeah. I just didn't know there would be such a big price to pay. I'm really not complaining though. It has certainly given me many opportunities most people don't get."

"Am I really sitting here having a normal conversation with Penelope Winters?" Faye said laughing.

Jesse appeared with their pizza and sat down next to his fiancée, planting a sweet kiss on her lips.

Penelope felt a yearning that she quickly tamped down. It wasn't her destiny. The natural gifts that had been bestowed upon her were also the very things that kept her from finding her one true love. It was a trade-off, but it had to be enough. She'd thought she'd found it twice and both times she'd been gutted.

She had vowed to herself after Noah that she'd focus on herself and her career and be thankful for what she had. If she had an occasional twinge of longing, that was only to be expected. She'd learned the hard way that most men weren't to be trusted or counted upon.

She concentrated on managing the cheese that was scalding her tongue and let the warm glow of conversation and alcohol numb her to the niggling voice reminding her of how lonely her life was.

hey rode home with the windows down and the song "Capital Letters" by Hailee Steinfeld and Blood Pop blasting through the speakers. Penelope danced in her seat, singing along. *"But then there was you...coming out of the crowd."*

"I love this song," she yelled over the music. "The sound system is amazing," Penelope said. When he smiled at her like that, she melted a little more each time.

"It'd better be," he said, laughing.

She grabbed his hand and squeezed it, "Thank you."

"The pizza wasn't *that* good."

"It wasn't that bad either. This was exactly what I needed after my run-in today. To be around normal people having normal conversations."

"If you can call any of us normal. Ty just about lost his shit over the selfie. Thanks for being so generous."

She leaned her head back against the car seat and studied Griffin's profile, feeling the beat of the bass pulsating through her body like another heartbeat. His dark hair was a wild mess and she loved the afternoon stubble on his face. It made him even sexier if that was possible. His lashes were unbelievably long and when he smiled his eyes crinkled. Damn him.

"Yes," she yelled, trying to control her windblown hair whipping across her face.

He turned to look at her, one eyebrow arched. "Yes what?"

"Yes, I'll go out with you this weekend."

"Hot damn. I knew Faye was my ace in the hole!"

"As friends. I could use a friend."

"That's as good a start as any." He pulled into her drive and turned off the engine. He sat for a moment without moving, waiting until the song ended, then opened his car door and came around to her side. He bowed and held out his hand. "My lady," he said comically.

"And Stew said you couldn't act."

"I'm crushed my lady. Remove thy beak from my heart."

"A Poe fan, no less."

"Not really, too depressing. Well this is it," he said depositing her at the front door.

"Bye, Griff, see you tomorrow. What time?"

"I'll pick you up at eight. Pack an overnight bag, just in case. Small planes are vulnerable to weather. You never know. I've been caught before."

She frowned, "We won't get stranded, will we?"

"I'll check the weather forecast again before I file the flight plan, we should be fine."

"Where are we going?"

"It's a surprise."

"What should I pack?"

"Pack a swimsuit, a change of clothes...wear a sundress, something casual."

"I can do that."

He reached out and ran his thumb across her bottom lip and her body responded like a thoroughbred at the starting gate. Pulse fluttering, lady parts throbbing, she turned and left him before she did something she'd later regret.

18

*G*riffin had completed his preliminary safety inspections and checklists and was waiting to be cleared for takeoff. Penelope was strapped in next to him, tantalizingly close and cozy in the small cockpit of his four-seater Cessna 172. He glanced over and their gazes locked, her eyes sparkling with excitement. They both had on their headsets with mics, which allowed him to communicate with both air traffic control and with her.

"Have you ever flown in a single-engine?" Griffin asked.

"No. I'm so excited." Her voice sounding slightly tinny through his headset.

"You'll feel more turbulence, so don't freak out."

"I won't."

"I'll do my best to make the trip as smooth as I can."

The headsets crackled as messages were relayed. He

smiled when he was finally cleared for take-off. "Just sit back and enjoy the view. Nothing beats it."

"I've never been to Savannah before," she held up her index finger, "however I want you to know that I did read Midnight in the Garden of Good and Evil. That has to count for something."

He smiled, "We'll be there in about forty-five minutes tops."

His hands skimmed confidently over the controls, his movements fluid and sure. The smaller planes were much louder than commercial jets, but the headsets buffered much of the noise. Once they were cruising, Penelope gazed out the window like an excited child. She laughed out loud when he banked the plane so she could get an even better view of the coastline.

He was happy that they had such great weather; the views from this altitude were stunning. Penelope's eyes were glued to the window and she pointed out something of interest every other minute. The inlets and white sandy beaches, the water sparkling like diamonds, the waterways, were all amazing to see from the air. It was magical.

"This is great! The rivers are amazing, all that lush vegetation surrounding them...so green," she said. Her enthusiasm was contagious and reminded him of how jaded he'd been feeling lately.

"Our company has a private jet and I'll choose this every time if the distance allows it. This has a four-hour fuel capacity. It's like a road trip only in the air."

He was acutely aware of Penelope's every movement. The cockpit was a tight fit and their thighs kept brushing against one another. Her smooth bare legs had him itching to reach over and feel just how soft they were.

The thin strap of her sundress had slipped down one shoulder. The back of his hand brushed up her arm and he hooked a finger underneath and pulled it up. When she moved, he caught tantalizing glimpses of her cleavage.

He liked this view even better than the one out the window. She had pulled her hair up in a high ponytail and as far as he could tell she had worn minimal makeup...if any. She didn't need it. She took his breath away. He couldn't wait to show her Savannah and was grateful that he had her all to himself for a whole day.

The landing was textbook perfect and in no time at all they were parked in the small aviation airport hangar and loading their totes into the rental car waiting for them.

Penelope seemed different somehow...lighter... free...Happy. He hadn't really noticed until now, but she usually seemed subdued on set. The contrast was breathtaking. Her face animated, her smile frequent and dazzling, her laughter sexy as hell. His heart felt like it was lodged in his throat, touched by her childlike delight. He wanted to show her how to play, how to have fun, make her laugh.

"I don't know about you but I'm starving," Griffin said.

"Me too."

"I have a great little place lined up for brunch. A chef friend of mine owns it. It's a Michelin-star restaurant. You won't find better food in the world than you will here in Savannah."

"I believe you. What are we waiting for?" She flashed him a wide grin. He put the convertible Porsche Boxster in gear and sped off.

Griffin regaled her with some of Savannah's rich history and pointed out historical points of interest as they wound through the old city.

"It's really beautiful. I love the Spanish moss and all the old statues. It's so mysterious. Makes me believe in ghosts."

"Is that even a question?" he said laughing. "They even offer ghost tours here." He loved the way her nose crinkled when she smiled at him. "After breakfast we can do the walking tour if that sounds good to you. Then we'll head on over to Tybee Island for some beach time. You know that's where they filmed *The Last song?*"

"I remember hearing that."

"You know what happened during the filming?" He winked at her. Her cheeks turned pink. She obviously knew he was referring to the love affair between the co-stars. He found an empty spot and parallel parked in front of a beautiful old red brick building. "Here we are."

The landscaping around the restaurant beautifully incorporated statues and a fountain with Koi fish swimming lazily at the bottom of the pool. The zinnias lent a riot of color and the purple coneflowers had bees and butterflies sipping the nectar.

He slipped his arm around her waist, resting his hand on the swell of her hip.

"This way."

They walked up the cobblestone pathway and

around to the back. A beautiful, covered courtyard with outdoor seating and not a soul in sight awaited them. Griffin pulled out a chair for her and said, "I'll be right back. I'm going to tell Pierre we're here."

"Okay."

*P*enelope took a long look around, marveling at how different the vibe was in the south compared to anywhere else she'd ever been. Her encounters since she'd arrived for filming had shown her that the southern hospitality, they were so famous for was the real deal. As much as she could tell anyway.

Her fame kept her apart and altered her experiences compared to what most people had. When she was in public, she often felt like she was looking through a glass window, with everyone else on the outside looking in at her. She could rarely let her guard down. Another reason why her Montana ranch was so important to her.

She watched as Griffin approached with a man in a white double-breasted chef's jacket. Griffin looked good enough to eat for breakfast, his faded jeans slung low on his hips with his white polo shirt tucked in. He hadn't shaved...just the way she liked him.

She bit her bottom lip when he threw his head back to laugh at something the chef had said. What was she doing here? This was a mistake that would cost her. He was way too desirable. Those annoying warning bells were going off in her head again like a fire alarm.

"Penelope, this is Pierre. He and my mom knew

each other back in the day, before they both moved to the States," Griffin said.

"*Mademoiselle* Winters, my pleasure," he said, in a heavy French accent. He leaned over her hand, planting a kiss on the back of it.

"So nice to meet you Pierre."

"When Griffin called to request a private dining experience, it was my profound pleasure to prepare a meal for such an honored guest."

Eyes wide, she put a hand to her throat. "Private?"

"*Oui, Mademoiselle*, I must return to the kitchen to put the finishing touches to your brunch." He bowed then backed away, leaving she and Griffin alone again.

"Griffin, this is way too much. You really shouldn't have gone to all this trouble."

He sat back in his chair and laced his fingers behind his head, giving her a great view of his muscular arms. As if she needed to be reminded. A sudden flash of their on-set lovemaking flitted through her mind and she felt her face heat up.

"Well, have I impressed you yet?"

"Griffin, I don't want to lead you on...friends remember?"

"I remember, but I don't believe you. I think you want me as much as I want you...which by the way, is a hell of a lot."

"Even if I were ready to start something, which I'm not, you're too big a risk. You're a player, Griffin."

"I'm not going to lie to you, I've never been inclined to settle down. The grass has always been greener on the other side. Always chasing the next shiny object...always fighting an inner restlessness...

but right now, from where I'm sitting, I'm right where I want to be. I'm in the greenest pasture I've ever seen."

She raised a skeptical eyebrow. "It always feels that way in the beginning. People think of me in a certain way, they assume that they know me because they've seen me in a film or two. But I'm not that person, it's a character I play. It's a big letdown when they find out that I'm just a normal human being, with the same foibles as everyone else."

"I understand that. And I am captivated, intrigued. But I want to get beyond that armor you've got up."

"Griffin, I'm the shiny object right now...I'm something new and interesting. It's a challenge and all that, I get it, but I just can't allow myself to be the new toy in your toybox."

"I could say the same about you. You're around all the glitter and glam, handsome leading men, fans swooning over you, men lusting...fantasizing. I'd be taking a risk too...but how will we know if it could be more unless we try?"

Penelope crossed her arms, eyes narrowed. "I've been with two men in my entire life. Can you say the same?"

His eyes widened in shock. "Really?"

"Yes really."

"Wow. Who'd have ever thought."

"See, that's my point. You see me in these torrid onscreen romances, then assume I'm the nymphomaniac of your dreams. Instead I'm just an ordinary person."

His blue eyes were bottomless as he boldly met her

gaze. "Hardly ordinary. I find you fascinatingly extraordinary."

A waiter appeared with a pitcher of fresh squeezed orange juice and two glass bowls of honeyed fruit salad. "Could I interest either of you in a Bloody Mary or a Mimosa?"

Griffin said, "I'm going to pass since I'll be flying us back, but why don't you indulge?"

"Yes, I'll have a Mimosa please."

"I'll be right back with that *Mademoiselle.*"

A different waiter appeared with a tray of flaky, layered French pastries. Penelope's mouth watered as she eyed them. She moaned audibly as he placed a plate in front of her. He'd barely retreated before she picked it up. She glanced up and caught Griffin staring. *Busted.*

"I love your enthusiasm," he said, his voice warm and amused.

Embarrassed, she defended herself, "I haven't had one bite to eat today."

"It's not a criticism. I mean it. I love watching you. It's like seeing a kid in Willy Wonka's Chocolate Factory."

"Gee thanks," she said, feeling slightly awkward.

"You're welcome."

She took her first bite of the pastry and looked up to see both waiters carrying enough food to feed the entire film crew. French crepes, classic French merguez —which, Griffin pointed out, were essentially fancy sausage—quiche, cheese slices, bacon, yogurt and granola, French toast with three flavors of syrup.

The minute they left, she said, "Oh my God! In two

days, I'll be naked in front of a camera again. What are you trying to do to me?"

"We'll walk it off."

"Are we walking all the way back to North Carolina then?"

"Dig in."

"Oh, I'm going to, you don't have to worry about that."

They both put their heads down and ate like it was their last meal.

~

*G*riffin glanced over at Penelope as they soared three thousand feet above the earth. She'd fallen asleep within minutes of them taking off. He'd wanted to get back home before nightfall, so they'd packed in as much as they could. After brunch they'd been too full to do much of anything, so they'd hit Tybee Island first and lazed around the beach for several hours before exploring Savannah. All in all, it had been an incredible day.

*H*e brushed his fingers up and down her arm. "Wake up sleepy head, we're here."

She opened her eyes slowly and stretched her arms overhead, yawning. "I slept through the landing?"

"Yep, alcohol at brunch sets the tone for the day, laid back and easy," he said.

"I'm sorry for this day to end," she said wistfully.

He tweaked her nose. "We'll do it again. Now I'll

deliver you back to your castle before you turn into a pumpkin."

"Willy Wonka, Cinderella, you'll make a great dad someday."

His eyes flickered inscrutably before he reached for their bags and opened the plane exit door. The drive home was a quiet one, both deep into their own thoughts.

At the door he dropped off her bag and quickly departed. No hug...no kiss. Platonic, like she'd requested. Then why was she so disappointed? Archie raced to greet her, jumping up enthusiastically. She picked him up and cradled him in her arms as he licked her face. She sighed, "At least I have one guy that loves me unconditionally."

She put him down and went to find Dolly. Thank God for friends.

19

*P*enelope's hands shook as she stared at the words written in garish red marker, scrawled across her face on the magazine cover. *Whore.* Nice. And the superimposed penis sticking out of her mouth was so original. Truly the work of an artistic genius. Way to start a Monday morning.

Someone had slipped it under her dressing room door sometime between last Friday and today. It had been sealed in a plain manilla envelope with her name printed neatly on the front. She didn't have to think too long or hard about who that someone could have been. Jack. Of course, he blamed her for getting fired; it was easier than looking at his own disgusting behavior.

She slipped her shirt off then stepped out of her jeans and underwear. She grabbed the satin and lace corset and pulled it on leaving the garter straps dangling, then slipped on the matching panty.

"Knock, knock," Dolly said as she entered. She'd

arrived to do her hair and makeup before the morning shoot.

Penelope grabbed the magazine and thrust it toward Dolly.

Dolly's brows drew together. "Where did this come from?"

"I found it about ten minutes ago, when I walked into the room."

"We have to find Stew. Can you text him?"

"No. I'm not going to bother him with this. I'm becoming a pain in the ass. Look, we know this is about Jack and his ego. He fucked up and now no one will hire him. He's got to blame someone."

"Stew needs to know."

"I'm ready to put that whole thing behind me. Jack is trying to pay me back by scaring me. I'm not partaking. I won't let him get to me Dolly. If I do then he's won."

Dolly glanced at her watch. "We'd better get a move on. You're due on set in forty minutes."

"Yeah, a big sex scene with Noah. Joy. He's been acting so weird lately."

"He's jealous and he knows how badly he screwed up. He's still in love with you, Penny."

Raking her hands through her thick blond hair, she blew out a long breath, "I know. Not much I can do about it."

"You're right. It's not your problem."

"He's trying to make it mine."

"My advice is to ignore him. Do your scenes, let him get his petty jabs in and move on."

"You're right."

"No wonder you hate men," Dolly said.

Penelope leaned over and pulled up the sheer black stocking, fastening it to the garner belt in the front. "Can you hand me the other stocking?" Dolly tossed it to her.

"Hurry up and finish getting dressed so I can get your hair and makeup done in time."

Penelope stood and attached the back garter straps to her nylons, then slipped on her silk robe, knotting the tie at her waist. "I'm ready. All I have to do is dig out my black stilettos and I'm good to go."

"Sit." She scrutinized Penelope's face and said, "I think I have the easiest job in the world."

"I'm aging as we speak. With the way things are going, I'll probably look thirty years older by the time we're done shooting."

"*C*ut!" Stewart said. They were filming at a rented beach house that served as the set home for Penelope and Noah's movie characters.

Thank God! Penelope didn't think she could take another second of Noah touching her. He'd taken a few liberties with the scene they'd acted out, enjoying their sexually charged fight far more than he had a right too. She quickly donned her robe and hugged herself, her body suddenly cold and shaky.

"It's a wrap. Good job. Only three takes. I'm sorry we had to redo the last one. I know these scenes are tough for everyone."

Penelope reached down and grabbed her shoes and

discarded corset from the ground and said, "Can I leave, Stew?"

"Yeah, take a short break but don't go back to the hotel yet. I'd like to shoot the scene with you in the kitchen after Noah leaves."

"Okay."

Noah followed her outside. "You seem a little off today. Everything alright?"

"Noah, you took advantage in that scene and if it happens again, I'll have no choice but to tell Stew."

"What are you talking about? Don't be such a prude. It was a sex scene. It's supposed to be hot; it's called improvisation...you know that thing we actors do to make a scene believable?"

"You were putting your hands in places they didn't need to go."

"I was trying to make the scene sensual...unlike you."

"What's that supposed to mean?"

"I carried that scene and you know it. You were practically flinching every time I touched you."

"Good thing my character hates her husband isn't it? I'll let it slide this time, but be on notice, you've had your one and only warning."

"What has happened to you? You've become impossible."

"If standing up for myself means I'm impossible, I'll proudly wear that badge." She held her chin up and put as much distance between them as she could. Fuming, she paced back and forth, doubting herself. Maybe it should be addressed with Stew immediately.

Why was she always so afraid to make waves? Why

did women always have to do the accommodating? She sighed. If she was looking for black and white, she knew she wouldn't find it. Life was mostly lived in the gray areas. She hoped her warning was enough and that would be the end of it. This would be her last film with Noah; now that was *one* decision that was crystal clear.

20

*I*t was nice to have the day off, but even after a morning jog, Griffin was still restless. His cell phone pinged, signaling an incoming text message.

> Courtney: Hey, its Courtney. I have a twenty-four-hour layover. Meet for a drink?

He studied the message thoughtfully, surprised at how indifferent he felt. How should he answer? Normally a romp with Courtney would be high on his 'yes please' meter, but today it fell surprisingly flat. He scrubbed his face with his hands and blew out a breath. Was this what his thirties were going to be like? Maybe he was becoming a dull and uninteresting bore. Not going to let that happen.

> Griffin: Yes. Yacht Club lounge, six o'clock happy hour?

Courtney: See you then gorgeous.

Griffin: Looking forward to it babe.

Settled. Giving up...not an option. Way too young to throw in the towel. Maybe Courtney was just what he needed to get Penelope out of his head. She had taken up a permanent residence there it seemed. In his whole life, everything had always fallen neatly into his lap. Never had to work for it before. Why should he start now? This distraction was perfect timing. He glanced at his watch. Now all he had to do was kill two hours.

A half hour later he merged onto the byway, straddling his powerful Ducati. Nothing like high speed to blow off steam. He'd skipped the helmet, needing to feel the full force of the wind against him. Talk about running against the wind...his gut churned with an unfamiliar yearning. He'd never really needed anyone before. Need...a small word for a big problem...was this what it felt like? Or was it simply a matter of not getting what he wanted...instant gratification was his normal modus operandi. Made sense that he'd be discombobulated by Penelope's reticence.

Leaning his torso low over the bike he went full throttle and stormed down the highway like the devil was on his heels.

❧

*G*riffin sipped his second martini, only half listening to Courtney excitedly prattle on about her latest traveling adventure. This was not going as planned. He was still bored. He couldn't keep his mind in the game. If he were in Vegas, he'd be losing big time.

Courtney grabbed his arm, "Griffin? Did you hear anything I just said?"

"I'm sorry. I was distracted. Tell me again."

"I just asked how it feels to be thirty? You did have a birthday, recently right? Does it have you thinking about settling down...maybe a kid or two?"

His brows snapped together, and sounding more irritated than intended, he said, "Why is everyone so interested in tying me down?"

"I was teasing. We're cut out of the same cloth I'm afraid. Just checking. No one special then?"

"I'm not dating anyone, if that's what you're asking."

"That's good then," she slipped her hand down to his thigh and snuggled it against his crotch.

Normally this would have been all he'd have needed to be settling the check and heading to her hotel. Instead he was detached, like it was happening to someone else. When she groped his cock firmly and squeezed, he knew it was time for his exit.

"Listen Courtney, I'm going to have to bow out here. Sorry, but I've got to get up early in the morning."

She studied him, "That never stopped you before. You don't have to stay the night. Let's just have a quickie and be done with it. I'm horny as hell. I've missed you."

"Not tonight Court, but thanks."

"Can't say I'm not disappointed, but at least we got a chance to catch up. Does this have anything to do with your leading lady?"

"Hardly."

"Just checking. She's certainly a force of nature, couldn't blame you for falling for her."

"End of conversation," he said. Settling their bill, he left the tab open on his charge for Courtney. He stood and she swiveled her bar stool to face him.

"Have a safe flight out tomorrow." he said, placing his hands on her shoulders. Leaning down he kissed the top of her head.

"You sure about this?" she said, looking up at him through her lashes.

He grinned. "I'll probably be kicking myself later, but yeah, I'm sure."

"See you around then?"

"Yeah. Drink up. It's on me. Order some food if you're hungry."

"You always were the consummate gentleman. Thanks." Winking at him she said, "Good luck with your leading lady."

He tensed, ready to snap back, then checking himself, he forced his shoulders to relax, "Nice try. See ya." And he left, wondering what the hell he was going to do for fun the rest of his life.

21

Griffin stuck his head inside Penelope's dressing room, "Hey how did the shoot go yesterday?"

"A barrel of laughs," she said, meeting his eyes from her vanity mirror.

"Was it that bad?"

"It wasn't fun, but whatever."

Griffin's eyes narrowed as he spied the defaced magazine on top of her vanity.

"What's that?"

She grabbed it and tossed it in the trash. "Jack's revenge."

He walked in and pulled it out of the trash can, studying it with a dark scowl on his face. "This is bullshit."

"Don't I know it?"

"Did you show it to Stew?"

"No, I decided to drop it."

"Don't think so babe."

"What?"

"I said no. You've got to report it."

"What is it with you men? You all say jump and I'm supposed to nod and ask how high? I said I'm handling it and I've decided to ignore it." She stood up and paced.

"Ouch. So now I'm the bad guy?"

"I'm just sick of it! I'm sick of all of you." She plopped down on the edge of the couch and covered her face with her hands fighting back tears.

Griffin shut the door behind him and sat down next to her. He put his arm around her, and she stiffened.

"Leave me alone."

"I can't...believe me I've tried."

Her voice sounded muffled through her hands. "Please just go."

He pulled her onto his lap and held her tightly against his chest. His lips brushed against her hair as he said quietly, "Penelope, you can call me a dick, control freak whatever you want, but I'm not leaving."

Her shoulders shook as she cried quietly into his tee shirt. "I'm a mess."

"Let it all out. You've received a few knocks; you're entitled to your tears."

She slowly relaxed against him, her body softening. She slid her arms around his waist then rested her head on his shoulder. His shirt was wet from her tears. Her breath hitched several times before she quieted. He stroked her hair back and inhaled, groaning inwardly at her intoxicating feminine scent.

She was all woman and her hands seared him

through the cotton fabric of his shirt. He shifted her weight on his lap hoping it would ease his arousal. Her fingers curled into his waist as her breath quickened, tickling his neck. The electricity between them suddenly became inescapable. She put her lips against his throat and his belly coiled with desire.

Cupping the back of his head she pulled him down to meet her lips. He held completely still, afraid to breathe. Was this really happening? She traced his bottom lip with her tongue then drew it inside her mouth sucking gently.

He pulled away reluctantly. "Whoa, Penelope, maybe we should dial it back a notch."

Her answer was to deepen the kiss. He gave in and opened his mouth to cover hers. He pushed his tongue inside, tasting, taking, exploring. He was acutely aware that there was only the thin fabric of white silk between him and her naked body. She seemed desperate as she clung to him. *Not now, not like this.*

His voice was husky with restraint. "Penelope as much as it pains me to say this, I'm not about to take advantage of your vulnerable state, not here, not now." He kissed her forehead. Softly he said, "I've fantasized about this moment a thousand times, I want to kiss every inch of your body. But the first time we make love is not going to be on the proverbial director's couch. I want it to be special and I want to be sure you're ready and it's not just a reaction. I promise you, I'm going to seduce you like you've never been seduced before."

Still breathless, her eyes soft, she brushed his hair back from his brow. "Tell me all about your fantasy."

"Soft music, candlelight, rose petals, hot oil," he murmured, voice low and sexy.

"More..."

"Me inside of you, making you crazy with desire for me, you on top of me, your lush breasts bouncing as you ride me..."

"Yes," she said softly.

He moved quickly and flipped her onto her back and began raining soft kisses across her face then her neck and shoulders, until she began giggling.

"Is that a promise?"

"Stop...that tickles." She squirmed underneath him.

"Promise me. Say it."

Breathless from laughing, she said, "I promise. It's a date."

"This Saturday."

"This Saturday," she agreed.

He relented and got up, pulling her with him. "I'm glad we don't have any sex scenes this afternoon," he said.

"We still have a scene to shoot together. But it's rated G. You'll be fine."

"I'm going to my room to take a cold shower. You have a scene with dickhead this morning, don't you?"

"Yeah, but it's only PG...swear words are involved."

"See you on set." He stared into her sparkling pools of green and knew he was lost. He grabbed the offensive magazine and rolled it up and stuck it in his back pocket. He left even though everything inside, screamed at him to stay.

22

_P_enelope watched as Stewart paced back and forth waiting for the rest of the cast and crew to show up for the impromptu meeting he'd called. Griffin sat slumped down in a chair, arms crossed, with an endearingly serious expression on his face.

"Am I the only one not worried?" she asked.

"You're taking this too lightly," Stew said.

"It's an intimidation tactic. It's not going to work."

"Penelope, we have to take all threats seriously. We don't know for certain who left this for you. I'm going to have everyone keep their eyes open for anything unusual. I should have had the meeting last Friday after the firing, but a lot of people had already left for the weekend."

After Stewart was satisfied that everyone available was present, he pulled out the magazine and held it up for them to see. "This piece of smut was slipped underneath Penelope's door sometime between Friday and this morning when she showed up for work. I don't think I need to emphasize the seriousness of this." He passed it around for them to get a better look.

"What many of you might not know is that I had to fire Jack Feldner on Friday for making aggressive and inappropriate physical advances toward Penelope. We have no evidence that he's responsible for this lewd display, only strong assumptions. However, he is no longer welcome or allowed anywhere near this building, Penelope or any off-site film locations. If anyone sees or hears from him, you are to report it to me immediately. Are we clear?"

Everyone nodded, some of them wearing shocked expressions. "Now, I'd like to hear from you. Did anyone see Jack anywhere near here after three on Friday?"

Someone from set design volunteered, "I saw him in the afternoon, not sure when. We spoke and he seemed normal, so I'm sure it was before he was fired."

Stewart nodded, "Yes, he was quite angry when he left. Stormed out in a rage. Just stay alert. We always need to be on the lookout, not just over this incident. It's important we look out for one another. If you see someone or something out of place, pay attention. That's all for now. Any questions?"

Everyone seemed concerned, a few shook their heads, and some stopped to offer their support to Penelope before heading back to their tasks.

Stewart sat down next to Penelope, "How are you feeling?"

"To be honest, I'm a little embarrassed over the

attention we're giving it. I think everyone is making a bigger deal out of it than it deserves. Don't get me wrong, I appreciate the concern and don't mean to sound ungrateful."

"You can never be too cautious. Doesn't hurt to have everyone looking out for anything out of the ordinary. With the pandemonium of production at times, the more eyes the better. It'd be easy to slip something by."

Griffin who had been quiet until now said, "Stewart, what do you think about hiring additional security?"

"I've thought about it and already made the call."

"I think she should have a guard stationed outside of her house."

"You can't be serious!" Penelope exclaimed.

"Dead serious," Griffin said.

"I have to agree. You're used to security on your publicity tours. It's not so bad. The peace of mind far outweighs any inconvenience. You won't even know they're there."

"Easy for you to say," she said, her lips tight.

"I know you think it's overkill, but I'm beefing up security...and someone will escort you to and from the set and be stationed outside your residence for now."

Griffin reached for her hand and she pulled it away.

Stewart quickly glanced at his watch. "We'll take a short break now, then we'll caravan to the beach location set. You've got fifteen minutes."

The door closed behind him and Griffin took Penelope's chin in his hand and said softly, "You okay?"

"Yes, I just wish you hadn't involved Stewart. It was high-handed."

"I tend to take threats against the people I care about seriously."

She looked up at him through her lashes. "I know you mean well, but there is so much in my life that's controlled by others...it's overwhelming at times."

"When you put it like that...I understand a little better."

"I hope so. I'm not trying to be difficult."

"I'm sorry Penelope, I shouldn't have gone to Stew behind your back. Forgive me?"

She bit her bottom lip and nodded.

"You're killing me, you know that don't you? I want you all to myself. I want to hole up somewhere for a solid week. Just you and me. Hell, *I* want to be your bodyguard."

"Sounds good to me...you can put in your application at the front desk." She smiled wanly, her face drawn and pale.

"Can you manage an overnight this weekend?"

"Yes," she said, without hesitation.

"Where I'm taking you, we won't need security."

"Where is that?"

"It's a surprise."

"Not even a hint?"

"Nope."

"I hate to bring this up, but Stewart took notice of you trying to hold my hand and I really don't want anyone speculating about us. I know he would never say anything, but I think we need to be discreet," Penelope said.

"I caught that too. I agree one hundred percent, but

any friend would have done the same. I wouldn't worry about it with Stew."

"I'm not, I just want to be extra careful."

"Absolutely, I wouldn't have it any other way."

She smiled. "Not that I won't be thinking about it."

He traced her lips with his finger before opening the door, "After you Ms. Winters."

"Thank you, Mr. Bennett."

"See you on set." He turned and walked purposefully away.

~

*G*riffin went back to his dressing room and made a quick call to his brother Kyle. Highhanded or not, he wasn't leaving anything to chance. Despite his apology to Penelope for taking things into his own hands earlier, this was different. He could justify this to himself.

He needed to find out everything he could about Jack Feldner. Did he have a record, a history of violence, anything they could dig up. Maybe even have them do a preliminary on the rest of the crew to see if anything jumped out. Kyle had many connections and had made use of private investigators in the past. He'd know who the best of the best was. Penelope might not be worried, but he was.

23

"Dolly are you sure you don't mind watching Archie overnight?"

"Of course not." Dolly's cheeks turned bright pink, and she said shyly, "Ben's coming over tonight to keep me company."

"Ben? Ben Donavan? When did this happen?"

"We've been hanging out some at work. He's really nice."

"Good for you. I like him."

"I'm going to make dinner for us then we're going to watch Netflix together. Where is Griffin taking you?"

"He's being all mysterious about it. He did say that where we're going, we won't be needing security for the night."

"Very intriguing and romantic."

Penelope looked off dreamily, "Yeah, he is that."

"Just take it slow. But you seem happy."

"Dolly this can't get out. I don't want anyone to know. Please don't mention it to Ben. Not that I don't trust him, I just don't know him that well. I've never worked with him before."

"My lips are sealed. The sharks would gather in a feeding frenzy if there was even a hint that you were seeing someone...especially if that someone was not Noah Davis."

She shook her head. "It would be a nightmare."

"I didn't tell Ben where you were going or with who, only that I had the place to myself tonight."

She heard the car pull into the drive and gave Dolly a quick hug. "Thanks, I owe you."

"Have fun."

Penelope stopped to talk with her security guard stationed at her house, who had already been informed that he wouldn't be needed until the following day. "Thanks Luke, I'll see you tomorrow."

"You're welcome Ms. Winters. Have a nice time."

"I intend to."

She climbed into the Audi as Griffin held the door. His eyes scorched her as they roved across her face. He threw her overnight bag into the back, then climbed into the driver's seat. Reaching across her body he grabbed her seatbelt, his arm brushing against her breasts. She inhaled sharply as she caught his heady scent, clean and fresh with a hint of aftershave.

"Hi," she said breathlessly.

"Hi back." His voice was husky and full of desire; his thumb stroked her cheek.

"Security is going to follow us until we get

launched," he said, nodding at the black SUV parked in the street.

She arched her brow. "Launched?"

His lips turned up. "Yeah."

"Does this involve water?"

"Yes. We're taking my yacht out overnight."

"That sounds fabulous!"

"It will be. We'll anchor once we find a spot offshore from one of the barrier islands; it'll be just the two of us...all night long."

She grabbed his hand and squeezed, "Heavenly. Thanks for arranging this."

He raised the back of her hand to his lips and kissed it, "You're welcome, but it's pure selfishness on my part."

He drove with a relaxed confidence, handling the vehicle easily like he did with everything he attempted. He was so sexy. She felt her belly tighten with need. He took that moment to glance over and his eyes heated, the blue darkening to almost cobalt. Her pulse fluttered erratically.

"How big is your boat?"

"Forty-one footer. It's a Bavaria, German engineering," he said, pulling into the Yacht Club's private parking lot. He jumped out and she watched as he spoke with the valet. When he returned, he grabbed their bags from the back and opened her car door.

"Come on, your sea-chariot awaits."

She admired the array of gleaming boats moored at the marina. Then Griffin stopped beside the one they were presumably going to be sailing out on.

"Here we are."

"It's beautiful."

"Wait till you see the interior." He tossed their bags on, then climbed aboard and turned to give her a hand.

Giving her the tour of the yacht, he pointed out features of the watercraft. It offered both shade and sun, a sunroof covered lounge that with the flick of a switch could be in full sun. There was a hydraulically lowered bathing platform, for water toys or toe dipping. She gasped at the opulence.

No details were spared as far as she could tell. The bow had bright comfortable cushions to relax on, away from the sun. The kitchen and salon were combined and sleek, and there was already a bottle of wine chilling in a bucket on the counter. And the entire view from inside was unobstructed, the huge glass windows letting in plenty of light. She was impressed by the beautiful teak wood, colorful upholstered fabrics, and the gleaming metal.

He led her below deck, and they peeked into the first bedroom which had a double bed and bath. Then he led her to the master suite cabin and her eyes widened when she saw the rose petals scattered on top of the duvet. She glanced over at him and found him watching her intently.

"I hope you remembered your oil," she said in a husky voice. His eyes flashed with desire. The king-sized bed and wood finishes were the lap of luxury. It had a lavish bathroom with a separate shower, and she gaped when she saw that there was even room for a sofa.

"I can't believe how much space there is."

"I think we'll be more than comfortable. Come here

you," he said as he pulled her into his arms. He tipped her chin up then scattered light kisses across her face, her cheeks and nose, then her chin. He moved to the curve of her neck, nibbling, then he licked the hollow of her throat. She gripped his biceps, enjoying the powerful feel of his muscles bulging beneath her fingertips. When he pulled her pelvis against his, she felt his erection. He was rock hard. *Mmm.*

He plundered her mouth almost desperately, and she met his tongue thrust for thrust. He backed her up against the bed, then gave her a slight push and she was suddenly sprawled on top of the duvet. He straddled her, his weight pinning her down. Pulse racing, she raked her fingers through his hair as he kissed her fiercely. She moaned against his lips, surprised that the sound came from her. He lifted his mouth then buried his face in her hair, his breathing ragged.

"Penelope, I don't know what's happening to me. You've cast some kind of spell. I'm half-crazy with desire for you."

She smiled, her lips curving into his soft hair. "Shouldn't we at least make it out of the marina?"

He groaned softly, "Killjoy."

He propped himself up on his elbows and gave her one last soft kiss on the lips before pushing himself up and climbing off the bed.

She scooped up a hand-full of rose petals and buried her nose into her palm, inhaling the sweet scent.

"I've never had anyone do something so romantic for me before."

"I find that hard to believe."

"It's true. I'm having a lot of firsts with you Mr. Bennett."

His eyes were intense and unfathomable as he stared into hers. "Me too." Like a switch had been flipped, he abruptly grabbed her hand and tugged her off the bed. "Let's get out on the water."

24

The water was calm, buffered by the saltwater sounds. There were inlets peppered throughout the North Carolina barrier islands, so boating was the perfect way to explore the coast. They had anchored offshore to enjoy their day out at sea. Griffin had lowered the deck bathing platform and Penelope sat on the edge, dangling her feet in the water.

"You ready to swim?" Griffin asked, plopping down next to her. His eyes skimmed across her face, then wandered slowly down her beautiful body. She was a goddess. His gaze lingered on her full breasts, continuing down to her flat belly and gorgeous thighs. He found himself getting aroused all over again. Fortunately, he had on his sunglasses, so he hoped he was getting away with the blatant perusal.

"Yes, if you are."

"Let's go," he stood up, took off his shades and dove in, making a big splash as he entered the water.

She carefully lowered herself in, inch by inch, and propped her elbows on the deck. Griffin swam up, his arms pinning her on either side, his lips an inch away from her ear, making him hot with desire.

His voice soft and lazy, he said, "Chicken."

"I'm just adjusting to the water temperature," she responded breathlessly.

"Liar," he whispered.

Her voice low, she said, "What are you doing to me?"

He chuckled, "Let go."

As he tread water, his legs brushed against hers, the sensation sent desire coursing through him. "Come on," he said. He pushed off and sank underwater, popping up several feet away.

She finally released her grip on the boat and kicked out. They swam around for a while, staying close to the vessel. Griffin pulled himself onto the deck and grabbed a couple of colorful noodles. He threw one to her then jumped back in with his. "This will keep us afloat so we can stay in the water a little longer."

They relaxed, floating on the water's surface until Griffin excitedly pointed to several dolphins less than twenty feet away.

"I see them all the time when I'm windsurfing," he shared. "It never gets old."

Her eyes went wide with surprise. "It's incredible!"

Her hair was plastered to her head which accentu-ated her delicate features and classic beauty. Her lashes had droplets of water clinging to them. Griffin lost himself in her sparkling green eyes while she watched them.

The dolphins swam in closer, appearing as curious about them as they were about the dolphins. They arced out of the water then disappeared only to reappear again.

Penelope's face was beaming. "They're playing," she whispered in awe.

"Yes."

They continued to circle for several minutes then swam off, seemingly without a care in the world. Penelope sighed loudly.

"Griffin, that was magical. Thank you!"

"I'm really glad you got to have that experience Pen. Ready to get out?"

"Yes, before I shrivel up."

~

*G*riffin had thought of everything from the rose petals and wine to the gloriously thick steaks that were currently searing on the built-in grill.

"I'm ready for a glass of wine, how about you?" he asked.

"Yes please. Do you want me to get it?"

"No princess, you look way too comfortable. Let me serve you, my lady."

And she was. Comfortable didn't even begin to describe it. She was sprawled belly-down on the deck cushions, under the canopy, half asleep. The combination of sun and water, and the lack of stress, had her body feeling like an overcooked noodle.

He trailed his knuckles down her back before handing her a glass of white wine. Her bikini left little to the imagination and most of her bottom exposed; she was happy that he took full advantage, leaning down to kiss one rounded cheek then the other. She squirmed, suddenly fully awake.

"Get rested up now princess, because I have big plans for you later that involve strenuous activity."

"I certainly hope so."

"That's my girl."

Her belly flipped at the casual endearment. My God, she felt like a sixteen-year-old who'd never been kissed. He turned her inside out without even trying.

They'd just finished dinner and Griffin raised his glass, "A toast, to the best day of my life," he said.

She clicked her goblet against his and sipped the dry sauvignon blanc, her tongue darting out to lick a droplet from her bottom lip.

"When you do that babe..."

"What?"

"Lick your lips," he said, his gaze hungry.

She felt like that juicy steak right now and he was about to devour her. An entire day of flirtation and near nakedness had them both hot with need.

"Let me clear the table then we can shower off the ocean water. What do you say?" he asked.

Her voice didn't even sound like her own when she answered; it was breathless and smoky. "Yes."

When they went below deck, his eyes burned with a passion so intense she almost had to look away.

"Let's wait on the shower. I need you now," Griffin said, grabbing her hand. She let him lead her over to the bed. After pushing the duvet cover off to the side, he lay her down on the crisp sheets that smelled of fresh linen and a hint of the rose petals. He pulled off his trunks and crawled in beside her, naked and fully erect. His warm body against hers filled her with desire.

As his eyes slowly roved over her nakedness, she quivered with anticipation. Now breathless with need, she whispered, "Griffin, you feel so good."

Untying her bikini top she felt the cool air against her breasts as they spilled out. She smiled as his breath hissed, then he leaned down and lapped at her nipple before drawing it into his warm mouth. He suckled until she was panting, clenching her fingers in his hair. Trailing lower he nuzzled her mound, kissing her through the fabric of the skimpy covering. She felt something deep inside of her begin to unravel.

Her skin felt scorched when his thumbs slipped under the elastic of her bikini bottoms and he slowly pulled them down the length of her thighs. Tossing them aside, he kissed his way back up her inner thighs, burying his mouth in her wet center as she rocked against him. A moan escaped as he licked and sucked on her labia, making her ache with need. When she was writhing under his expert tongue he lapped at her clit before scattering light kisses between her legs, nibbling her inner thighs, then finally returning to her sweet spot. He licked his way back up to her belly, and she gasped when he dipped his tongue into her navel before rubbing his erection against the wetness between her legs.

As she bucked beneath him, he reached into the bedside table and pulled out a foil packet. Ripping it open with his teeth he kneeled, straddling her as he slipped the condom over his engorged penis. His eyes were hooded, glazed with arousal as he spread her thighs wide and positioned himself on top of her.

"Yes," she said, feeling the tip of his hardness push against her tight opening.

Hands cupping her breasts, he kneaded and massaged, his thumbs rolling over her erect nipples. Her need was almost more than she could bear, she had to feel him inside her. He rubbed his shaft against her sex, stimulating her, gliding, rubbing, circling his hips.

Her voice quivered, "Griffin, please...I...please." She was ready. She felt as if she'd been waiting a lifetime for it. "Please," she begged.

He finally thrust, hard. Filling her, stretching her. He withdrew partially and paused, then thrust again, slowly, tantalizingly, all the while circling his hips, between each thrust.

She loved the feel of his weight pressing her into the bed. She wrapped her thighs around him and met him thrust for thrust. His tempo increased, the heat between them building. The sound of his pelvis slapping against her sent her to the edge.

They both burst into climax at the same time. Her eyes were squeezed tightly shut as she raked her fingers down his back. He collapsed on top of her and buried his nose in her hair. "Holy hell Penelope." His words sounded like a caress.

They lay spent, their breath slowly returning to normal. He rolled off and she felt a moment of loss, but then he pulled her on top of him and cradled her to his chest. He kissed the top of her head and she was content again.

She may have dozed but she became aware of Griffin's teeth biting her earlobe and him whispering, "Let's shower then go up and do some star gazing. You won't believe what a night sky is like, so far removed from light pollution," Griffin said.

She stretched lazily and sat up.

He eyed her hungrily. "I don't think I can ever get enough of you. You're addictive."

She smiled like a Cheshire cat with the cream. "I'll bet you say that to all the girls."

Looking suddenly serious, he said, "Never, until now."

Her warm body tingled. He led her into the shower, and they took turns washing each other. He squeezed some shower gel into his palms and began massaging her shoulders and arms then her hands.

"Turn around," He said softly, as he poured more of the lavender scented bath gel onto a washcloth. He lathered her back and her bottom, then the backs of her thighs. She sighed, *heavenly.*

After he finished, she returned the favor. When they stepped out of the shower he said, "Let me dry you."

She wrapped one towel around her head turban

style and handed him the other one. He rubbed her skin briskly. After they were both dried off, he took her hand again.

"Come with me. I want to give you the moon and the stars."

*T*hey ended their night on deck, naked on the lounger with Penelope's back snuggled against his chest, her hips sandwiched between his thighs. He ran his hand down the soft skin of her arm, then her belly, his feather light touch branding her.

"Not sure I like feeling this out of control," he said softly.

Instead of answering, she pulled his head down for a kiss. In the moonlight his face was shadowed but eyes blazed with heat, penetrating deep into her psyche. She was lost and incapable of resisting her attraction.

The only sounds were their breathing and the gentle waves and water lapping at the bow. An unexpected meteor shower gave them plenty of chances to wish upon the stars. *Magical.*

riffin sat in the parking lot without starting the car, his face set in an unreadable expression.

Penelope reached over and squeezed his shoulder, "Is there something wrong?"

Still staring straight ahead, he said, "Stay with me tonight. Don't go home."

"But Griffin, we both have to be on set early tomorrow morning, and I haven't studied my lines. I have Archie to think about too."

He turned, his eyes burning with intensity. "Won't Dolly watch him for another night?"

He caught a flash of longing flicker across her face, "I'm not sure it's such a good idea...this is moving too fast. I wouldn't trade our time yesterday on the boat for anything in the world, but now it's time to get back to reality."

He turned in his seat to face her, then reached

across and brushed his knuckles along her jaw, "Too fast for who? Not for me. I want to be with you. I want you in my bed tonight."

"Griffin, where do you think this is all going to lead?"

"I'm not thinking about that, I'm thinking about now. I'm thinking about you curled up next to me, in my arms all night long."

"All I can see are the reasons we should be putting on the brakes," she admitted.

"I get that, but can we just see where this takes us? Baby come home with me, be with me, I need you tonight."

Penelope bit her bottom lip, obviously weighing her choices. She lifted her gaze, meeting his eyes and slowly smiled, "You win. I'll call Dolly; if she's okay with it, I'll come home with you."

He grinned broadly before starting up the car. As the powerful engine roared to life, she made the call.

~

*A*fter dinner they decided to watch the sunset from the beach. The last sliver of the orange globe had just sunk into the sea. "That sunset was incredible, like a wildfire in the sky," Penelope said. They had spread a blanket out on the sand to watch the spectacular show of fiery reds, oranges and yellows, as colorful as any artist's palette.

"Let's take a walk," Griffin said.

He jumped up and reached down, hauling her to her feet. He didn't release her hand, just intertwined his fingers through hers. The soft sand was still warm from the sun, and the stars emerged as night fell. It was high tide and they wandered to the edge where the waves kissed the shore.

"Griffin, where do you see yourself a year from now?"

"I have no idea. Before this film came along, I'd been restless...thinking about a change of address."

"To where?"

"Again, not sure. I've thought about moving back to the South of France. I lived there for a few years after college. My mom still has family there. It's easy since I'm fluent in French. The work I do for my nonprofits, I can do from anywhere."

"Did you ever think of working for your dad's company?"

"I tried. Don't have the stomach for it. I prefer my freedom. Another strike against me with my father."

"I'm sure he wants what's best for you."

"Maybe. But much to my old man's disappointment, none of us have followed in his footsteps. No one's interested in carrying his torch. My brother Kyle is an attorney and takes care of his legal stuff. My sister Faye and I sort of coasted along. Dad's still on the Board of Directors. I think he's holding out hope that one of us will change our minds someday. But the company doesn't need us."

"What was it like growing up with everything you could possibly need right at your fingertips?"

"Besides the fact that my father was busy running an empire, and mother was a self-centered billionaire's wife, big into high society and the privilege it afforded her? Honestly, I didn't know any different until I struck out on my own. I might sound bitter but I'm not, thanks to my siblings."

She squeezed his hand. "I envy you your relationships with you brother and sister."

"In fairness to my mom, she loved us, did the best she could considering her own childhood. Growing up, she relied on her beauty to get ahead and had a phenomenally successful modeling career. Then she met my dad and followed her heart and the money."

"I'm afraid everyone is winging it when it comes to parenting."

He grinned at her. "I'm her baby, so of course when I did get her attention, she spoiled me, but it was of the smothering variety."

"I was lucky in the mom department. She was my best friend," Penelope shared.

"In a lot of ways, Kyle served in more of a parental role than my parents. We had to stick together. We were shipped off to the finest boarding schools, weren't exposed to any other way of life. Then I went to Columbia University. I liked that it was in New York City; I thirsted for a bigger life...more action. It was there that I got a glimpse of diversity...a look at privilege and poverty living side-by-side."

"That must have been an eye opener."

"Yeah. It was profound."

"What did you major in?"

"Non-profit Management. Pretty demanding curriculum." He grinned. "Cut into my party time, but academics seemed to come easy for me."

"I'm intrigued."

He smiled, "Good, that's right where I want you, completely captivated. What about you? What makes the beautiful Penelope Winters tick?"

"Well you already know about my mom and that I have no brothers or sisters. I never knew my dad. I'm kind of a loner anyway. Not sure if that's because of my career choice or my nature really." She smiled up at him. "I've always had a few great friends which made up for the lack of siblings. In high school I couldn't wait to get away from the small town I grew up in. I waitressed and saved up my money to move to Hollywood and chase my dreams."

"You moved all by yourself?"

"Yeah, it was pretty scary."

"Makes me feel like a sheltered prince."

"That's because you are one," she said, laughing.

Griffin's forehead furrowed. "You're joking, but I look at my brother and sister and see how happy they are. They've both found their mates...their niches. Recently I've been wondering about myself...what's wrong with me? Why don't I have any ambition? Why do I avoid commitment like the plague? The more I think about it, the more I realize that I've been running."

"From what?"

"From myself."

She looked up at him under the brilliant star lit sky. "Do you know why?"

"I've reached the conclusion that I don't like what I see if I slow down for too long."

"What do you see?"

"A man without a purpose, one who is hiding...

hiding behind his privilege...a man who's alone. I think I've mistaken being needed or needing someone as too much responsibility. A loss of freedom. You know, a while back you said you've only been with two men in your life. Truthfully, I've been with lots of women, but I've never let anyone in."

"You've never been in love?"

"Nope."

"That's so sad."

"I'm not normally given to introspection, but lately it seems like I can't avoid it. I've been pondering life's meaning," he said, trying to laugh it off.

"Maybe it's just the natural progression of things," she said. "The twenties are for exploring, adventure, finding out who we are...separate from our families, ya know?"

"Maybe. But lately it feels like there's a void in my life. If I didn't know better, I'd have to call it loneliness."

"I've certainly felt lonely...as cliché as it sounds... even in a crowd," Penelope said.

His thumb caressed her bottom lip. "What I'm feeling with you is all new to me. I feel contented when I'm with you. That scares the shit out of me. I'm afraid of these feelings you're stirring up."

She studied his beautiful face, so earnest. "Griffin, I'm very drawn to you as well...but I'm certainly not ready to dive into anything serious."

"I know that. I respect that, but I'm trying to be one hundred percent honest with you."

"I appreciate it."

"I'm not asking for anything more than a chance to see where this attraction leads us." He pulled her into his arms. Bending down he kissed her softly. "You're different from anyone I've ever known."

"How?" she asked, her voice husky.

"I can't put it into words. There is something other-worldly about you. Like you somehow float above us mere mortals," he bit back a laugh. "I know that sounds stupid. I get the sense that there are many layers and a depth to you that leaves me yearning to know more. I feel like I've barely scratched the surface."

She sighed, then murmured, "Kiss me again."

This time he hungrily covered her mouth with his as his hands slid down to cup her bottom. She reached under his shirt and her hands rode up his abdomen and settled on his chest.

"Let me make love to you. I want to take you home and kiss every inch of you," Griffin said, his voice rough with need.

"Yes," she said, against his mouth.

When they reached Griffin's house, he picked Penelope up and carried her inside, not putting her down until they were in his bedroom. They made love and fell into a deep sleep.

~

Sometime in the wee hours of the night, Penelope awoke to the soft sound of a piano. She wrapped a sheet around herself and, lured by the beautiful notes, went to investigate. She found Griffin at his piano, completely absorbed in the music he was creating. The backdrop of the waves crashing to shore made the whole thing feel as if she were in a dream.

His upper torso was bare, and he had on a pair of gray sweatpants, his hair the usual unruly mop. She stood quietly, leaning against the wall admiring his beauty. As if sensing her presence, he glanced up from the piano keys and met her gaze. His eyes were dark and intense with some inner firestorm she could only guess at.

"Don't stop on my account," she said softly.

He paused from the haunting melody he'd been playing to segue into the soulful ballad, "Don't Let Me Be Lonely Tonight," by James Taylor. Her breath caught when he began to sing. His voice was warm, the tone cozy and mellow with perfect pitch. Her pulse fluttered and as if on its own volition, her body moved to stand behind him. She rested her hand lightly on his shoulder and leaned down to touch her lips to his hair. *Her lover.*

Her heart was ready to burst. He seemed so vulnerable, in complete contrast to the man she'd painted him to be. Had it only been weeks ago? He laid down the final notes then swiveled around to face her. He pulled her to him and held her, resting his head against her belly as she cradled him.

"That was so beautiful. Thank you," Penelope said.

He didn't answer, just stood and picked her up into his arms and carried her back to bed.

———————

26

*T*he following morning Penelope awoke to the smell of bacon frying. She opened her eyes and stretched out like a cat. Her face flushed remembering their lovemaking from the night before. She'd never had multiple orgasms until now. Griffin was an incredibly attentive lover and her body felt sore in a good way.

After brushing her teeth, she found one of his tee shirts in the dresser drawer and pulled it over her head. Slipping on her panties, she followed her nose to the kitchen. As she passed by the baby grand piano, she ran her fingers lightly over the keys, evoking the magic from the night before.

"How long have you been playing?" she asked.

"My whole life. We all play. Our mother insisted. Not to brag, I mean I wouldn't want to intimidate you or anything, but when I was fifteen, I started a band at boarding school. I played lead guitar and we played together all through high school. We called ourselves the Outsiders. All the fourteen- and fifteen-year-old girls were in love with us." He grinned broadly, as he dropped four slices of bread into the toaster.

His mood was light this morning, the melancholy of the dark hours of the night seemingly quelled. "So, you're telling me you were some catch, even back then," she said, laughing.

"Something like that. How do you like your eggs?"

"I'm not picky."

"I'll scramble them then."

She sidled up to the kitchen island and sat on the tall stool. Griffin placed a mug of steaming coffee in front of her. "Cream or sugar?"

"Cream please."

"Tell me when."

When it was the color of caramel, she said, "That's good."

"Do you want to shower here, or do you need to go home first?"

"I need to go home. I need a change of clothes *and* we can't show up together."

He buttered her toast and placed a plate with a mound of scrambled eggs and way too much bacon in front of her. "Thanks Griffin, looks delicious."

"Not as luscious as you look, all sleep tumbled, soft dreamy bedroom eyes, I wish we didn't have to leave the house for the next week."

She sighed, "Me too."

She dug in and in no time at all was polishing off the last bite of bacon and pushing her plate aside.

"Looks like I won't have enough time to do the dishes. Too bad." She grinned, not the least bit sorry.

"As if..." he dazzled her with his smile before kissing her full on the lips. "Man, those lips were made for kissing."

Her eyes flickered with desire. "We'd better leave soon, or we'll never make it out of here."

"I'm ready, I'll drop you off and come back to shower."

Once in the car, they held hands all the way to the beach house. After he dropped her off, Penelope felt an ache in her chest. *What was happening to her?*

∾

*P*enelope was practically floating from the weekend, so when she and Dolly pulled up to work, she was mentally unprepared for the small crowd of tourists loitering around the front entrance. So far, production had been successful in keeping their filming locations under wraps. The non-disclosures had been effective. No leaks. Until now. Because the location was off the beaten path, most paparazzi wouldn't waste their time. But it was bound to happen, and when she spied a couple of professional photographers in the group, her thoughts immediately went to Jack. *Damn.*

Penelope slid way down in her seat, practically sitting on the floor, and pulled her cap low over her forehead. Glancing at her watch she noted that they were still a half hour early.

"Can we sneak in the back door?" Penelope asked.

"I'll drive around and check it out. Stay down."

The paps weren't stupid and when they saw a car slow down, then suddenly change directions they pursued. "Shit shit shit!" Dolly said. "They're following."

"Just turn around and pull up close to the front door. I'm afraid the back door will be locked. I'll hop out and run in and you can park the car."

Dolly parked right in front and said, "Now!" She giggled as Penelope contorted her body like a crab to try and escape from the car without being discovered. "Hurry! They're descending upon us."

"Easy for you to say." Keeping her body below the window height was damn near impossible. She managed to open the door and fell out of the car. Dolly was snorting with laughter as Penelope scrambled quickly to her feet and ran for the entrance.

The tourists had their cells out snapping photos and selfies with Penelope darting inside as their backdrop.

Still breathing heavy from her sprint, Penelope swiped her card and entered her dressing room, flipping on the overhead lights. She stepped on something crunchy and looked down to see another manilla envelope under her foot. Filled with dread she bent over to pick it up.

She took in several deep breaths. Her hands were shaking so badly, she wasn't sure she could open the envelope. She examined it closely, looking for a return address or any clues that could point to the sender. None. Same neatly scripted writing as before. How had Jack managed to slip past security? *Did security even stick around on the weekends?*

Her heart pounded in her chest as she slid her finger under the flap and ripped open the envelope. She reached inside and pulled out a handful of photographs. The room spun as her stomach lurched. She threw the photos down and ran to the bathroom making it just in time before she began to retch.

Kneeling in front of the commode, her breath came in rapid shallow bursts as she fought to control the anxiety and her gag reflex. Who had sent them...and why? She had so carefully buried her past. Why now? *Slow deep breaths*...her nausea dissipated.

When she was sure the sickness had passed, she splashed her face with cold water and brushed her teeth. She had to hide the incriminating photos before Dolly arrived.

She picked up the offending pictures, her face heating with shame as she shuffled through the half dozen photographs. Her on the arms of various powerful men. A lifetime ago, but now the memories rushed back like it was yesterday.

She fought as the bile rose again, burning the back of her throat. She looked so young and innocent. *Well, that's because you were, Penelope, you were barely nineteen years old for God's sake.* She heard someone outside the door and quickly stuffed the photos back into the envelope and hid it in her bag.

"I brought you a coffee and a donut from the buffet," Dolly said, handing her a to-go coffee container and a white paper bag. Penelope tried to smile her thanks, but it was half-hearted at best.

Dolly looked at her friend with concern, her forehead furrowed, "You look like you've seen a ghost. What's wrong?"

"Nothing, my stomach is upset. I'm sure it's from the narrow escape."

"Are you sure that's all it is? Your face has absolutely no color. Should we call the doctor?"

"No, I'll be fine. I just need a few minutes."

Dolly's eyes narrowed, "You were fine when you spilled out of the car. What happened between then and now?"

"Please, just drop it," she said, more sharply than she'd intended to. Dolly winced. "I'm sorry, I didn't mean for that to come out so bitchy."

"No worries. You've had a lot to deal with lately."

"There is something I'd like to confide with you, but not now and not here. I've got to get it together for the shoot this morning. I promise we'll talk tonight."

"Okay...if you're sure it can wait."

"I'm sure."

Dolly stared deeply into her friend's eyes, then slowly nodded her head.

"Let's get that makeup plastered on then," Dolly said.

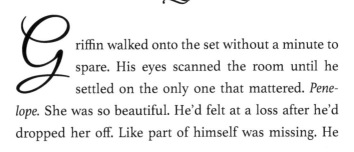

*G*riffin walked onto the set without a minute to spare. His eyes scanned the room until he settled on the only one that mattered. *Penelope.* She was so beautiful. He'd felt at a loss after he'd dropped her off. Like part of himself was missing. He hated the feeling. It was another brand new experience, compliments of Ms. Winters. This craving he had for her wasn't welcome.

He walked over to Penelope and she barely glanced at him, keeping her eyes lowered.

"Hey, you ready for the big fight scene?"

She shrugged one shoulder, not meeting his gaze, "I guess."

"Something wrong?"

"Just not feeling very well this morning."

"Why don't I believe you?" He said, frustrated by the limitations of keeping their relationship under wraps. He wanted to grab her by the shoulders and make her look at him. Instead she abruptly turned away, leaving him staring at her backside. *Fuck me.*

"Is this how it's going to be? One step forward two steps back?" He knew he sounded aggressive, but in that moment, he didn't give a shit. He'd allowed himself to be vulnerable with her and now she was shutting him out.

Quietly, she said, "Quit pushing me, I said I'm tired, drop it."

He came up close behind her and whispered in her ear, "Really Penelope?" He felt her stiffen.

"What am I missing? Because when I dropped you at your door an hour and a half ago, you were anything but detached."

"We can talk later, okay?" she said, not bothering to turn her head.

His jaw clenched and he was ready to argue with her some more, but Stew called out "Places," and it was showtime.

. . .

"Sydney, look at me." She kept her head lowered; arms crossed tightly over her chest. "Your husband is on to us. I'm sure those threatening messages came from his camp."

"We don't know that for sure."

"I'm sure enough. We need to stop seeing each other."

Her eyebrow arched, "And you can do that so easily?"

"Don't twist it around. For God's sake Sydney, this isn't some game. Your husband is a very powerful man. A United States Senator...with connections and access to surveillance that we could only imagine."

"Is that all that I mean to you? Was I just some pathetic lonely politician's wife you felt sorry for? Someone you saw needed a good fucking?"

"You know it was more than that...so much more," Bryan grabbed her chin and tilted her head up, gazing intently into her eyes. "It was for me anyway."

Her eyes welled with tears and she impatiently brushed them away. "I want to leave my husband. I just don't see how! But I can't do this anymore. I want to be with you. I love you."

His heart lurched in his chest...for real...you're Bryan dude...not Griffin...

"I love you too Syd, you've got to believe me, but I don't want to break up your marriage and I really don't want to be on some politician's hit list. That threat was real."

He pulled her into his arms and pressed his lips to hers. The passion ignited, going from zero to sixty in a breath. Bending her back over his arm, he plundered her mouth. She clenched her fingers in his hair, groaning against his lips. He lifted his mouth and buried his face into her neck.

"We can run away. Hide out until it's blown over. Don't leave me Bryan."

Bryan's eyes darted around the room. "I'm getting so paranoid, I'm afraid we're being recorded right now."

Her eyes filled with tears again. "Hold me Bryan, just hold me." He held her tightly against his chest while she cried.

"When does he go out of town next?"

"Next week, he'll be campaigning with the presidential nominee, and it's possible they'll announce that he's the VP pick."

"Text me after he's gone, and we'll set up a meeting time. Somewhere safe."

"Yes, thank you Bryan. We can make this work, I know it!"

"I love you Sydney, no matter what happens, I always will."

"I love you too." She brushed his hair back from his brow, kissing him softly on the lips. "I'll text you the minute I can. Please stay safe and watch your back. I don't think he'd ever follow through with those threats, but I need you to be safe."

"Believe me, I'm on high alert. I'll see you next week. I think its best if we don't make any contact until then."

"I agree, but I don't like it."

He kissed her one last time and exited the room.

· · ·

"Cut!" Stewart called. "Brilliant! You guys are on fire. You're making my job easy."

Griffin came back through the door, and stood apart, leaning against the door frame, waiting for further instructions from their director.

He studied Penelope; she seemed so off, aloof, guarded, walls up, untouchable...yet she still put in an amazing performance. Real tears and all. Even though he was pissed as hell, he was still impressed with her acting chops.

He wasn't about to let her get away with this blow-off without an explanation. He'd corner her soon. This was bullshit. He deserved a 'fuck you get lost' at least. He'd take that any day of the week over this cold, unresponsive ice maiden.

"If there's nothing else Stew, I'm out of here."

"Sure thing, see you tomorrow morning."

Penelope didn't even look at him as he turned on his heel and left fuming.

27

Penelope was sitting outside when Dolly found her. Handing her a glass of wine, Dolly sat down next to her on the wicker couch, curling her feet up beneath her. Penelope had been dreading this conversation all day. Other than her mom, she'd never told a living soul about this dark stain on her past.

Dolly touched her arm, "Hey, if this is too much, we can postpone it until you're ready."

"No, I need someone to talk to. I'm scared Dolly."

Dolly's face was etched with concern. "Okay, I'm listening."

Penelope hugged herself tightly, her bottom lip trembling. "I don't know where to start."

"Take your time, breathe."

Taking a steadying breath, she began, "I guess I'll start at the beginning. I left Ohio for the bright lights of Hollywood when I was eighteen. Big dreams. I'd saved all my tip money from waitressing the summer before senior year. I had two thousand dollars to my name." She bit her lip.

"You were so young, just a baby," Dolly said. "How brave you were."

"Mom had just remarried, and I couldn't wait to get out of the house. I felt like an interloper, not that they tried to make me feel that way, a new marriage...they needed time alone, just as a couple."

"Makes sense to me."

"We didn't have the money to send me to college and I had my heart set on acting anyway. I'd always landed every leading role in high school and community theatre. I got cast in my first play when I was eight. I got bit by the acting bug early."

"I can see a little adorable tow-headed Penelope, nailing her performance."

Penelope smiled sadly. "Yeah, always determined."

"So, then you landed in LA?"

"Yes, I stayed in a youth hostel, posting everywhere looking for a roommate. Found one the first week, Camille was her name, also an actress from Missouri, she was twenty-one and so cool." Penelope rolled her eyes. "So much older and wiser than me."

"I went to every casting call I could find, walk-on parts, extras, stand-ins you name it. I found a job waitressing at a trendy LA diner, made great tips but not enough to cover the cost of living in LA." Penelope paused, taking a deep breath. "This is where it gets hard."

"It's okay, I won't judge."

"One night Camille came home all excited. She had

been approached at the bar where she worked by some big-wig from one of the major studios. He had a proposition for her, said she could make great money, one to five thousand dollars for a few hours of work."

Penelope paused, her throat tight with unshed tears. "I'm not sure I can go on."

Dolly reached for her hand and held on tight. "You're trembling! Oh honey, there is nothing you could say that would make me change my opinion about you."

She impatiently brushed at her eyes. She whispered, "I don't know what I'm going to do."

"No matter what it is we'll figure it out," Dolly said firmly. "Why don't you try again?"

Penelope sat up and grabbed a tissue from the side table and blew her nose loudly, which made them both smile.

"Where was I?"

"Your roommate met with a studio head...that's as far as you got."

"Right..." Sighing, she tentatively began again. "The executive told her all she had to do was accompany some of his friends, clients, benefactors, he was running a little side business...perks if you will. When they needed an escort, he supplied them. Basically, all she had to do was to be their date, get wined and dined and come away with a boatload of cash, under the table of course."

"If it sounds too good to be true..." Dolly interjected.

"Exactly, but she was twenty-one years old...from Missouri! I was just shy of nineteen and backward.

Small-town syndrome." Her gaze took on a faraway look, remembering. "She was over the moon. She promised if it went well, she'd put in a good word for me."

"And I'm guessing it went well?"

"More than well, she was making a ton of money and having fun doing it. Going to parties, campaign fundraisers, film premieres, I mean she was a gorgeous young girl. They often specifically requested her."

"Did she get you in then?"

"Yeah, after a couple of months she introduced me to the studio exec. He liked me and asked me to work for him."

"I can imagine he thought he'd hit the jackpot when he got a look at you."

Penelope bowed her head, "Actually, I thought I had. It seemed like a dream come true at the time. I trusted that Camille wouldn't steer me wrong."

"I'm sure she wouldn't have intentionally," Dolly said. "But you were both young and dumb."

"Yes. One of the conditions...was...um...that, you know, I had to act the part, pretend to be their girl-friend, lover whatever. I figured this was Hollywood and could be my shot at meeting someone, my big break."

"Let me guess, lecherous old men..."

"Some were, then there were the gay men that needed cover, those were the dates I loved. We laughed and partied...I had several gay guys that called on me several times a month. I got to meet a ton of actors and directors by the way, so I figured eventually it would pay off, I'd be discovered." Penelope grimaced, recalling her naiveté.

She took a sip of wine, "I had begun noticing a change in Camille. Subtle at first, she would get irritable and moody, snap at me over nothing. Then she became depressed and withdrawn."

Her phone pinged again, she glanced at the message and frowned, then continued. "I was having my own problems. I had several incidents with a couple of my clients. One guy became obsessed with me. He was a total tech geek, one of my wealthiest and most frequent clients. Then there were the rich dirty old men I'd accompanied. A few came on way too strong in the back of their limos. One of them got rough. I went to the boss and he told me to lighten up. He suggested I could make a hell of a lot more money if I did put out."

Dolly's eyes widened and she put her hand over her mouth. "Oh my God! That's terrible. He sounds like a pimp!"

"Yes, I told him he'd better do a better job of screening my clients or I'd quit. I'm ashamed to admit, but I had let a few of the men I'd escorted kiss me, no biggie, but that's as far as it ever went, I swear! You may be wondering why I didn't quit? Stupidity and bills. Plain and simple, I was making so much money it was hard to give it up."

"Oh Penny," she looked so sad that Penelope teared up again.

"Fast forward...the billionaire computer nerd, Josh, began to get possessive and demanding, wanting me all to himself. He offered me everything short of the moon. He wanted me to quit and marry him. He said I was too sweet and innocent to be escorting lecherous old men for money."

"What was he like? Any sparks there?"

"God no! He freaked me out. He was obsessed with me. Ironically, the very last escort date with him changed my life. It was a political fundraiser. He was a big donor to the senator up for re-election. Huge fancy gala. Celebrities, the governor, the who's-who list in attendance."

"I'm scared to hear what's coming next."

"I fell in love."

Dolly gasped, "That's definitely not what I expected to hear. I thought you said there were no sparks?"

"Ha! No, not with Josh. There was this up-and-coming, might I add, young, gorgeous and ambitious, district attorney at the party. From Nevada. He had his life mapped out, grand plans for his political future. His dream was a senatorial run."

"We hit it off immediately. He was intelligent, funny, charming, and completely smitten with me. He sat next to me at the dinner...we couldn't take our eyes off each other. We laughed and talked; I was half in love by the end of the night. It was mutual."

"What did your date think of all this?"

"He was furious. At first, he was so busy schmoozing with the elite that he didn't notice I wasn't paying any attention to him. When he finally did notice, he practically dragged me out of there, then berated me the entire trip home. That's when I decided to quit. Done!"

"What happened to Mr. Dreamy? Did you have time to exchange numbers?"

"No, but the next day three dozen long stemmed roses were delivered to my home, followed by a phone call. He'd managed to get my name and number from the host. He also found out I was an escort, but he didn't care. He wanted to see me again."

"I said yes. On our third date we made love. He was my first. Of course, he was stunned to find out that I was a virgin. We fell hard for each other, dated for about six months whenever he was in town. By then some small parts were trickling in, my name was getting out there. It was an exciting time. Then..." Penelope bit her knuckles. "I got pregnant."

"What?" Dolly's eyes widened.

"Yes. It was a shock. I was terrified...but I was kind of excited too."

"How did he take it?"

"Not very well. He said he wasn't ready to start a family. He wanted me to get an abortion. I refused." Dolly looked so sympathetic that Penelope choked up for a minute before continuing.

"We continued to see each other when he was in town. He had promised to pay for my medical costs and to financially provide for the baby, but that it was important for his political aspirations not to be linked with me or the child."

"Bastard!"

"Looking back, I can't believe how naive I was. A small-town dumbass simpleton. I'd taken everything at face value and thought I knew it all and was savvy enough to handle anything thrown my way...not."

"One day there was a knock at my door...it was Mrs. Emily Warren, his wife. To say I was upset is an understatement, I was devastated. She had photos of us, even one of us entering the OBGYN office together. I was obviously pregnant, my belly swollen, his arm around my waist. She also pulled out pictures of his kids, all three of them."

"Oh Pen, I'm so sorry."

"I was shattered. I loved him so. There I was, nineteen, pregnant in LA, and alone. Emily Warren made me promise not to tell Graham about our meeting. I had to promise I'd never reveal how I found out about his double life. If I didn't go along with that, she would ruin me. I was to break up with him and never make contact again."

She took a deep breath then continued, "When I confronted him about his marriage, he begged me not to end it. He swore we could still have it all. He claimed I was his one true love. And that his marriage was a sham. I told him I wouldn't share him or break up a family, I couldn't add homewrecker to my list of sins. I ended it and told him I never wanted to hear from him again."

"A week later I lost the baby. I was almost six months along. I thought I'd never recover. But the worst of it was the tiny speck of relief I'd felt—that nearly destroyed me. I was sure that it was karma...for being with a married man, for escorting men for money, that I'd somehow killed my baby...like I'd willed it because I really wasn't ready for a child."

Penelope reached for an envelope on the side table and handed it to Dolly. "I found these in my dressing room this morning."

Dolly slowly pulled back the flap and reached

inside the envelope. She pulled out the 5 x 7 photos and her jaw dropped. A very young Penelope Winters was in every shot, looking seductive and caught looking questionably intimate. In one shot she was laughing up at an older man while he stared leeringly at her breasts, in another photo she was sitting on the lap of a much older man wearing a tight skirt that rode up her thighs.

Penelope grabbed the pictures from Dolly and laid them out side by side on the glass coffee table. She went down the line, pointing, "This one married, this one married, this one a very powerful politician..." She got to the last one, an incredibly handsome man in his early to mid-thirties. She picked up the photograph, touching the image with her fingertip, "This is him, Graham Warren."

Dolly gulped, "*The* Graham Warren? The same one that just announced he's running on the Republican ticket for president?"

"Same."

"Oh my!" She studied the photograph. They were holding hands with the backdrop of Rodeo Drive behind them. They looked like any other beautiful couple. Stunning, happy, in love. "How many years ago was this?"

"Thirteen."

"Wow!"

"Yeah, you can say that again."

"What are you going to do about this?"

"What can I do? Wait and see what's coming next. I'm sure it's going to be a real riot," she said. "The funny thing is," Penelope said, picking up the picture of her and Graham, "I've seen this photo before. This is the same one that Emily confronted me with all those years ago. I'd never forget it. It's burned in my memory."

"What the hell? Why would she be bringing this up now? You know what? Fuck it! Today, nobody is going to care what you did thirteen years ago."

"I'm not so sure about that. An affair with a married man, especially one with three kids is still frowned upon. Plus, what about Graham? This would ruin him. Not to mention the other men in the photos. What about their wives? And children and grandchildren!"

"You have to take care of yourself. Don't worry about those bastards."

Penelope waved her hands up in the air, "Headlines, *Penelope Winters...dark past revealed...she was once an escort for the rich and famous including the presidential hopeful, Graham Warren.* The tabloids will devour me and him. It sheds a whole new light on the magazine cover that was left for me though. Where does Jack fit in, if he even does? Did someone hire him?"

Dolly's eyes narrowed. "I wonder."

"Is it a coincidence that they just announced Graham was running on the Republican ticket, and this resurfaces?"

"What a mess!" Dolly said.

"The more I think about it the more I'm thinking there is a connection between his run and these photos."

"But why bother with you? If they're blackmailing him why go after you? It doesn't make sense."

"I don't know, but I think I should try to talk with Graham. Obviously, I no longer have his contact information. I'll have to leave a message with his staff and hope he receives it."

"Yes, I think you have to."

"Dolly, I've been carrying this alone for so long, it's a relief to finally talk about it. My mom knew some of it, but not all."

"Make the call today."

"I will."

"Whatever happened to Camille?"

Grief danced across Penelope's face, "She overdosed. Gone. She'd moved out of our apartment and moved in with some guy. About a year after she left... she was dead."

"How sad."

"Now that you know all of my dirty little secrets, do you think I'm a terrible person?"

"Hell no, now I understand why you hate men! Makes me want to kill someone!"

Penelope had to laugh at the vision of her sweet-natured friend killing someone.

"Thank you," Dolly said.

Surprised, Penelope put a hand to her throat, "Thank *me*? For what?"

"For honoring me with your trust."

Penelope threw her arms around Dolly and hugged her tight, "You are such a dear friend. It's only because you made it feel safe that I was finally able to open up."

They'd been enjoying unseasonably warm temperatures for early October, allowing them to take advantage of their heated pool, even after the sun went down. "Let's get in our suits and float around for a bit."

Penelope's phone pinged, signaling another text message.

"Griffin?"

Penelope nodded. She silenced her phone and put it back in her bag.

"Don't do this Pen."

"I can't talk to him about it right now."

"I think you need to talk to him. He's crazy about you Penny, and I've never seen you this gaga over a guy. Don't shut him out."

At Penelope's warning glare, Dolly held her hands up. "Okay, I'll drop it for now. Go put on your suit."

"Okay. And thanks for understanding."

"I didn't say I understood. Griffin is a good guy. Even if you can't talk to him about this yet, don't shut him out from the rest of your life. You know what? To hell with wine...it's a tequila kind of night my friend."

"Couldn't agree with you more."

28

Griffin wanted to punch something. Why wasn't she returning his texts or phone calls? What bullshit was this? They'd both let their guard down over the weekend and it had exceeded every expectation he'd had. She'd been open, funny, sensual, uninhibited, free, what the hell had changed from the time he'd dropped her off until now?

Less than twenty-four hours ago they'd made love and now he'd been summarily dismissed. He knew it was late, but what the hell, he was going to get to the bottom of this. Grabbing his car keys, he headed out the door.

He put in a call to Kyle en route to Penelope's. "Hey big brother, any bites on the investigation?"

"Jack Feldner is still in town. It appears that he hooked up with a local woman and is crashing at her house. She waitresses at a bar in town, which I assume is how they met."

"I was hoping he'd catch the first flight back to LA, but apparently no such luck."

"How far do you want to take this?" Kyle asked.

"I'm not sure. Does he have a record?"

"None on file. He's either never been caught or hasn't been formally charged with anything. He was let go from another film project he worked on several years ago, but no reason was given. You've got to be damn careful about what information is divulged these days. People can sue for anything."

"Let's give it a couple more days, keep our eyes on him and see if he does anything suspicious. Maybe it wasn't even him that sent the rag."

"Yes, it's all conjecture at this point."

"What about the rest of the crew, any red flags?"

"None so far. I'll keep you posted. One interesting sidebar, not pertaining to any of this just some trivia, you know the guy that threw himself into the presidential race, Graham Warren? His nephew Ben is working on your film. Small world."

"Nice kid, I won't hold that against him. Can't choose your family. Thanks bro. I owe you one."

"How's the film coming along? Are you going to bring an Oscar to the Bennett family portfolio?"

He scoffed, "I'll be lucky to get through it."

"Faye said things are going well so far."

"It's complicated. I may have screwed up big time by getting a little too personally involved with Penelope."

Kyle chuckled. "Some things never change."

"I thought this one might be different, but now I'm not so sure."

"She may be just what you need. You need a woman

who can go toe to toe with you. You've been way too comfortable in your Lothario role. One of these days you're going to meet *the one* and settle down. I'll pay big money for a front row seat to that."

Griffin's lips tightened, "You were no saint yourself before you met Ella."

"Not even a close comparison to you, but I'm not here to bust your balls. I'll keep the PI on retainer until you say otherwise."

"Thanks. Later." Griffin pressed a button on his steering wheel and disconnected just as he pulled into Penelope's drive.

*D*olly opened the door holding Archie, and Griffin could swear he saw pity in her eyes, "Hey Griff, what's up?"

"Where's Penelope?"

"By the pool. Um Griff, this may not be the best time for a visit."

"Maybe not," he said, as he pushed by her, "but ya know what? I don't give a shit."

Her eyes widened. "Well then..." She stepped out of his way. "We've been drinking Margaritas since six, a glass of wine before that. I quit a while ago...but not Pen...Do you want one...a glass I mean?"

"No thanks."

Dolly grabbed his arm, "Go easy on her, there's a lot you don't know."

"Enlighten me then."

"That's not my place. Just have patience...give her time."

"I'll take that into consideration."

"I'll give you two some privacy. I'm going to bed. I'm taking Archie with me."

"Thanks Dolly."

When Griffin saw Penelope's red nose and puffy eyes, his anger dissipated substantially. She appeared so vulnerable sitting there, her head bowed, sipping her drink through a straw.

"Hey Pen," he said quietly, taking the seat Dolly had occupied earlier.

"Griffin, what are you doing here?" Her voice slurred slightly, and her nose crinkled adorably as she tried to focus.

"I'm here to find out what's going on with you."

Her eyes flooded with tears. "Nothing."

Griffin rubbed his thumb across her cheek catching a tear as it escaped.

"You expect me to believe that? What the hell happened between when I dropped you off and when I saw you less than two hours later?"

"I'm sh..orry, I'm just having a bad day."

"That's bullshit and you know it."

Penelope pouted, "Don't be a meany..."

"It feels like you're backing off. I'm normally the one terrified of any hint at commitment, so I get you...but... this is different...what we have, I mean."

"You don't even know me...you think you do...but you don't you know...you don't have a clue," she attempted to set her glass down and almost missed the table. Griffin's quick reflexes saved the glass before it crashed onto the cement patio.

"I'm trying to remedy that but, sorry to say, I haven't mastered mind reading yet."

She swatted at him and snickered, "You're sho...so funny."

Griffin checked himself. He wanted to pick her up and carry her off to his lair. He'd never experienced anything like it.

"Penelope, I'm not judging, but perhaps you'd better lay off the tequila. I think it's served its purpose."

"Your normal high-handedness I see...just what I'd *spect* from you. I'll drink whatever...whenever...I want." To prove her point, she picked up her drink and sipped from her straw, draining the entire glass in one noisy slurp.

She looked around, her eyes narrowed and unfocused. "Where's Dolly?"

"She went to bed."

"I'll have to have a talk with her...she's got some *splainin'* to do," she giggled.

"Pen, obviously we'll have to have this discussion another time. Please just do me a favor and go to bed now. You've got a full day of filming tomorrow."

"Overbearing much?" she said, glaring.

"I call it caring...and being truthful. But yeah, in this moment I am feeling like throwing you over my shoulder and taking you home for your own protection."

"Ooooh, I like my men saucy."

"Stay right here, I'm going to go get Dolly."

She fell back against the cushions and closed her eyes. "The room is spinning. I feel like I'm going to be sick."

He sighed heavily, "Hold on, let me help you." He scooped her up into his arms and carried her inside. "Where's your room?"

Her arms wrapped around him, her face burrowed into his neck and she nibbled and licked his skin, driving him crazy. She whispered, "Down the hall and right." She hiccupped and giggled again. "My Sir Galahad."

"Do you still feel like you're going to throw up?"

"No. But I'm *shill* lightheaded."

"I'm going to have you sit down on your bed for a second." She sat on the edge of the bed and Griffin kept one arm tightly around her while he pulled back the coverlet.

"Your suit is still damp, so I'm going to take it off, okay with you?"

"Shh...ure...you know me, just a hussy." She giggled then squeezed her eyes shut. A second later she broke into tears.

"Awww, Babe." He sat on the bed and hauled her against his chest. Kissing her brow, he murmured soothing sounds as he held her tight.

"Griff?" Her voice sounded so tiny.

"Yeah?"

"Can you stay with me?"

It was difficult to keep up with her sudden twists and turns and he was doing his best to navigate. "Maybe I should go get Dolly to keep you company."

"I *jush* want you to hold me."

"I can do that," he capitulated, since it was what he wanted to do anyway.

He pulled the ties on her bikini top and removed it,

then tugged her bottoms off. "Don't move," he said, then went over to her dresser and rooted around until he found a tee shirt.

"Put your arms up," he commanded, she swayed as she held them out for him. He pulled it over her head then lay her down, covering her.

"Don't leave me," she said, sounding panicked.

"I'm not, I'm just taking my pants off." He kicked his shoes to the side and stepped out of his jeans. Then he took off his shirt and crawled in next to her with only his boxers on. He sighed. *It's going to be a long-ass night.*

He spooned her from behind and pulled her tightly against him. Inhaling her scent, he took pleasure in her warm soft body melting into him. Within minutes her breathing was quiet and steady...she was asleep. He kissed the back of her head and much to his surprise he found himself getting sleepy.

As he drifted off, he remembered her calling herself a hussy; what was that all about? She'd said she'd only been with two men...hardly promiscuous. He'd question her about it when she was sober and rested. His last thought as he drifted off was...*so elusive.*

*P*enelope snuggled sleepily into the warmth enveloping her from behind. Her eyes shot open when she felt a hard stiff rod pressing into her bottom. Suddenly she was wide awake. She wiggled her butt against Griffin and his arms tightened around her. His lips rested against her neck for a moment, then he sat up, leaving her filled with a longing for his touch.

"Where are you going?" she asked. She rolled onto her back and watched him pull on his pants.

"Home."

"Why?"

"Penelope, we have a few things to work out before we jump back into sex again."

She sat up scowling. "You're blowing me off?"

"No, I didn't say that."

"It sure sounded like that to me."

"You'd better get out of bed and get ready for work Ms. Tequila Sunrise or Stew will have your head. Do you have any aspirin around here? I'll bring you a couple before I take off."

"In the bathroom." She watched his broad shoulders and muscular back as he strode toward her ensuite. "I suppose you undressed me and put me to bed?"

He returned with two pills in his palm and a small glass of water.

"Here."

She popped them into her mouth and swallowed.

"How are you feeling?" he asked.

"Too soon to tell. How bad was I last night?"

"Let's just say I got here in the nick of time...you were a hairbreadth away from passing out."

She looked at him from under her lashes, and felt her cheeks grow warm, "Did I say anything that I should, A...apologize for or B...be embarrassed about?"

He smiled down at her and took her chin in his hand. "Your secrets are safe with me."

She stiffened and all the color drained from her

face. "Wh...wha...what do you mean by that? What did I say?"

"Hey, I was just kidding. Penelope? Are you alright?"

"I guess I'm more hung over than I thought. You can go now," she said, jerking her chin from his grasp.

"See you on set." He turned abruptly and stomped out of the room.

Her hands shook as she tied the sash of her robe. She felt terrible. Instead of thanking him for taking care of her last night, she had hurt him. *How am I supposed to work today?* But they were depending on her and she would have to suck it up. Nobody's fault but her own. Coffee first, then she would get it together.

29

*G*riffin grabbed his cup of Joe from the coffee bar and turned as Penelope approached. "Hey," he said.

"I've been looking for you."

He stopped in front of her and his eyebrows rose as he waited. She licked her lips which sent desire coursing through him.

"Griff, I'm sorry. I had some unexpected news yesterday and I was trying to wrap my head around it. I didn't mean to push you away. Forgive me?"

He tilted his head. "Are you alright now?"

"Yes. I have some things to deal with that I'm not ready to talk about just yet, but I'm handling it."

"Is there anything I can do to help? I've got very broad shoulders you know."

"Just be patient with me."

"Patience is definitely not my strong suit, but I'll do my best."

A smile lit up her face, and her eyes sparkled. "I'd appreciate that."

"I'd like to whisk you away for another quick trip. After tomorrow, we don't have any scenes for a couple of days."

"Can I think about it?"

He reached down and stroked her face, "Do I have a choice?" Her eyes closed as she rubbed her cheek against his hand. Griffin sighed, "Right now, all I can think about is you pressed against me in bed this morning. I want to kiss you breathless right now. This distance at work is killing me."

She dissolved into laughter, "What do you think would happen if we came out? That we'd be making out all day between sets? We'd still be in the same boat. We have to keep things professional."

He grinned salaciously. "Says who?"

"Me. I've got to find Stew. I have a couple suggestions for my next scene. I'll get back with you later about the getaway."

"I saw Stew in the meeting room right before I came for coffee."

She met his gaze, "Thanks, I'll see you later."

It was taking an extreme amount of self-control to keep his hands off Penelope. He craved her. If her burning gaze was any indication, he wasn't alone.

"Later." He watched her disappear around the corner then headed to his dressing room. He needed to hit up Dolly for a favor. He was hoping to enlist her help in surprising Penelope. That is, if Ms. Winters said yes to his suggestion. They needed time to play together...she needed to forget about whatever demons she was fighting. Dolly was the best ally he could think of.

~

*P*enelope and Stew had hashed out some scene details and now she was pacing in her dressing room gripping her phone, summoning up the courage to make the call to Graham. She knew it was ridiculous to be nervous. There was no way she'd reach him today and she had a slim chance that he'd return her call at all. *Well here goes nothing.*

She dialed the number for his local office. "Yes hello, my name is Penelope Winters and I'd like to get a message to Senator Warren; it's important that he return my call."

"You must get teased a lot for having the same name as the movie star," the receptionist said good-naturedly.

"You have no idea," Penelope said.

"I can try to make sure that he receives this message, but he's in DC and out of this office until the end of the week. No guarantees. I can make sure his assistant gets it though."

"That will have to do. Will you personally follow up on it for me?"

"Absolutely, now what is the message?"

"Please tell him that I have some old photographs that he might be able to use for the campaign. Tell him to call me. I know he'll be interested. Here's my number." Her hands were shaking as she rattled off her number. He promised to follow up with her after he delivered the message and they disconnected.

It would be perfect timing for a getaway with Griffin. She needed the distraction, or she'd drive herself crazy waiting for the return call. Penelope glanced at her watch. She'd better get a move on if she didn't want to be late.

Like they were in perfect sync, Dolly knocked at that exact moment and popped her head in the door.

"I'm here. Sorry I'm a little late, Griffin cornered me."

Penelope arched a brow, "Did he now?"

"Yes, and I promised to twist your arm about his surprise trip. Can I just say, he is so romantic! You'll love this itinerary."

"Spill."

"I can't, I promised. But I do have a job assigned to me after I get you to agree."

"You're playing it that way, are you? I had you pegged as the loyal type."

"I am. I know what's best for you."

"I was going to say yes anyway. I called Graham and left a message with his local office in Nevada, but he'll be in DC until the end of the week, so he probably won't get it until then."

"Perfect. You'll get to take a break with that gorgeous hunk, and no more mysterious packages to freak you out while you're away."

"How will I know what to pack if you two won't tell me where I'm going?"

"That's part of my job. Pack for you and find a great costume disguise so you won't be recognized."

"You're kidding right?"

"Nope. I'll make it easy, so you won't have to spend hours on it."

"I take it I won't be going as an alien then?"

Dolly snorted, "No, I'll make you just as beautiful as you normally are, I promise. A good wig will probably be enough."

"Can I make guesses and you can tell me if I'm hot or cold."

"No. Quit digging. My lips are sealed."

"For now. I'll get it out of you."

"Now sit so I can do your makeup. Look at those rosy cheeks, Griffin is good for you."

"I really like him Dolly, I just keep reminding myself to be in the moment. Nothing is promised."

"I don't know...I have a feeling about this one."

"What about you and Ben?"

She blushed, as she applied foundation to Penelope's face using a moist sponge, "We're friends. I'm taking it slow, but I like him."

"He seems sweet. I've never worked with him before, but he seems dedicated."

"He loves his job. He is also funny as hell, which is like kryptonite to me."

"You'll have a couple nights to yourselves with me gone."

"Pout your lips," she said, holding up the lipstick tube. "It hadn't even crossed my mind."

"And I don't believe you."

"Finishing touch. You're good to go. I managed to cover those dark worry circles under your eyes. I'm a miracle worker. You're welcome."

"Marvelous job. Thanks. I'd better high tail it out of here."

"I'm thinking red."

"What?"

"Your disguise...for your getaway with Griffin."

"I've always wanted to be a redhead."

"That should be enough to disguise you...that and sunglasses whenever possible."

"Right. See ya." She ran out the door to the set which was on location today. She wouldn't see Griffin again until late afternoon. They were reshooting a short scene that Stew thought needed a few changes. She didn't have any nude scenes for the rest of the week. For that she was thankful.

She determinedly put aside analyzing the puzzling photographs. There was nothing to be done about it for the time being. She'd focus on work then she planned to throw herself into the trip. A flash of Griffin's sexy smile made her lips turn up at the corners. She'd be happy as a clam to hole up in a bedroom for the entire time. That would be quite alright with her.

30

When Griffin saw Penelope, he had to do a double take. If she hadn't been standing at her own doorstep, he wouldn't have recognized her. "Damn, Dolly is good."

"I heard that," Dolly said, stepping around the corner. "I think she makes a gorgeous redhead, don't you?"

"She does indeed. Those eyes...green-eyed redhead. Instant boner."

"TMI," Dolly said, plugging her ears.

"Hey, you two, I am standing right here you know."

Griffin swooped down and planted a kiss on her full lips, "You look ravishing."

"Thank you. I'm kind of enjoying the red hair."

"It suits you."

She slipped on her sunglasses and Griffin grabbed her suitcase.

Dolly followed them to the front door holding

Archie. "You guys have fun and forget about everything."

Penelope kissed the top of Archie's head. "I'm always leaving you...my poor baby."

"He'll be fine. Go!"

"Thanks for your help, Dolly," Griffin said, over his shoulder.

"Welcome."

He held Penelope's door and she slid into the luxurious Audi. Jogging around, he jumped in and fired up the powerful engine.

"Mmm these seats are sinfully sensuous," she said, sinking into the soft leather bucket seat.

"What do you want to listen to?"

"Bruno Mars? With your sound system it should be awesome."

"Sure, sounds good."

"Now will you tell me where we're going?"

"I'll give you a hint, Mickey and Minnie."

She squealed, delightedly. "We're going to Disney World?"

He looked over at her and nodded, his throat tightening seeing the joy on her face. Her smile was devastating.

"You approve?"

"I've never been! I feel like my life kind of skipped that part."

"Stick with me, I'll show you the world," Griffin said, then realized that he meant it. He wanted to give her everything she'd ever wanted.

"Oh my God! This is perfect. Thank you."

"We're flying down in the company jet. I've booked

two nights at the Four Seasons. After we check in, we're going to go insane for a couple of days."

*P*enelope detected a bit of jealousy coming from Natalie, the flight attendant. She was pleasant enough, but she could sense a coolness. Penelope couldn't help but notice the way Natalie looked at Griffin, as though she'd like him to be her next meal. Who could blame her? He was rocking his designer stubble and always managed to pull off a sexy, carelessly cool look. Faded blue jeans hung low on his hips, a Vee-neck white tee shirt molded to his body, biceps strong and tanned, check...check...check...all her boxes. *Damn him!*

The disguise seemed to be working since neither the pilot nor Natalie had recognized her until Griffin had introduced them. She had to promise the pilot a selfie before disembarking. Natalie was less impressed. Penelope bit back a smile, she certainly didn't expect her to be asking for an autograph any time soon.

Griffin was acting as excited as a little boy and he pulled out his laptop to show her the things he wanted her to experience while they were at Disney World.

"Number one priority is Haunted Mansion. It's dark and we'll ride through it on *Doom Buggies*...get it? *Doom buggies*," he said.

She laughed. "I get it. Is it scary?"

"It's just fun and silly...nothing jumps out at you. It's my personal favorite thing there. Sparks my imagination."

"How many times have you been?"

"At least a half dozen." He flashed her that killer grin. "What can I say? I'm a big kid."

"I love this side of you," she said, her heart melting in her chest. Griffin got real still and looked at her so intently that she had to look away. She swallowed then asked, "What else?"

"Indiana Jones Stunt Spectacular, which is a wild stunt show with the Indiana Jones movie theme. Now that's a job I could get into. Then there's the Kilimanjaro Safari, it's like going on a real African safari tour. The scariest is Expedition Everest...high speeds, drops, creatures jumping out, backward plummets, a train careening up the mountain. It's a blast! They closed my previous favorite, the Twilight Zone Tower of Terror, but they've replaced it with Guardians of the Galaxy, and it will be new for both of us. You aren't afraid of heights, are you?"

"Why?"

"Just answer the question," he said.

"No."

"Afraid of the dark?"

"No, but should I be starting to worry here? I know you're the adventurous sort."

"Hey at least I'm not asking you to parachute or ride in a glider plane."

"Do you do that?"

"Guilty. Didn't I mention that I'm an adrenaline junkie?"

"I may have missed that memo."

"I'll take good care of you."

"I trust you...I may be crazy, but I do," she said, and he smiled so warmly at her that her heart was no longer melting in her chest, but was now lodged firmly in her throat. A wave of longing surged through her. Was she falling for this guy?

"Quit looking at me like that or I won't be responsible for what happens next," he murmured.

His eyes scorched her right before his open mouth came down on hers. As his tongue plunged inside her, she felt a dampness between her thighs. She moaned against his lips.

"I want to kiss your entire body..." he said.

She rode a wave of desire, forgetting time and place until he lifted his head and, grasping her chin, said, "To be continued."

Her breathing fluttered fast and shallow as his thumb traced her bottom lip. *"Vous êtes si belle,"* he said softly. "I'm falling down the rabbit hole."

"Griffin, I..."

"Can I get either of you anything else?" Natalie asked.

"Pen?" Griffin asked her.

"No thank you."

"Me either. Thanks Natalie."

"Just buzz me if you need anything, but we're only about twenty minutes from landing."

"That went quick," Penelope said.

"Yes, thank God! I could only hide my hard-on under the laptop for so long."

"You're so bad."

"And you're so impossibly good."

31

*P*enelope screamed at the top of her lungs as the roller coaster dipped straight down and Griffin couldn't breathe, he was laughing so hard. "Are you going to make it?" he yelled, his face alight with amusement.

Her eyes bright with excitement, she said, "Bring it on!"

"That's my girl," he said, then grabbed her hand and held on tight as they went into a sharp curve.

As the coaster climbed at an impossibly steep angle, he grinned in amusement seeing her tightly closed eyes. "This can only mean one thing," she said, shuddering.

"Hang on babe, it's about to get real."

As they plummeted, she squealed, all the while wearing a huge grin plastered across her face. Something inside of him stirred at seeing her so carefree and in that instant, he realized that he was consumed by Penelope. He wanted to share everything with her. He wanted to be the one to light up her world, to make her smile, to please her, to bring her body to ecstasy again and again.

As they exited the ride, Griffin wondered if he'd ever be able to use his fingers again, she had squeezed his hand so tight.

"Oh my God that was intense!" she said, laughing.

He raised the back of her hand to his lips and said, "You're so much fun to be with."

Still breathless from the rush, she dazzled him with her smile. "What's next?"

Griffin pulled her against him and leaned down to bring his mouth down on hers. "This," he said, and kissed her hard, like he'd never get enough. He felt her body melt into his. Gruffly, he said, "Pen, all the times I've been here...and on that ride, with you, it came alive in a whole different way. It's like everything is new...and brighter...I don't know." He felt a little embarrassed, not sure how to express what he was feeling.

"I feel it too," she confessed.

His arms tightened around her, pulling her even closer to him. "I've got to admit, this is all new to me."

She ran her fingers through his hair and pulled his head down toward her lips. "Kiss me again."

His lips lightly touched hers and lingered before he reluctantly pulled away. "Let's head over to the Safari ride, we need a little calm after the storm."

He checked out the map, pointing to where they currently were and where they were heading. Interlacing his fingers with hers, they went to find their next adventure together.

~

*A*s they exited the restaurant after their romantic dinner, the skies opened, and a torrential rain came down. Penelope grabbed the hand Griffin held out, and they ran laughing and breathless through the downpour. They were drenched to the bone by the time they reached the car.

It was a short drive back to the hotel and they were still dripping wet when they reached the lobby. The water trickled down her face and hair and between her breasts. Griffin looked soggy but delicious, and that made her smile. She wanted to lick the droplets from his neck.

The minute the elevator doors closed they were in each other's arms sharing a wet steamy kiss. Her tongue entangled with his as he grasped her hips, pulling her hard against his erection. Her knees buckled as she got lost in a swirl of passion. The elevator dinged, signaling they'd arrived, and the doors quietly swished open right into their penthouse suite.

His eyes smoldered as they probed hers. He removed her soaked wig and tossed it aside, then slowly undressed her, never taking his gaze from her body. Unclasping her bra, he slid the dainty straps down her slim arms, his fingers brushing against her sensitive skin, sending shivers throughout her body. His lips found the sensitive spot at the curve of her neck. He licked and nibbled as she threw her head back and grasped his shoulders for support. He pulled her panties down and she stepped out of them.

Without a word he picked her up and carried her to the bed. He held her arms above her head while he nuzzled the vee between her breasts, his weight pinning her down. The feel of his hard muscles against her skin made her insane with desire. The friction from the light covering of hair on his chest, brushing against her nipples caused her core to throb. He drew her rosy pink nipple into his mouth and sucked hard...pulling and tugging as she arched beneath him. Her fingers tangled in his hair.

She was already wet and juicy as he slipped a long finger into her tight entry. Plunging his finger, he inserted another inside of her, stretching, teasing her into a frenzy. "Griff," she moaned, "Let me pleasure you."

She wiggled out from beneath him and shifted her body so that she was now on top, tempting him with her full breasts, mere inches from his mouth. Rubbing against him, she loved the way his body felt against her skin...rough, soft, hard, warm. His hardness pressing against her clit as she pleasured herself by rubbing against his cock. Her tongue darted out and flicked his nipple, and his body bucked in response. Raining kisses across his chest she nibbled and licked her way down to his throbbing manhood.

She took him inside her mouth and teased him mercilessly, drawing him in and out, licking the tip of his shaft before enveloping him again.

"Penelope, sit on my cock, now!"

After slipping on a condom, she positioned herself

over him and mounted, straddling him she slowly sank down. He filled her completely, his warmth stretching her, as she took him in all the way and felt him press against her womb.

His muscles were hard and taut under her fingers as she braced them against his chest. She rode him slowly at first then as her own desire increased, she rocked faster and faster. Every time she lifted and sank down, she circled her hips, rubbing, stimulating herself against him, again and again. She gasped with pleasure when he pinched her nipples and cupped both her breasts in his hands.

He bucked underneath her as he began to come. Near to climaxing herself, his mating groans were her undoing and she erupted in an orgasm that swept her away.

"Damn, Penelope, you feel so good," he said hoarsely, as his body shuddered against hers.

Burying her face in his neck, she felt his breath against her skin. His scent...a heady mix of musk...and sex. She lay there taking in all of the sensations, her breasts pressed against his chest, the warmth of him lying under her, the rise and fall of his breath stirring her hair. A wave of emotion hit her, and she waited for it to pass.

"*N*o," she whispered, as he rolled onto his side, taking her with him. "I wasn't ready for you to leave me."

Griffin propped up on one elbow to study her. He

brushed her hair away from her face then traced her lips with his finger.

"I didn't want to leave. I could stay inside you forever. Feel your warmth hugging me. Penelope, you feel so good. I don't know what's happening here, but I've never experienced anything even close to this before."

"Griffin, let's not talk about it, let's just enjoy each other."

"That's supposed to be my line," he said.

Her eyes sparkled with amusement. "Funny. You're used to being in total control of your emotions, aren't you?"

"Yes." She squirmed under his light touch as he caressed her belly. "I never knew it could be like this."

She touched his face, her fingers searching as if reading braille, tracing across his eyebrows and lids, his nose, his lips, his jaw. She dipped her finger into his mouth, and he sucked on it. His eyes blazed with heat, penetrating deep into her psyche. *Could he be any more beautiful?*

He shifted onto his back and hugged Penelope tightly to his side. She flung her arm across his chest, her nose nuzzled against his neck. With her thigh flung over his legs, she felt a primal response to the feel of their bodies intertwined, his hard muscles making her insides coil.

"This might be the best day of my life, thank you," she whispered against his chest.

He kissed the top of her head, smiling into her hair, "I'll never forget your blood curdling screams for as long as I live."

She nipped him.

"Ouch!"

"Sorry."

"Sure you are," he said, his voice sounding sleepy.

"Goodnight, Griffin." She wasn't even sure that he heard her softly spoken, "Sweet dreams."

32

When they were at cruising altitude Penelope fished her phone out of her bag. She had forgotten to turn it on until now and saw that she had six missed calls. She frowned as she read a text message from Stew. "Griffin look at this," she said, passing him her phone.

"Shit."

Stew: Why aren't you answering my calls? Heads up, here's a snapshot from TMZ. Some upstanding citizen must have submitted it. WTF? What is going on with you two? There are at least a half dozen reporters camped out at the Butler. Call me!

"I probably should have given him some warning that we were involved," Penelope said, pressing a hand to her forehead. "I feel bad."

"I was on the same page as you were. I felt like it

was better to keep our personal lives to ourselves for as long as possible," Griffin said, resting his warm palm on her thigh.

She pinched the screen to enlarge the photograph of them embracing on the safari bus. Then another of them kissing. On the close up zoom of her face, the wig and sunglasses hadn't been enough of a disguise. Her breath caught seeing how happy she looked.

Griffin chuckled over the headline, *Has Benters replaced Winoah?* "They're creative I'll give them that."

"It is going to be a shit show from here on out. I'm not kidding."

"But the Carolinas are off the beaten path."

"It won't matter now that there's something juicy worth stalking over. The tabloids have been pushing the Noah and Penelope reunited narrative, but this will be even more salacious. All of us on the same film. A triad. Perfect storm."

"I'm sorry," he said quietly.

"It's not your fault. It comes with the territory. Don't say I didn't warn you. It's about to get messy. You may as well have a taste of it sooner rather than later. Kiss your privacy goodbye."

"What can we do?"

"Nothing but lay low and make no public comments."

"Do you think Stew is pissed?" he asked.

"His nose is probably bent out of shape because we left him out, but this can only help the film. It's free publicity. He'll be happy about that."

Penelope dreaded the fallout from this. Griffin had no idea what he was now caught up in. With everything she knew about him, he was going to hate this loss of freedom. His life had just been split open like a pair of tight pants. After all this time, it was a part of her life, but she'd never gotten used to it. In fact, she hated it. How could she expect him to stick by her or this budding relationship with all the baggage attached?

"Griff, I'm the one that's sorry. I won't blame you if you decide that it's all too much."

Griffin reached for her hand and brought it to his lips, "Let's take it as it comes. I'm not worried."

Her lips twisted, "You're too innocent to be worried." She had no doubt that he thought he understood what was about to happen, but she knew differently.

"Don't let this ruin your mood. I'm going to focus on the positive."

She sat there for a moment before responding. "Griffin, no matter what happens, I want you to know that I had the best time I've ever had in my life with you."

His voice was husky as he responded, "There is so much more I want to share with you. Don't give up on us so easily Pen."

She stretched up and planted a soft kiss on his cheek. "I'll work on that."

"I'll text Stewart and have him send a car to the airport for us. I'll call ahead now and get clearance. They can drive right up to our plane after we land," Griffin said.

"Perfect," she said.

∼

*T*hey'd been successful in avoiding detection at the airport and their driver had dropped each of them off at their own homes. Griffin was now sprawled out on his couch watching a PGA tour on TV, his concentration continuously disrupted by remembering how good it had felt to be with Penelope.

He understood why she was worried about the unwanted attention and what it would do to them. It was unsettling. He felt protective of her and of his growing feelings for her. But this fell under the *I have absolutely no control* category, and he knew he had to shut down his worry. They'd figure it out...or not. Only time would tell.

Maybe it was time he admitted to himself that it was much more than a wild sexual attraction...or that he was more awake than he'd ever been in his entire life...it was also like feeling he'd been out in stormy seas and had finally found safe harbor. Did she feel it too?

~

"*Y*ou're just going to have to tighten up security and assume someone is always watching. I'm afraid we've all gotten used to a certain level of freedom here. That's probably all about to change," Dolly said.

"I know. Lots of films have been shot around here and they've managed to keep it under the radar for the most part. I'm hopeful this will blow over after a few weeks," Penelope said. "Especially if they don't get any new material! If those photos from my past are made public..." she shuddered.

"Don't even go there. Nothing back from Graham I take it?" Dolly asked.

"No. I didn't expect to so soon. Maybe I'll hear from him tomorrow. How can I be sure he'll even get the message?"

"I'd keep leaving messages until you hear back," Dolly suggested.

"I suppose you're right."

"What did Stewart say when you talked to him about the media?"

"He was upset that I hadn't warned him about Griffin and me. I told him we hadn't said anything because it wasn't serious."

"Most everyone on set had an idea. They're not blind or stupid. He had to have had an inkling."

She softly kicked Dolly who was laying at the other end of the couch, "Is that supposed to make me feel better?"

She grinned, "Of course. Fuck 'em. It's nobody's business."

"Speaking of...how'd it go with Ben?"

Dolly blushed, "Good. I like him. It seems mutual."

"It's about time."

"Yeah, I'm not getting any younger."

Penelope snorted, "You're only twenty-six, but it's been two years since you've been serious about a guy. I just want to see you happy. But my advice, don't marry anyone before you're thirty. How old is Ben anyway?"

"He's twenty-five."

"He seems older."

"I know." Her eyes were unfocused and dreamy.

"I'm happy for you."

"Thanks. I'm happy for *Benters,*" she said, giggling as Penelope playfully glared at her.

"On that note, I'm heading for bed," Penelope said. "Night."

33

*P*enelope hung up the phone, relieved that Stewart was over his snit. He was sending a car to pick her up in an hour. Her phone immediately rang again, and thinking it was Stew, she picked up.

"Hey Stew, what'd you forget?"

"Penelope."

A male voice on the other end, warm, seductive and even after thirteen years of absence, very familiar. She froze, her throat constricted.

"Pen, are you still there? It's Graham."

Finding her voice, she said quietly, "I know, thanks for calling back."

"It's so good to hear your voice. It's been so long. Why did you phone me?"

There was a long pause while she tried to regain her equilibrium, surprised by her visceral reaction. It was like she was right back there, thirteen years ago.

"I'm sorry to bother you but have something I thought you should know about."

He sighed heavily into the phone, "I'd like to think this was a friendly call, maybe to congratulate me, but I'm sure it's more ominous than that. You mentioned in your call something about photographs?"

"Yes, from our past."

His breath hissed, "Penelope, did you have something to do with them?"

"What are you talking about? Do with what? I am the one who received photographs last week, a couple of them featuring us. Why would I send myself photos?" she snapped.

"I have no idea what you're talking about. I don't want to discuss this over the phone, but we must talk."

"When?" she asked.

"I'm sitting in front of your house right now. I took a detour and came straight from DC."

This time she gasped, "How did you know where to find me?"

"Penelope don't be so naive, I'm a United States Senator. My assistant thought your message might be important; it was unusual to say the least, so he forwarded it to me."

"You of all people would know about my naiveté wouldn't you Graham?" she said.

"Let's not discuss this over the phone. Can you come out to my car right now?"

"I'll have to make arrangements with my director first. Then I'll throw on some clothes and be right out." She hung up and called Stewart back. He was confused but agreed to work around her. She scrambled into her jeans and a tee shirt and grabbed the envelope with the photographs from her desk on her way out.

She called to Dolly, "Guess who is waiting out front in their car for me...this very second?"

"Griff?"

"No, Graham Warren!"

Her eyes widened in shock. "What? He must know something about the photos then."

"Yes, there's something going on. Watch Archie for me, okay?" She asked, swooping him into her arms and kissing the top of his head. "Stay with Aunt Dolly and be good."

"What about work?" Dolly asked.

"I called Stew. He was confused but understanding."

"Are you sure you'll be safe with Graham?"

"I don't have much of a choice, but yes, I'm sure. But I'm glad I told you everything...at least someone will know who I'm with...just in case. But don't worry."

"Yeah right."

She ran out the door and into the waiting SUV with the dark tinted glass.

*H*e looked as handsome as ever, just older, the gray hair only adding an element of authority, which certainly didn't hurt his political image.

"You still take my breath away," Graham said, his dark eyes burning as he stared at Penelope. He looked hungry, there was no other way to describe it. "You're even more beautiful now than you were back then. There hasn't been a day that's gone by in the last thirteen years that I haven't wondered...what if."

She raised a skeptical brow. "You have no right to even talk about our past Graham. You broke my heart into a million pieces."

He reached out to touch her and she recoiled. "Don't you dare touch me."

"I'm sorry. You're right. I'm going to drive for a while to make sure we're not being followed. Then we can stop to talk."

Penelope had a sudden chill go up her spine and shivered, "Followed? What's going on here Graham?" She rubbed her hands briskly up and down her arms.

"I'm only being extra cautious. I'm not taking any chances. Are you okay?"

"What do you think? No, I'm not okay!"

"Stupid question." They rode in silence, until curiosity got the better of Penelope.

"Congratulations by the way. Wow, running for President, go big or go home, I guess. I always knew you were ambitious, but I didn't realize how much. Was it all worth it then?"

"That's debatable. Speaking of big...what about you? Superstar. You've certainly done well for yourself. Of course, I've followed your career closely over the years. Is it everything you'd thought it'd be Penny? You had such big dreams."

"All I can say is that it's a good thing we can't see into the future or we'd never leave the house."

He laughed wryly. "I can vouch for that."

After driving for about a half hour, he pulled into a small rest area off the highway.

"There's a picnic table back by the tree line. We'll talk there."

Penelope felt as if she was acting out a bad script as she followed Graham, who kept looking over his shoulder as if he expected someone to pop out of nowhere.

"As long as they didn't slip a bug into our shoes or aren't hiding in the trees, I think we're safe," she said, her tone snarky.

"You sound cynical. Not like the girl I once knew."

"Guilty as charged. You may have had a little something to do with that."

"Penelope, I'm sorry. You asked if it was worth it— truthfully, if I had to do it all over again, I would make a different decision this time...many of them. I was already in too deep with three kids. I didn't expect to fall in love. I never loved my wife. Ever."

"I feel sorry for her. She was the real victim here... not me and definitely not you."

"It was a marriage of convenience and opportunity. A modern day arranged marriage. She's no victim. Don't waste your pity. She wanted to please her daddy and she wanted a powerful husband. Her father had big plans for his future son-in-law. He needed me in power to push his own agenda. She might have fancied herself in love at one time, but by the time I met you, there was no love lost between us."

Penelope played with her watch, thinking about what he'd just revealed. In some strange way, it assuaged her guilt an infinitesimal amount.

"I guess it's never black or white, is it? In the end, we were all victims. You know Graham, I may not sound like it, but I have forgiven you, really I have."

"I've never forgiven myself. You were my one true love, Penelope."

Seeing the sadness dance across his face made her chest ache. She allowed herself a fleeting memory of their time together...before she'd found out the truth.

"Well, let's get down to business," she said, handing her envelope to Graham. "I found these on set, in my dressing room. Someone had slipped them under the door."

His expression was disturbingly serious as he traded his pictures for hers. She flipped through them, confused. These were completely different shots than the ones she'd received. The content of hers had filled her with shame...these were like a knife in the heart.

They all captured her and Graham at various stages of their relationship. Almost a montage, chronicling their time together from the beginning until the last photo of her, six months pregnant, swollen belly and Graham's arm around her waist. One she'd seen before, so many years ago. That would have been right before she'd lost her baby. Unconsciously she held a hand protectively over her abdomen.

Their eyes met, and he looked as puzzled as she felt. "Were these sent from the same person?" she asked. "Could it be just by chance that we both received photos for completely different reasons?"

"Highly doubtful. And the timing is suspect...immediately following my presidential run? I don't believe in coincidence."

"But why involve me?"

"I'm not sure yet."

"I'm scared Graham."

"I wish I could say I'm not shaken by this. For me, I thought it seemed obvious that I was being threatened by a political rival, but now? Why did you think to call me?"

"I don't know. I wondered if you might know something about it and I wanted to warn you in case they got leaked."

"There is something..." She pulled out one of her photos, the one of them on Rodeo Drive. "I never told you how I found out you were married in the first place. It was your wife. Emily confronted me with evidence of our affair. She had pictures. I have no idea how she got them. She threatened to expose me if I let on to you that she knew about us. This is the exact same photo Emily showed me when she confronted me all those years ago."

His brows drew together, "Emily? What?"

She reached for another photo from his pile, the one picturing them together with her pregnant swollen belly. "She showed me this one too. Then she made me promise that I wouldn't tell you."

"I'm supposed to believe that she's known about us all along. For all these years?"

"It's the truth."

"And you're sure these are the same photographs?"

"Positive, I could never forget something like that, Graham."

"Jesus!" He raked his hands through his hair, then stood up and began pacing. "My wife has been adamantly opposed to me accepting this nomination. She doesn't want the additional scrutiny that my holding this office would bring to our family. She has come to resent what she calls, 'sacrificing her life,' for my career."

"Could she have sent them?"

There was a long stretch of silence before he answered, "Anything is possible, but isn't it strange that all your pictures target your," he cleared his throat, "Your...um..."

"Just say it, me with my clients. And yours are all of the two of us."

He pinched the bridge of his nose, "Rather than gaining clarity, I'm more confused than ever. When we talked on the phone, I wasn't completely honest with you."

"What do you mean?"

"I have a nephew, Emily's sister's son, who coincidentally is working on your film. He's been facetiming us and I've had to suffer through hearing about you and my wife has never let on anything. She's listened to him sing your praises without a hint of emotion."

Her eye's widened in shock, "Oh my God! Who is your nephew?"

"Ben Donavan."

"Ben? Are you sure he doesn't know about us?"

"I was before. He was just a kid then."

"But he is Emily's nephew and has access to my room. As a matter of fact, he's gone out with my roommate several times. Could he be using her to get at us?"

Graham blew out a long breath, "I'll have to question Emily and get back with you. We'll get to the bottom of this."

"If these photos get out, it will destroy your career and at the very least my reputation."

"I'm aware of that," he said grimly. "I'll give you my private number and you must let me know if you hear any more. Don't let on to Ben that you know about his connection to me until I have time to sort this out. I've known Ben his whole life. He's a good kid. I'm sure this is all innocent and nothing but a bizarre coincidence. If I'm wrong, he and my wife are the ones who should be on the big screen. They'd be up for an Oscar."

Penelope nodded her head, "I'll go along with that for now, but don't take too long. I'm worried about my friend. I really think I need to say something to her, at least."

"Can she hold a confidence?"

"Absolutely. I trust her with my life."

"Do what you think you need to. I guess we should head back. My people are on this. I'll stay in touch. Are you alright?"

"Yes," she said quietly, keeping her eyes lowered.

"Penelope, I'm sorry for everything. I never meant to hurt you...most of all, I'm sorry that I never got the chance to tell you how badly I felt that you lost the baby. I'm sure you were devastated. I never had any intention of abandoning the baby financially. I just wanted you to know that."

She smiled sadly. "Hard to believe our little girl would have been thirteen years old this November."

"Yes, it is. In some ways it feels like yesterday."

On the drive home, both were lost in their own

memories and the atmosphere held emotional under-currents of all the things left unsaid. The second the car pulled into her drive, Penelope said a brief goodbye and hopped out. Without a backward glance, she ran into her house.

34

A cacophony of people yelling and cameras flashing greeted Penelope as she was hustled from the SUV into the Butler House. She kept her head down and even with her sunglasses on and hair tucked up in a large floppy hat, they were neither fooled nor deterred.

"Penelope how does Noah Davis feel about your relationship with your co-star?"

"Penelope, does this mean it's really over for you and Noah?"

"Is it true that you got the part for Griffin Bennett?"

"How does Griffin Bennett feel about sharing you with your last lover?"

The guards formed a wall between her and the small crowd and after she made it inside, they locked the door behind her.

Dolly rushed over, "Quite the welcome committee."

Rolling her eyes, she said, "I've missed them so."

"It was great while it lasted."

"Have you seen Ben yet?"

"No. Don't worry, I can fake it," Dolly said. "I know he has nothing to do with any of it."

"I agree. I don't think he's behind any of this either, but on the slim chance that he is, we have to be careful."

"I know, I get it. Aren't you shooting the boat chase scene today?"

"Yes. We're going over the scene in the conference room then we'll caravan there. Security is tight and they have everything blocked off on the set."

"I've got my kit all packed up."

"I'll see you after the meeting."

She hadn't seen Griffin since he'd dropped her off yesterday and a flutter of anticipation had her belly doing flip-flops. He was the first person her eyes landed on and her breath caught in her throat. He was so damn sexy. His eyes were a deep blue today, bright and animated, he looked so happy. She smiled and he grinned back, nonchalantly stretching his arms over head as he tipped his chair back on two legs. She was unsure where to sit. Now that they'd been outed, it complicated everything. She chose a chair across from him, opting for discretion.

She hated holding secrets from him. She had wanted to keep her past buried, but that was impossible now. Her history had finally caught up with her. She had to fill him in on what was going on. Would he understand? She hoped so. She felt eyes boring into her and glanced at Noah. He was glaring...as if he had every right to. Unbelievable.

Stew said, "I'll say one thing about the tabloid fiasco then we'll move on. No one is to speak to the press about anything that goes on behind the scenes. No comment...burn that line into your brain. We want to contain this from becoming a circus. Everybody understand? If I find out there are leaks, you'll be summarily dismissed. I had a small meeting with the rest of the crew this morning and everyone has been warned."

"It sucks that we have to deal with the fallout," Noah said, arms crossed, glaring at Griffin.

"Hopefully there will be little fallout."

"Yeah right, dream on. It's embarrassing for me... makes me look like the loser," Noah said.

Penelope spoke up before she had time to think, even as the words left her mouth, she knew she shouldn't have taken the bait. "Embarrassing? You're embarrassed? What a joke! Getting a small taste of your own medicine. How do you think I felt when everyone but me knew you were sleeping around on set...behind my back? Embarrassed doesn't even come close to describing it."

"Is that what this is then? Revenge? Penelope, you don't have to do this."

"Oh my God! Could you be any more self-centered? Unbelievable."

"Enough you two!" Stewart said. Griffin's jaw was clenched, and Penelope feared he was going to punch Noah.

"Back to business. I met with the stunt men an hour ago on site and the extras in the next scene are already there. Griffin, your nephew Tyler is there going over his scene. I think he's been bitten by the acting bug. He's catching on quick. They're going through the blocking right now."

"He's psyched to say the least. Or as he'd say, he's *lit.*"

"Heads up, there's quite a crowd gathered on the other side of the tape. The Yacht Club has been more than cooperative with security, but there's only so much they can do."

"Good to know," Penelope said.

"A shout out to Griffin, our so called 'novice' actor. He's a real badass. His rehearsal of this scene was spot on. We won't need any body doubles for the boat chase until right before the crash scene. I'm proud of you. I wish I had your balls," Stewart said, making everyone laugh. "Anybody have any questions before we head over?"

"Should we make time after the shoot to sign a few autographs?" Noah asked.

"Up to you. The way it's set up you should be able to do that safely from the Yacht Club parking lot. It's all cordoned off, but you can mingle along the perimeter if you want to."

"Have to keep the fans happy," Noah said.

Under her breath Penelope said, *yeah and your ego.*

"Okay, the vehicles are parked around back. We'll meet and caravan as a group in ten minutes."

35

*P*enelope loved action scenes. It was a pure adrenaline rush. She was glad that she and Griffin got to share this moment together. They were almost done filming. She couldn't believe that they only had a few more scenes to shoot and that the wrap party was next week.

Griffin's eyes shone, he looked so confident...a man in his element. They had just filmed a shootout scene on the pier and now they were getting ready to film their getaway.

Tyler rushed to greet them, his eyes blazing with excitement. "Griff, dude, are you going to be able to stick around to watch me do my scene?"

"Wouldn't miss it."

"Stew gave Faye and Jess permission to watch. They'll be here any minute."

Griffin smiled affectionately at his nephew, "Stewart says you're a natural."

Ty's eyes widened, "He did? What else did he say?"

"Said you were catching on quick."

"That's dope!"

"I'm proud of you Ty," Griffin said.

"You've been hanging out with Aunt Faye too much," he said. His lips tugged up at the corners, a shy smile flitting across his face. A tell that he was uncomfortable with his uncle's praise. "Griff thanks. I really appreciate you putting a good word in for me."

"I can say I knew you when. Just make sure you don't forget about us when you're a Hollywood bigshot."

"Man, you're straight off the cob dude."

Penelope laughed out loud, "Ty, I love you."

He flushed and shrugged his shoulders, "Awkward."

She hugged him and said, "You're just going to have to live with my displays of affection. You should be used to it by now."

"We'll hit you up after this scene," Griffin said.

"Places everyone, action!"

*B*ryan *grabbed Sydney's hand and pulled her along. "Faster!" he said. She lost her balance and tripped, nearly falling. He wrapped his arm around her waist and held her to his side as he pushed them forward. Glancing over his shoulder he spied two men coming towards them, guns drawn.*

"There's two more, they're close. The next boat on our left is mine. We don't have time to fuck around Syd. Jump on."

He helped her onboard then untied the boat, throwing the rope inside the craft. He revved the boat and backed out before gunning the motor full-throttle, heading to open water. He couldn't afford to look behind them.

"Sydney, can you see what's happening?"

"Oh my God! They just threw someone off their own boat and they're coming after us."

His face grim, he said, "Hang on. I'll lose them."

He turned sharply and changed directions breaking all the rules as he went full speed in the no wake zone. He swerved around other craft, barely missing them as he and Sydney ran for their lives. The speed was dizzying, and Sydney had to hang on for dear life to keep from being thrown from the boat as it zig-zagged dangerously. Bryan's hands gripped the wheel tightly and the wind whipped around him, almost taking his breath away.

As shots rang out, he yelled, "Get down now!"

Sydney hit the floor of the boat, crying and screaming at the same time, "We'll never make it. My husband is too powerful. We may as well give ourselves up and be done with it."

Yelling over the noise of the craft and the wind, he said, "Easy for you to say. You'll return to your gilded cage, but at least you'll still be alive. I'll be wearing cement shoes at the bottom of the ocean. Fuck that. Too late to turn back now."

"If you slow down enough for me to jump out, I'll do that. They'll pick me up and you can keep on going. Please Bryan. I can't bear to see you killed. I love you," she said, sobbing as more shots rang out.

"We're in this together. I love you too, only you."

. . .

*T*he stunt man and woman who were doubles for Griffin and Penelope pulled up to take over for the rest of the scene and subsequent crash. The next scene would have some dazzling acrobatics with the boat jumping across land and landing safely back in water with a crash scene at the end. Way beyond what the studio would allow Griffin to tackle.

Griffin's stunt advisor Jeremy had coached him for the chase scene they had just shot, and he was beaming at Griffin. "You were just like a pro. Damn dude!"

Griffin idled the motor to talk with them before the shooting continued. Penelope went to stand behind Griffin placing her hands on his shoulders. They hung out for a few minutes talking and laughing while the boat with the camera operators prepared for the next scene. The helicopter hovered over them waiting for the cue.

The camera crew signaled they were ready for action. "Break a leg," Griffin said as Jeremy sped away. Penelope sat in the seat next to him and propped her feet up on the dash lifting her face to the sun.

"Heaven," she said.

Griffin said, "I'll take it slow on the way back."

"You were incredible. It felt like we were shooting a Bond film."

"It could be addictive."

He looked so relaxed, with his designer shades and graceful movements. She'd never witnessed him off balance or awkward, all of his biomechanics were smooth and confident. Penelope couldn't take her eyes off him. He was fit and tanned, strong and capable, and he was her lover. She was in deep...almost over her head if she were being honest with herself. Today was even more poignant because it was their last scene together.

She sighed. It was time to have that talk with him. It wasn't fair to keep him shut out. She had neatly compartmentalized her life, but she was no longer comfortable keeping secrets from Griffin. She didn't know when it had happened, but they had somehow passed an invisible line...into what she wasn't sure, but it was no longer in the casual zone.

Taking a deep breath, she dove in, "Um Griffin, I have something important that I need to talk with you about. How about dinner tonight?"

"What's up?"

"I really don't want to discuss it now. I'd rather be alone, drinking some wine, just the two of us. Okay?"

"Sounds rather mysterious, is everything okay?"

"There's something I've been putting off talking about. That's all I'm going to say right now."

"My place then?"

"That would be perfect," she said. "Can I bring Archie?"

"Of course. I need a little bonding time with my man."

"He's definitely feeling neglected. After they drop us off at The Butler, I have to pick up a couple of things from my dressing room, then I'll have my driver take me home to pick up Archie. Is there anything else you want me to bring?"

"Your beautiful self, that's all I need. I've got the rest covered."

He docked the boat smoothly and they jumped off; the crew took over from there. He slipped his arm casually around her waist and she liked the feeling of intimacy. They went to look for Stew and found him in deep discussion with Noah who was about to shoot a scene.

Looking up Stew spotted them and called out, "Reports are you got it on the first take. Good job. You're done for the day."

Penelope bobbed her head towards Griffin, "This guy's a natural."

"I'm glad my instincts paid off," Stewart said. Noah nodded his head in greeting and made a point of staring at Griffin's arm around Penelope's waist.

"You're both too kind," Griffin said.

"Your sister and Jesse are somewhere around here. Ty is about to shoot his inside bar scene."

"That's where we're headed now," Griffin said.

"Take good care of Ty, Stew. Break a leg Noah," Penelope said.

"Thanks," Noah replied, his tone clipped.

When they were a safe distance away, Griffin said, "Are you sure there's nothing still going on between you and Noah?"

"Are you serious? Why would you ask something like that?"

"He certainly seems proprietary where you're concerned."

"We were together a long time. I know he has feelings for me...and I'll always care about him, but I'm not in love with him...if that's what you're asking."

"That's what I'm asking."

"You don't have a thing to worry about there. How about you? You're used to variety, no strings, are you seeing anyone else?"

He turned to her and pulled her towards him framing her face with both hands. He gazed intently into her eyes, "Penelope, there hasn't been anyone else since the moment you scorched me with your fiery gaze and blew me off."

She smiled up at him, "I'm glad to hear that." Wrapping her arms around his neck, she pulled his head down to meet her lips, "Kiss me."

~

"*T*yler lit up the set. Not only is he drop dead gorgeous, but even with his few lines, he managed to pull me in," Penelope said.

Griffin shook his head, smiling, "I hope this doesn't change his mind about college. He was higher than a kite."

They held hands as they made their way to the getaway van, managing to make it under the fans' radar. The driver dropped Penelope off at the studio and took Griffin home.

36

*G*riffin opened the door to Penelope's light knock and stepped back to let her enter. When she'd mentioned *the talk*, he'd felt a ripple of uneasiness. Seeing her worried expression now did nothing to dispel his anxiety.

"Come on in. You look juicy." He leaned down and brushed his lips against hers. He eyed her appreciatively. He liked the way the white tube dress hugged her curves in just the right places. Her toes were painted a bright pink to match her flip flops and her hair was falling loose around her shoulders. He wanted to touch her soft skin, feel it against him. The sun had lightly tanned her skin; it was almost the color of pale honey.

"Ready for that glass of wine?"

"Yes, please."

"I think I'll join you. Why do I get the feeling I'm going to need it?"

"I don't mean to be so mysterious. I feel like I'm being cruel, it's just a hard conversation for me."

"I understand, at least I think I do. Make yourself at home, have a seat here at the kitchen island. I've got most of our dinner pulled together, just have a few finishing touches."

The glass clinked as he set her wine on the granite in front of her. Leaning over he rested his hands on the counter.

"What's going on Penelope?"

She took a big gulp of wine then coughed as it went down the wrong way.

"I'm sorry," she managed to choke out.

There was something in her eyes tonight that he couldn't quite put his finger on. She was off balance, but it was more than that...fear? Embarrassment? Sadness?

"Why don't we eat first then have this *hard* conversation after dinner. Sound good to you?" Her cheeks turned pink and she nodded. He jammed his hands in his front pockets to keep from touching her.

Returning to the salad he was throwing together, he added croutons and tossed it with a lemon vinaigrette dressing. As he carried it to the dining room table, he questioned why he'd even bothered with candles and soft jazz music. It felt off...didn't fit the scene. *Oh well.*

"Come on over and have a seat at the table. I'll grab the bottle of wine then we can eat."

He watched her out of the corner of his eye as she sat. His desire for her hadn't dissipated with time—in fact, it grew stronger every time he was with her. He not only wanted her, he felt fucking freaked out that he might actually need her.

She played with the food on her plate, and as far as Griffin could tell, she'd only managed to consume a few bites. But at least she'd finished her salad.

"We'll just leave everything here, I'll clear the table later," Griffin said. "Let's move outside to the deck."

"Okay."

The ocean breeze stirred her hair and she brushed it back. She looked so vulnerable and scared that all Griffin wanted to do was pull her into his arms. She rubbed her temples then took a deep breath, began talking, and the bottled-up words spilled out.

Griffin sat back and listened to her pour her heart out. The more he heard, the more his body tensed. He was all over the place. Protectiveness, shame for being a man, sadness, helplessness, but the overriding feeling was incompetency.

He was in way over his head. He wasn't a psychologist. He didn't have a clue how to comfort her...what to say. He was momentarily blindsided. He couldn't care less about her history, but how was it that she was so afraid to trust him? How was it that all this had been going on and he hadn't even had a clue? Was he really that self-absorbed?

She got through it all without crying and maintained an impressively dignified countenance. When she was all talked out, she wrapped her arms around herself and looked at him, her eyes flickering with doubt.

"Say something," she said, quietly.

"I don't know what to say. It really sucks. You've

been through so much. I'm really sorry all of that happened to you."

Her eyes narrowed, sensing something was off. "I didn't tell you to burden you, I just felt like you deserved an explanation. It's all such a mess."

He blew out a breath. "That's an understatement."

"Thanks," she said, grimacing. She began nervously toying with her hair, her gaze now lowered. "Griffin, I can tell that you've pulled back. Are you upset with me?"

"No, why would I be? None of this is your fault."

"I'm sure you think I'm some kind of moral degenerate or something."

"You were young and innocent. It wasn't your fault. Look, I have no place to stand on the moral high ground."

"And yet, it's hard not to judge, isn't it? When you haven't walked it yourself."

"I'm not judging you. It's just...I'm not sure how to help you. I've spent a lifetime steering clear of my emotions...avoiding   complications...skimming   the surface, and now, this is a lot. I'm concerned for your safety, worried about the threats...I must confess that I had my brother hire a P.I. to check out Jack and the film crew...for peace of mind. I found out about Ben and his connection to the Senator, but it didn't mean anything at the time."

She bit her lip. "You did that for me?"

"Yeah, I thought you'd be mad."

"I might have been before, but not now. Listen, it's important that we act the same with Ben as we did before we found out all of this. Don't let on that we know anything about him. Graham needs to follow up with his wife first."

Griffin flinched at the mention of her ex-lover. "It's a lot to take in Pen. I'm not going to lie to you, I'm not good at this part."

She tilted her head, frowning. "And what part is that exactly?"

He squirmed under her penetrating stare. "The complicated part...the feelings part."

A flush crept up her face. "You mean the messy part?"

He ground his jaw. "No, it's not like that Pen. I don't know what I mean or how to say it. You've been with-holding a huge part of your life...like you've compart-mentalized chunks of yourself and I'm tucked in some neat little corner. I don't like the feeling. I can't explain it to you right now."

"You don't have to. For the record, I can fill in the blanks. Too much baggage. I get it and I don't blame you. I tried to warn you in Savannah." She stood up. "You know all I wanted was for you to hold me and tell me everything was going to be alright. Instead all I'm hearing is that it's too much for you...I'm too much. I get it. I'm truly sorry for that. Now if you'll excuse me, I won't burden you any further."

He reached for her, "Penelope...you've got it wrong...I..."

She raised her chin, then held up her hand, "No! Don't say another word. Listen Griffin, I understand. Who in their right mind would want to have their private lives dragged through the mud? I don't blame you for pulling back."

"Pen, please don't leave. We can get through this. You have to take a leap of faith at some point and trust me."

Her eyes were shiny with unshed tears. "I just did and look where that got me."

"What the hell is that supposed to mean? I'm trying to be honest with you and you're twisting my words into something else. Why are you being so stubborn right now? It's frustrating as hell. What else can I say?"

"Griffin, there is nothing more to be said and you don't owe me anything."

"I get that you're hurt and scared, but don't slam the door shut on us."

"I need some time. Let's just leave it for now."

He knew it was pointless to try to get through to her. He needed a minute and she needed some space to process it all. Right now, she was a fortress and she had barricaded herself inside...apparently something she was a pro at. Griffin followed her to the door. *What the fuck was happening here? It's a runaway train.*

"I'll let myself out. Goodbye Griffin. See you on set."

～

*P*enelope made it to the car before bursting into tears. She pounded the steering wheel with her fists, mentally berating herself for getting involved with him. It cut deep. She could feel his judgement of her from a mile away. An affair with a married man, escorting strange men, blackmail, all her secrets exposed at once. No wonder he had pulled back. She couldn't blame him, but her heart ached with disappointment.

Later as she tossed and turned in bed, she had a moment of self-doubt. Was she projecting her own shame onto him? Was it fair to keep ignoring Griffin's calls? She knew she should respond, but she felt like she couldn't handle anything more. It was all too much. The thought of her past being exposed for the entire world to see was horrifying. To see her reputation being smeared was bad enough, but it was hardly fair to drag Griffin through it. Their relationship was too new and too vulnerable to withstand that kind of assault. She felt horrible for Graham as well. His entire career was about to implode, and she was partially to blame.

Adding to her despair was Griffin's first response, which had been to withdraw. His gut reaction had been flight...not fight. In her opinion, one's first reactions were the most honest. That was all she needed to know. It was true that she couldn't blame him, however she was not willing to be with anyone that didn't love her, imperfections and all. She also cared enough about him to let him go. Nobody deserved to be dragged through her mess.

37

*P*enelope's heart raced when she saw the caller ID number on her phone. *Graham.*

"Hello?"

"Penelope, are you alone?"

"Yes."

"It's Graham. How are you?"

"Just finished up filming. Nothing more to report from this end. What did your wife say?"

"I've discussed everything with Emily, a very painful but revelatory conversation. It wasn't her. She doesn't know anything about the photographs. I believe her. Ben is completely off the hook. As a matter of fact, he had flown home on the weekend in question. He's completely in the clear. He doesn't even know about our past."

"If Emily can keep the fact that she's always known about us a secret from you, what makes you think she isn't lying about this?"

"I just know. She worked too hard to bury it. She's a bitter and unhappy woman, but not for the reasons you may think. All she's ever cared about was keeping the family intact. Emotionally, she didn't even care about the affair, she just didn't want to be publicly humiliated."

"What about her objections to you running for president?"

"I told you before, for her it's always been about things, lifestyle, status, prestige...that means everything to her. Though she says she doesn't want to live in the fishbowl as First lady, part of her relishes the idea. It will give her another thing to blame me for, but the status will be intoxicating to her. Her false accusations that she's squandered her life for me, my career, ring false."

"So, you're ruling her out because of her ambitions?"

"That and the fact that she didn't even know where the original photographs came from. She didn't take them herself, nor did she hire anyone to spy on me. She received them anonymously. Up until that point, she had suspicions that I was having an affair, but was clueless about us until she received the photographs. She never cared as long as I was discreet. The pictures changed that. I suspect that the same person that sent them to her all those years ago, may now have sent them to us. Any ideas of who that might be?"

"None. It happened before I had any name recognition. So not a crazed fan."

"How about any of the men you worked for back then...um...dated."

"No. I quit right after I met you...months before your wife confronted me. The guy, Jack, who got fired from this film, has an alibi for the weekend the magazine showed up and was back in LA when the photographs were delivered. Plus, how would he have gotten ahold of them in the first place? He seemed a likely suspect for the tabloid, but not this." She blew out a breath. "I just don't know."

"All I can tell you is that we're working on it. My people will be in touch to get the names of your clients from that time. The more you cooperate the better chance we have. I'm not saying it has anything to do with you. We haven't ruled out that it's a political hit job, but we have to look into every possibility."

Penelope's voice was thick with unshed tears, "I understand, but I don't want anyone else hurt by my past."

"They will be discreet. I promise."

"I'll get the list together...as much as I can recall."

"That's all I can ask. I see the tabloids have you linked with your new co-star."

"Don't believe everything you read," she said, her tone acerbic.

"I just want you to be happy. You deserve that Penelope."

"Do I? I'm not so sure about that. Besides, I have a successful career, freedom from financial fears, I have more than most people."

"But you've always lived from your heart. I hope you find your happily ever after, Penny."

"Thanks, but right now I'm not looking. Let's just concentrate on finding out who is threatening us."

"I intend to. Nothing is going to stand in the way of me getting what I've put my entire life into accomplishing. And nobody threatens you and gets away with it. Not if I have anything to say about it."

Penelope's lips twisted at the irony of her first love, who'd smashed her heart, now gallantly proclaiming he'd protect her unfailingly.

"Should I call you with the list?"

"Yes, get back with me as soon as possible."

"Will do. Goodbye Graham."

"Goodbye Penny."

38

Griffin looked around the ballroom of the Butler, where the wrap party was currently in full swing. The filming had ended ahead of schedule. Pretty impressive. It was possible that they'd have to reshoot or add some scenes later, but it was early November and for all practical purposes his part was done until the time came to promote the film. Now the project would go into post-production for a projected late spring release. He smiled looking around at the people celebrating. He couldn't believe it was over. Time had flown by. He'd met some great people and picked up a few friends along the way. He was sad to see it coming to an end.

Where was Penelope? Since she'd dropped the bomb, she'd completely ghosted him. He couldn't penetrate her armor. Confusion didn't even come close to describing how he felt right now. He was angry that Penelope could so easily toss out their relationship and frustrated that she refused to talk to him outside of work. In fact, it was as if it was all his fault.

Talk about feeling powerless. Had he reacted? Hell yeah, he had. It had taken him a minute. So what? It had been a lot to take in. But contrary to what she assumed, he didn't feel the least bit turned off or judgmental. He just felt ill-equipped. He'd been happily skimming along the surface his whole life. This was like jumping into the deep end without swim lessons or a life jacket.

He'd never been in love before. *Love.* When and how had that happened? Sometime between the first scene and the final shoot. That's about all he knew. One minute he was a confirmed bachelor, enjoying lots of beautiful women, the next he had met one he wasn't sure he could live without. He'd only been half awake before she'd come into his life.

He might be inadequate, but he'd sure as hell do his best to figure it out...if he was given the chance. With any luck he'd be able to get through to her today. He walked over to the bar to grab a drink.

"I'll have your best bourbon on the rocks," he said.

The bartender winked at him suggestively and grabbed a glass, adding ice, then filled it with the amber liquid. "I can't wait for the film to come out. Our very own local on the big screen."

"I'm pretty excited about it myself."

"I just read an article about you in *People.* It said you'd never acted a day in your life before this movie."

Griffin grinned, "Yep, guilty as charged." Griffin turned as Noah called out a greeting, with Penelope by his side. Griffin's hand tightened around his drink at

Noah's smug look of satisfaction. *Really Penelope? This is how you're going to play it?* Pretty low to use Noah as her shield now. Hiding behind her ex.

Griffin tipped his glass then downed it. "Penelope, Noah, here we are, crossing the finish line." He tried to meet Penelope's gaze, but she kept her eyes lowered.

"Yes, we'll have a little time off, then the whirlwind of promoting the film begins. Late night talk shows, interviews, podcasts, it's exciting," Noah said, turning to order his drink. Griffin only half listened as Noah made idle chitchat with the bartender while she mixed his drink.

"Penelope, can we go somewhere to talk? I've been blowing up your phone."

"I can't. I've got too much going on right now. I wouldn't want to burden you with my problems."

Griffin leaned in real close and hissed angrily in her ear, "You're being ridiculous Penelope. I don't deserve this."

"I didn't deserve to be left dangling in the wind when I needed you the most. You showed what you're made of."

Griffin grabbed her arm and hauled her off to a private corner. "Maybe so, but you weren't going too deep yourself, were you? Couldn't take the risk of being honest, letting me in. The truth might be too much...... for you or for me? Maybe you're the one who has trouble looking in the mirror."

Her face paled. "How dare you."

"I dare alright. I'm calling out your bullshit. You're the one who's ashamed...and you're making me out to be the bad guy! I told you that night, I have no illusions about my moral standing, I've led a pretty selfish life. But at least I'm honest with myself that's more than I can say for you."

"If you're so honest with yourself then tell me what you're so afraid of? That you might actually need someone? Or even worse, that they might need you? Or maybe it's that they'll abandon you like your mother did?"

"Maybe. Probably all of that. I'll admit that I'm still a work in progress, but I do know that I'm willing to look under the rock. It might not be pretty, but I'll have a go at it. You didn't look under yours until you were forced to, by circumstances beyond your control. Now you want to use me to punish yourself."

"Grow up. You dropped the ball and now you're making excuses."

"I'm sorry that I didn't get your script before your little tell-all. It would have been helpful to know how you wanted me to act and exactly what you wanted me to say."

"This discussion is over." She turned on her heel and returned to Noah's side, her back intentionally facing him. Griffin set his empty glass down and stormed out of the party. Nothing to celebrate here.

39

*P*enelope stayed another hour after Griffin had stormed out, just for appearances. She had a headache, not to mention the ache in her chest. Her throat burned from holding back tears. She had hated the look of pain she'd seen in Griffin's eyes, but she'd had to stay strong for his sake. If he had sensed the least bit of hesitation on her part, he would have jumped on it.

She knew only too well the double-edged sword of being famous. It was hard to deal with the scrutiny on a good day but throw in a juicy scandal and it was pure misery. They would never survive it so why not let go now, before it became even harder.

Dolly and Ben were whooping it up, and Noah was flirting like crazy with the gorgeous bartender. His attentiveness had faded quickly after Griffin left the party. She could safely leave now without drawing too much attention to herself.

. . .

*L*uke walked her up to the door and waited while she unlocked. "Thanks, Luke."

"No problem Ms. Winters."

"I'm in for the rest of the evening. Relaxing is the only thing on my agenda. I don't think there's any need for you to stick around."

"I have orders. You won't even know I'm here," he said smiling. "I'm going to take a look around the premises and go through the house quickly if you don't mind."

"Of course. It's such a nice night I think I'll sit out on the deck and listen to the waves crash."

He left to walk the perimeters of the property. She reached down to pick up an exuberant Archie, who was jumping in his excitement. "Hey Boo Boo."

She walked straight to her bedroom and took a couple of aspirin and changed clothes. She grabbed a sweater on her way out. Stretching out on the lounge chair she was asleep within minutes. She sat up suddenly, startled awake by Archie's ferocious bark. He'd never sounded like this before, which made the hairs on her neck prickle.

"What is it Archie?" He stared at the house, alternately barking and growling. "There's nothing there, buddy. It's okay."

Archie was not to be consoled so she picked him up and carried him inside to prove a point, that there weren't any boogie men. As soon as she set Archie down he raced to the back of the house. She heard a loud yelp and went to investigate. When she rounded the corner, she stopped dead in her tracks. There was a man standing in front of her bedroom, holding Archie and a gun.

"It's been a long time," he said, dark eyes glittering. He had aged, but other than that and his gray hair, he looked the same. "Don't look so scared. I'm not going to hurt you Penelope."

A chill went down her spine. "You! It was you who sent the photos." Her eyes widened as it hit her. "You're the one who took them all those years ago. You were stalking me."

"Hardly stalking. We were dating. You make it sound like I'm some crazed fan. I was trying to protect you."

"Protect me from what?"

"Predators like Senator Warren for instance."

"And yourself?"

"It pains me to hear you speak like that."

"I can't have a normal conversation with you holding my dog and a gun. Please put them down."

He continued as if he hadn't heard her. "Actually, I can't take credit for those photographs. I hired someone to follow you. After you dumped me, I had to keep an eye on you for your own good. You were much too trusting to be alone in the world. Was I wrong?"

"Josh, I didn't dump you. I quit the escort business. We had a business relationship that ended. And that was almost fourteen years ago! Surely you've moved on by now."

"You've never really left my mind Penelope. How could you? We had such memorable times together. I felt like a prince with you on my arm. I was always with the most beautiful woman in the room. When I saw that filthy pig Warren was running for president, I became enraged all over again...it brought it all back as if it was yesterday. Him, married with three children, violating an innocent woman, no more than a child really. He stole the only person I've ever loved right out from under my nose. Used you then discarded you like you were a piece of garbage. And now he might become the most powerful person in the world? I saw an opportunity to get back what's mine!"

His words filled her with dread. "I was never yours or anyone's to steal. I made my own choices."

"Don't try to protect that cheating bastard. You can't lie to me. He broke you. You lost your baby and you're still going to stick up for him? I don't blame you for leaving me. I blame him. He fooled you. I loved you then and I still do." He pointed his gun toward the living room. "Let's move out of the hallway." He put Archie down and the dog immediately ran to Penelope.

Penelope walked slowly down the hall, her mind scrambling to figure out a strategy. Where was Luke? Her body was trembling so badly she was afraid her legs would give out. Her voice quavering, she said, "Let me get you something to drink. We can sit and talk normally. No guns. Please."

His response was to wave his gun in the air to emphasize his next declaration. "I woke up one night with a sudden realization! You can still be mine. It doesn't have to be over. I can save you...rescue you from making movies that are practically porn. Selling your body. You're better than that. You won't have to prostitute yourself when you're mine."

"Sex isn't dirty! My films are beautiful love stories. I make millions of dollars. I'm hardly a victim."

"You're blinded by fame because you haven't been able to distance yourself from it. Eventually you'll thank me. I wouldn't waste my breath arguing. I'm telling you; I expect you to come away with me, willingly. If you do, I'll let the senator off the hook. If not... well, I'll really have no choice but to expose him for who he is." He shrugged, "Unfortunately your reputation will be collateral damage."

Fighting panic, she said, "Surely you must see how crazy this sounds. Listen to me! You want to destroy his innocent children...his wife, all the people who count on him for their livelihood? Why? You say you love me —that isn't how you treat someone you love. You've got it all wrong Josh. I loved Graham. Was I young and foolish? The answer is yes, but he didn't force me to love him, it just happened. Neither of us expected or planned on the baby."

"He tricked you and he stole from me! You loved a liar and a cheat. I know you had feelings for me in the beginning, if he hadn't interfered, we'd be together now. If you can't accept this, you'll both pay." He scowled menacingly.

"I love my career. It's all that I ever wanted to do! Let this go and I'll pretend it never happened. It's not too late Josh...Please! Your fantasy of me accepting this is delusional."

His eyes glittered with rage as his expression darkened, "Careful Penelope, you're naive if you think I haven't planned this out carefully. You'll come with me or he'll pay for what he took from us. I won't let him win everything. We can't get back those years we lost, but we can still have our happily ever after. I know you loved me once. I'm *going* to have you. We'll live on my private island. Just you and me and my staff. You can have anything and everything you want. I'll save you from those crazy fans, the constant scrutiny and rumors. I'll take care of you."

"Josh, listen to me, put the gun down. You think trapping me on some remote island is the way to teach me how to love you? Can't you hear yourself?"

He screamed at her, "You're not listening to me! We were robbed and now I'm going to rectify that."

"Josh it's not that simple."

"It is that simple. Admit it, you're miserable. You're a virtual prisoner in your own life. Your fame has you trapped. You can't make a move without being followed or photographed. You make lousy choices in men. Look at your last one. Please, Noah Davis? He's weak. Even from a distance I could see that. I wanted to scream at the TV every time I saw you together. On the red carpet, with that vain egotistical twit. I could have spared you the pain. He was obviously a player, in love with himself. Whatever made you think he was the one? That he could be a substitute for what we had?"

Penelope changed tactics and schooled her expression, softening her eyes as she forced her mouth to curve up in a smile, "Josh...I think I understand what you're trying to say. And what we had *was* special. Maybe you're right. Maybe we could have it again. But not like this...not right now."

"Shut up!" he waved the gun around erratically. "Don't say that."

Penelope's entire body trembled, and her hands were clammy with sweat. "Okay, I'm sorry. We'll do it your way."

"You're so beautiful..." He caressed her cheek with the barrel of his gun. "He was your first, wasn't he? That maggot senator took your virginity. And to think it was because of me that your paths crossed in the first place. I've had to live with that."

Penelope stayed silent.

His face reddened and he screamed, "He had you first. Didn't he!"

She nodded her head slowly, "Yes."

"That son of a bitch. I should have stopped him back then."

"You can't control who someone else loves, how do you think you could have stopped us?"

"You only thought you loved him because he conned you...he took advantage of your innocence."

"I'll admit that I was young and stupid, but I was an escort for God's sake. That hardly made me a saint."

"Oh, but you were, you were my angel. I should have acted back then. I let the wolves strip you. I could have prevented it. He made you into his whore. I would have treated you like the priceless treasure that you were."

"Josh, please, listen, I know you love me but you're scaring me right now."

"There is no need to fear me if you just do what I say."

Penelope fought to keep from hyperventilating. Her voice sounded weak and wavering as she tried to reason with him. "I can't go with you right now. It's an incredibly generous offer, I know you're trying to look out for me, but I'm in the middle of a project, I can't let everyone down. At least let me finish what I started. Then we can see where this takes us. We have a lot to catch up on."

"Are you in love with that billionaire co-star the tabloids have been linking you with?"

"No!" she said sharply, not wanting him anywhere near Griffin.

His lips twisted, "Did I strike a nerve?"

"No, I just don't want anyone hurt."

"They won't be, as long as you cooperate. Their fate is in your hands now Penelope. Make it simple. Do the right thing. Come with me."

Penelope's stomach roiled. She was sure she was going to be sick. Summoning up all her acting skills and courage, she made another attempt to reason with him, praying for a miracle. "After I finish with the film, we can start making our plans together. Even though it sounds like a dream to up and walk away, I can't be spontaneous." Her mind was going a mile a minute, turning over escape plans that she quickly discarded as futile.

"This offer is non-negotiable. I'm not stupid, Penelope."

She looked up at him through her lashes and smiled, "Are you kidding me? I know how brilliant you are. Owning a billion-dollar tech company before you were even thirty? That's amazing."

"I'd suggest you grab a few things for the trip. Just enough to get you through the next day or so. I'll buy you whatever you need after that. I have my private jet on standby, waiting for us. Be quick, it's time."

Penelope saw a movement on the back patio. *Griffin. Be careful*, she said silently. She got up and started pacing to keep Josh distracted.

"Quit pacing and get your things, now!"

He pointed his gun toward the hallway, "Let's go."

He followed her to her bedroom.

40

*G*riffin couldn't shake a feeling of dread as he paced his living room. *Fuck it, I'm going back to the party and force her to talk.* He ran out the door and jumped into his Audi. He felt a sense of urgency that he couldn't explain.

*W*hen he arrived at the Butler house the party was still in full swing. His eyes searched the room, but he couldn't find Penelope. Spying Dolly, he made his way over to her.

"She left. Said she had a headache and was going to take some aspirin and relax by the pool," Dolly said.

"Thanks."

"Griffin don't give up on her. She's worth fighting for."

His lips tightened, "I'm trying."

"Go get her, and good luck," she said, smiling sympathetically.

On his way out, Noah grabbed him. "Leaving again?"

"Yeah, I'm heading over to Penelope's. That alright with you?" he said sarcastically.

"Better than that because I need a ride. Can you give me a lift? I've had a little too much to drink."

"I suppose."

"Great. Ready when you are."

Griffin forced himself to relax. He really didn't hate the guy. In fact, he'd had some good conversations with Noah and had it not been for the tension over Penelope, they might have even become friends.

"What's with you and Penelope? On or off?" Noah said.

"I could ask you the same question."

"Definitely off, but through no choice of my own. I'd take her back in a heartbeat. I'm still in love with that woman. She's really something isn't she?"

"Yes, she is."

Noah clapped Griffin on the shoulder, "Look, I know we've not always been on the greatest of terms, but I think you're alright. It's unfortunate that we happened to be vying for the same girl. You've been nothing but professional on the set, learned your lines, amazing acting, you're the icing on the cake of this film. I have a good feeling about it."

Griffin's lips turned up slightly, "High praise coming from you. Thanks."

"No problem. Whoever winds up with Penelope is one lucky man. I totally fucked up. But, fair warning, I haven't completely lost hope," he chuckled, "almost... but may the best man win."

Griffin pulled into Noah's drive frowning, his unease returning when he saw an unfamiliar car parked in Penelope's drive. He recognized Luke's vehicle but not the other sedan. "Whose car is that?"

"No idea," Noah replied. He hopped out and headed for home. "See ya around."

Griffin parked on the street then decided to walk around to the back. Dolly had said Penelope would be hanging out there. The ocean was calm this evening, the temperatures had been steady, only dipping into the mid-sixties at night, unusual for early November. As he rounded the corner, he saw Luke, sprawled on the ground unconscious. His hands were tied behind his back and he was gagged. He squatted down beside him and checked for a pulse. It was strong. He untied his hands and removed the gag. Then he heard a male voice shouting and froze.

"Shut up!" he saw the intruder waving a gun. "Don't say that."

"Okay, I'm sorry. We'll do it your way."

Griffin saw him rubbing Penelope's cheek with the barrel of the gun and wanted to storm inside and kill him.

"He was your first, wasn't he? That maggot senator took your virginity. And to think it was because of me that your paths crossed in the first place. I've had to live with that."

"He had you first. Didn't he!"

"Yes."

"That son of a bitch. I should have stopped him back then."

Griffin broke out in a sweat. Penelope was in big trouble. He pulled out his phone and texted Noah.

Griffin: Call the police. Silent approach. Penelope is in trouble. Armed intruder, possible hostage situation. At least one man. Not sure if there's more. I'm going in. Security knocked out and unconscious southeast side of house.

His phone immediately buzzed back.

Noah: I'm on it. Wait for me. Don't go in alone.

*G*riffin silenced his phone then headed back. He flattened himself against the wall, inching his way slowly. He wasn't about to wait for Noah. When he reached the corner, he peeked his head around and could see that the man had his back to the window and was waving a gun in the air. Penelope sat on a bar stool facing the patio.

He hoped he could get her attention without her giving it away. With the outdoor patio lights on, he would be visible if she was looking. If she saw him, she might be able to keep the intruder distracted long enough for him to approach. He made his move and quickly dashed to the arbor, crouching down behind the hot tub. Peering over the top, he couldn't be sure, but he thought that maybe Penelope knew he was there.

He waited for a second and then she stood up and began pacing, ensuring that she had the full attention of her assailant. Good. She knew he was there.

"Quit pacing and get your things, now!"

He pointed his gun toward the hallway, "Let's go."

He followed her, his gun pointed at her back.

Griffin spied Noah and motioned him over. This was a lucky break. They had one shot at it. There wasn't time to wait for the police.

Speaking softly, he filled Noah in. "One man, as far as I could tell, he has a gun trained on Penelope. From what I could gather, he's taking her hostage and they went to her bedroom for her to gather things. I'm going in."

"Shouldn't we wait for the police?"

"No. We have the element of surprise. I think Penelope saw me, so she'll be working with us. If we get inside, we can hide in the great room until they come out then try to overtake him."

"I'll follow your lead."

"Once we get inside, when I nod, you'll know I'm about to go for it. I'll try to disarm him. We have to make a silent run for it. Now!"

They made it inside and ducked down behind the sectional sofa. They could hear faint voices that were getting louder as they approached. Griffin looked at Noah. Both now running on adrenaline, Griffin knew, like any junkie, that he had to make it work for him, not against him. He took several deep slow breaths. Penelope was no more than ten feet from where they were crouched. His breathing sounded loud to his own ears and he wondered if they could hear it.

He took a risk and lifted his eyes above the couch and saw that the man was turned slightly away from him. It was now or never. He nodded to Noah and sprang from behind the couch, the element of surprise giving him a momentary advantage. They rolled around fighting for control of the gun. Noah jumped in and a shot rang out. Noah went down. Griffin couldn't spare a glance.

"Oh my God! Noah!" Penelope cried out.

Griffin had the man's wrist in a vice grip and was twisting it with all his strength. The gun fell to the ground, and the scuffle continued.

"Grab the gun Penelope," Griffin yelled.

"But Noah!"

"Penelope, just grab the fucking gun!"

She was now crouched by Noah's side. Griffin could hear her crying, but all he could focus on was the gun lying two feet from his reach. It was anybody's game at this point. This guy was strong. He felt an elbow slam into his head and his vision swam for a few seconds. Just enough time for the other guy to get the upper hand. Next thing he knew he was being hauled upright in a headlock; a gun jammed against his temple.

"Penelope, if you don't want me to blow your stud's head off, I suggest you come to me. We're leaving now."

"Don't listen to him Penelope. If you do, we don't stand a chance," Griffin said.

"Shut the fuck up or I'll off you anyway."

"How far do you think you'll get?" Griffin said, trying to get under his skin.

"Let's see, my own jet, a private island out of US jurisdiction...if I were a betting man, I'd give it ninety percent."

"Josh, I'll come with you, but you have to let me call an ambulance for Noah and you have to promise to let Griffin go."

"You come over here and help me tie this piece of shit up and we'll call after we're in the air."

"No! He'll bleed out by then," Penelope said. She was as pale as a ghost and her teeth were chattering.

"The longer you argue the longer he bleeds."

"Okay, what do you want me to do?"

"Grab some twine, rope, cord, anything we can use to tie him up."

She ran to the kitchen drawers and ransacked them looking for anything that could work. Suddenly police stormed the house their weapons trained on Josh.

"Put your gun down now."

Josh tightened his grip around Griffin's neck. "You want to see the billionaire's head blown off?"

"We've got the house surrounded. You aren't going anywhere."

"Is that so? Because right now, seems like I've got the ace in the hole, or should I say ass." He chuckled at his dark humor.

Griffin was waiting for any opportunity to knock the fucker to hell and back. He never dreamed he had such a murderous rage inside of himself...but he did. If he got the chance to kill this man, he'd take it, with no remorse. Griffin knew he had one shot and now was the time. He slammed the back of his head into Josh's face as hard as he could and connected with his nose, satisfied when he felt the bone shatter.

It was the momentum that allowed him to break away. As Griffin pivoted around to disarm him, a shot was fired from a distance and the intruder fell, dead before he hit the ground. Penelope screamed then ran over to kneel by Noah's side. He was deathly pale. It looked like he took it in the leg, probably an artery, judging by the amount of blood.

A police officer sent instructions through her radio as she walked to the front to unlock and open it. Returning, she said, "An ambulance is waiting outside. The first one already left with the injured security guard."

"Luke!" Penelope said.

"He appeared stable. They're taking him in for observation."

The paramedics entered quickly and loaded Noah onto the gurney. Penelope looked over at Griffin, her face devoid of color and her eyes glistening with tears. "Thank you. I'm sorry...for everything. I have to go with Noah." She held Noah's hand as she walked along-side the gurney to the waiting ambulance. And then she was gone.

41

Griffin hung up the phone after talking with his sister-in-law Ella, who had used her connections with the hospital to get an update on Noah's condition. He had been upgraded to stable. The surgery to repair the nicked artery had been successful and he would make a full recovery.

Griffin could hardly wait to get away from here. Tomorrow morning he'd be on a jet, flying to the south of France. The paparazzi were driving him crazy; he never knew when they were going to be waiting outside his house. The crazed fan storyline they'd sold to the public was being played out on all the entertainment shows and tabloids. Good for the film, bad for him.

Was it the same for Penelope? He'd heard from Stew that she'd been staying with him since the shooting, hanging around an extra week until she was sure Noah was stable. He had no idea how she felt since she was still ignoring him. He'd given up trying.

He heard a knock at the door and checked the security camera. A limo sat in his drive and a man in uniform stood next to Penelope on his front porch. His throat tightened, the momentary flicker of hope dashed when he opened the door and saw her face.

"Hey, come on in," Griffin said.

She tentatively stepped over the threshold and stood nervously wringing her hands. The driver stepped away. "I'll be waiting in the car, Ms. Winters."

His gut clenched as his eyes raked over her face. He took in every detail wanting to memorize it, sensing there would be no happy ending for them. Griffin shut the door and motioned for her to have a seat.

"No thanks, I'm not staying. I didn't want to leave without saying goodbye."

Griffin gently removed her sunglasses and revealed two pools of green, glossy with unshed tears. He framed her face between his hands. "Pen, talk to me." A tear escaped and he brushed it away with the pad of his thumb.

"I'm not here to talk Griff, I'm here to say goodbye."

Griffin winced. "That was to the point."

"I'm not trying to be a bitch, I'm still in shock over the events of the last week. I'm not in the right emotional state to be opening up. I'm way to vulnerable."

"You think I'm not?"

"Right now, I can't make it about you or anyone else. For once I have to put myself first."

"I can hardly argue with that, now can I? Not unless I want to sound like a selfish asshole."

"I know you're anything but that. I wanted you to

know, you didn't do anything wrong. It's all my fault. Because of me, Noah got shot. You could have been killed. I couldn't have lived with that."

"You aren't responsible for someone else's crazy."

"Griff, you were right about me. A part of me is shut off. I held back because of shame from my past, my guilt about the baby. I can't give myself completely to anyone, because I'm still trying to forgive myself."

Griffin grasped her upper arms, "You were right too. I didn't want anyone to need me, and even more than that, I never wanted to need anyone. I still don't. But the only way I know to fix that, is to dive in and live. I can't fix it in my head. I've got to walk through the fire and experience it, make mistakes, continually course-correct, just like sailing. The wind blows you, you adjust the sails, work with the wind, instead of fighting against it. Can't we work through this together?"

She smiled sadly, "Beautiful metaphor...I have nothing to give. Not right now. I'm heading back to my ranch to do some soul searching and get rest. I know I'm running, but it's the best I can do right now. I'm sorry."

Griffins voice was thick with emotion, "Can I call you in a few weeks?"

"It's better that you don't."

"That's it then...have a nice life? Does this self-imposed exile apply to Noah Davis as well?"

Her face flushed, "Thanks for making this a little easier. Goodbye Griffin."

"Penelope, wait, I'm sorry, I shouldn't have..."

She jerked away and ran out the door not bothering to shut it behind her.

Griffin slammed the door and went to pour himself a shot. *Blew it again asshole. You managed to put the final nail in the coffin. Bravo.* But she'd had her mind made up well before she came to say goodbye. Maybe she'd never had any intentions of it being more than a fling. He should know about that...he'd orchestrated his entire life the same way. Karma's a bitch.

Tomorrow couldn't get here fast enough.

42

_J_osie shook her head, tsking her disapproval. "You're too skinny. You must eat something."

"I'm not hungry. I'll make myself a sandwich later."

"I'm worried about you."

Penelope gave Josie a tight hug. Her lilting voice and the sing song rhythm always managed to sooth Penelope's nerves. Josie was like a second mother to her and she desperately needed that right now.

"I'm leaving Archie here while I go for a ride on Raven," she said.

"You and that horse. Chica, what am I going to do with you?"

"Just love me," she said, her lips curving up.

"Oh, I love you alright, but I want to paddle you sometimes."

"I'll be back in a couple of hours."

"You be careful. I will prepare you a big supper, and

you will eat it. You hear me? And Thanksgiving, it's next week already. Walt will have to get supplies and I have to plan the menu."

"Is your family still joining us?"

"Yes, and Walt and his new lady friend."

"Dolly and Ben haven't committed yet, but I'll try to pin them down tonight."

Josie's warm brown eyes stared at her with so much compassion it was nearly her undoing. Her voice choked with tears, "Thanks Josie."

She shooed her out the door, "Go...go...before we both cry."

*P*enelope let Raven have her head; they galloped through the barren meadow, the air cold and crisp. It was a sunny day which helped her mood immeasurably. Walt had tacked Raven up for her, but she hadn't escaped without another round of troubled admonitions. It was both comforting and annoying at the same time. She wanted to lick her wounds in peace...thank you very much. She needed a minute.

She'd felt exposed with Griffin; he'd somehow penetrated her carefully erected walls. She'd let him in and was now paying the price. But was the answer to wall herself back in again? Had she learned nothing? It had felt warm and good and true to let her guard down with him.

Rather than feeling confined by the relationship, she'd felt free. Fully alive for maybe the first time in her life. That's why she'd been so shocked and disappointed by his response to her confessions. She'd overcome such a personal hurdle to confide in him, and then to have him hold back, well, it had been devastating.

A sudden jolt went through her body as it dawned on her just how big a part fear had influenced her actions...the fear that their budding relationship couldn't endure the pressures of fame, fear that she was too much, that she was unlovable, but the most troubling was her fear that he'd leave her. Her belief that men couldn't be trusted and that they'd inevitably abandon her, had helped create the very reality she'd been avoiding. Had he abandoned her? His reaction had been honest and heartfelt, he'd just expressed it out loud at her most vulnerable moment, but that was hardly a crime.

Penelope transitioned from a canter to a walk and Raven snorted out her nose.

The thing now keeping her awake at night was that she was three weeks late with her period. She'd been blaming it on stress, but she had to face facts, she could be pregnant. Then what? She knew she'd have it but... did Griffin need to know, or would he even want to know? She understood all too well that a person couldn't change overnight. He'd said point blank that he didn't want to be needed. Being a dad was certainly about as needed as you could get.

She unconsciously put her hand on her belly and held it there. *A baby*. Her chest ached, a burst of pure joy, quickly chased by fear. She didn't think she could survive losing another baby. But...like it or not, if she was pregnant, she was committed to seeing it through.

She'd ask Walt to drive her to town in the morning to pick up a test. If she was pregnant, she'd call Griffin. It was up to him how much or how little he wanted to be involved, but he had a right to know.

*T*he following afternoon, Penelope stared at the thick line on the test stick not knowing whether to laugh or cry. She managed to fit both in. Archie tilted his head sizing up his mistresses' mood.

"Mama's okay. We're going to have a baby to take care of Archie." He lowered his head onto his paws, brow wrinkled.

"Don't worry, you won't be replaced."

Before she lost her nerve, she punched in Griffin's number and braced herself to give him her prepared speech. When she reached his voice mail she was thrown off; she hadn't anticipated that one.

"Um...this is Penelope, can you call me when you get a chance? You've got my number."

Her hands shook as she disconnected. Now all she could do was wait.

~

*G*riffin woke up with a slight hangover. He'd indulged in a little too much red wine last night. Since arriving in Saint-Tropez, he'd been burning the candle at both ends. If he could manage to drag himself out of bed, he'd walk to town and get an espresso and a cream-filled brioche to eat by the beach.

There was a knock on his bedroom door and Amelie popped her head in to see if he was awake yet. *Shit*, he'd forgotten about her. He'd insisted she sleep over since she'd been drinking, but much to her disappointment, he'd not invited her to share his bed.

"*Cheri, es-tu réveillé?*"

"Barely," he said as he stretched, yawning loudly, then crawled naked out of bed.

"*Homme sexy.*"

"I feel like roadkill."

"*Je ne comprends pas.*"

"Roadkill means...*Ce n'est rien!*" Forget it. His head hurt too bad to explain. "*Retrouvez-moi dans le salon.*" He closed the bathroom door behind him. He'd meet her in the salon after he showered, shaved and downed a couple of aspirin.

After showering, he toweled off then dressed, grabbing his cell phone on the way out. He saw that he'd missed a call that had come in around one in the morning. He'd been passed out by then. His heart skittered when he saw the number. *Penelope.*

If she'd called from Montana, with the eight-hour difference, it'd be around seven p.m. there now. He listened to her message three times. She sounded casual. Not much to go on. *Call me.* Something about the film maybe?

He scrubbed his hands roughly over his face. Why now? He'd have to think about it. He was here to forget. She could have been a little more informative. At any rate, he wasn't ready to call her back...if he even did return the call. At this point, what was the point?

Amelie was waiting for him in the salon and they

left together. As they walked the cobbled streets of the old fishing village, all he could think was that he wished it were Penelope beside him. She would love it here. He had to snap out of it, or he'd drive himself crazy. She wasn't here, her choice, and the beautiful Amelie was. The aspirins were finally kicking in, thank you Jesus. He was going to forget about that call for now and seize the day. Carpe fucking diem.

*P*enelope didn't know what she'd expected, but she was heartbroken that Griffin hadn't bothered to return her call. It had been a week. If he was going to call, he would have by now. At least she'd given him a chance. A nagging voice in the back of her mind told her that she was copping out, but she ignored it. She could almost convince herself that she was relieved...almost but not quite.

~

"*M*y son will say grace," Josie said. They were gathered in the dining room, around Penelope's massive oak table. Josie's two adult sons and their wives had come. She only had one grandchild, a three-year-old named Angelica, and she sat in her booster seat between Josie and her daughter-in-law Ana. Her niece Malena, who had just moved here from California was also there.

Dolly and Ben had made it in time for the Thanksgiving feast, having flown in the day before. Walt's eyes sparkled, and he couldn't keep them off his date Emma. Of course, Archie was on standby for any scraps that might come his way.

They all bowed their heads while Luis prayed. They then began passing the food around, everyone but Penelope heaping their plates high.

Josie frowned, "Why aren't you eating?"

"I'm feeling a little nauseous. I'm so sorry, everything looks so good."

"That's an excuse. I expect you to try a little of everything. How long are you going to mope around after a man?"

Dolly said, "You tell her Josie. She never listens to me."

"I'm hardly moping. I'm riding Raven every day, I'm painting again, I'm reading, basically I'm on retreat."

"*Lo que sea*, you can say that, but you can't fool Josie, I've got my eyes on you," Josie said, shaking her head. "I'm happy that *almost* everybody here likes my cooking." They all laughed.

Penelope took a deep breath and blew it out. "I'm grateful to all of you for being here today. You're my friends, but really, you're my family. I have something to share."

Everyone stilled, since Penelope wasn't prone to grandstanding.

She felt all eyes boring into her. "This cannot go any

further, you all have to promise." Everyone nodded their heads, looking more curious by the second.

"I'm pregnant."

There was a long pause, then everyone started talking at once.

Josie said, "Oh Dios mio."

"Penelope! When did you find out?"

"A week ago. Walt remember when I had you drive me to town?"

He nodded his head, "I was wondering what was so important that ya yanked me away from stacking hay. I can't wait to teach 'em how to wrangle."

Penelope laughed, "I would be disappointed otherwise."

"I will make homemade baby food. None of that processed stuff," Josie said.

"Can I be the godmother?" Dolly asked.

"Yes!"

Penelope felt her burden lift. She was not alone. She had everything she needed. Financial security, a home, and her friends. She could do this. For the first time since she had left Griffin, she knew in her heart that she and this baby were going to be fine. And this baby would have heaps of love.

❧

*A*s Penelope was brushing her teeth there was a knock at her door. "It's Dolly."

"Come on in." She rinsed her mouth and went in and sat on her bed.

Dolly plopped down beside her. "Hey, I'm excited that I'm going to be an auntie!"

"You'll be a fabulous aunt. What about me? Do you think I'll be able to do this mom thing?"

Dolly snorted, "Are you kidding me? Archie, what do you think? Is she a great mom or what?" Penelope laughed at Archie who had cocked his head to the side at the mention of his name. "All kidding aside, you're going to be a great mom."

"Are you happy for me?"

"As long as it's what you want, I'm ecstatic."

"It is. After the initial shock wore off, I'm really excited. I always thought I'd have kids but after I lost my baby, it never seemed like the right time...I guess not everything has to be planned."

"I wouldn't be your friend if I didn't ask—what about Griff?"

"I called him right away."

"And?"

"He didn't pick up or return my call."

"Let me guess, so you took that as a sign that you should drop it. You did your due diligence?"

"Dolly, you make me sound terrible. Listen, one of the last fights we had, Griffin admitted that he struggled with being needed or needing someone. He didn't like it or want it. A baby is the biggest commitment there is."

"That's not fair to him and it's taking it out of context. I don't know what he said or how he said it, but he wasn't responding to his child in your belly."

Penelope cupped her abdomen and looked down at the ground. "I hear what you're saying."

"Call him again."

"I don't know."

"I do!"

"And then what, guilt trip him into getting back together? What if he wants parental rights but doesn't want me? Can you imagine that nightmare? Him on the east coast, me on the west?"

"Penelope, it *is* his baby too. You can't control everything. You'll work it out. Have a little faith. If you search your heart, I think you already know what kind of guy he is. I think he's legit."

"I wasn't going to bring this up but hold on." Penelope went over to her nightstand and opened the top drawer pulling out a magazine.

Rolling her eyes, Dolly grabbed it from Penelope. "The gossip rags strike again. *Oh shit!*"

"Yeah, oh shit," Penelope said.

It pained her every time she looked at it, Griffin and the famous French model splashed on the cover, frolicking together in Saint-Tropez.

"He didn't waste any time returning to his playboy lifestyle," Penelope said.

"You know as well as I do that you can't believe most of what's in these stupid magazines. They already have you and Noah back together. Wounded hero, rescuing his true love, the beautiful Penelope Winters... finally back together. The way it was meant to be," she said theatrically.

"If I call him again, I'll wait until the second trimester. I don't want to put us both through all that and then lose the baby."

"I guess that makes some sense. Promise you'll try again?"

"I promise."

"Good enough for me. I'll drop the subject. Now what about names?"

Penelope laughed, "I've got a list a mile long. We'll work on that."

Standing, Dolly yawned loudly, "I'm off to bed. Thanks for inviting us. We're having a blast. And the guest house is perfect."

"Thanks for coming. If either of you want to go for a trail ride tomorrow, I'll take you out."

"Deal! I would love it."

"See you in the morning."

"Night."

Penelope snuggled in with Archie. And now there were three. She already knew this baby. Reaching up, she switched off the lamp and immediately fell into a deep sleep.

44

*G*riffin tucked the white formal dress shirt into his trousers. He'd decided to wear his slim-fitting, black, hand-tailored suit and a textured black and gray tie. They were kicking off the first premier of *Die for You* in LA followed by the UK premier in London, then on to Tokyo. The film would be released the first Friday in May. He'd been interviewed by Jimmy on the late talk show last night. He shook his head, *crazy*.

Today, he'd see Penelope for the first time in almost six months. He wondered how she'd act and what it was going to be like to see her again. Other than the tabloids linking her with Noah, Penelope had kept a low profile since filming wrapped, letting Noah and him carry the load of promoting the film. He didn't blame her after what she'd been through. Her name was enough to sell the film anyway.

His old life no longer fit, but he had yet to figure out

what that meant. She was probably still furious, or even worse hurt, that he'd never returned her call all those months ago. He just hadn't been able to make himself do it. Now here they were.

Since Ty was in the film, he'd brought him along. He was practically jumping out of his skin with excitement.

"Hurry up dude," Ty said pacing.

Ty was the perfect date. He didn't need the speculation about his love life right now. Truth be told, other than casual dating, he had no love life. He finished adjusting his cuff links then he and Ty headed out the door. His driver was waiting. It was going to be a star-studded evening with the entertainment talking heads out in full force.

"Let's go," he said.

They climbed into the back of the limo and the driver whisked them away. He nervously adjusted his tie and stared out the window as they made their way to the historic Grauman's Chinese Theatre in Hollywood. Everyone was familiar with the footprints and handprints and signatures of movie stars imprinted in front of the building. It was a huge tourist draw. But a lot of people didn't know that many of the movie premiers were held here.

The limo pulled up to the pandemonium of crowds, traffic and arrivals. Security was tight and the fans were cordoned off from the red carpet. He had cut his arrival as close as possible. Griffin and Ty stepped out to the sound of screaming fans pointing and calling out to Griffin. Was he actually stepping on to *the* red carpet? It was like a dream.

"Man, I need to up my swag. This is amazing. I just saw Brad Pitt!"

Griffin couldn't believe that people actually recognized him. Fuck, the film hadn't even released yet but there was already Oscar buzz. The recognition didn't come as a complete shock; he'd done numerous interviews solo as well as alongside Noah. The film had also been featured in *People Magazine* and he'd even landed on the cover of *Vogue* and *GQ*.

He stopped to sign a few autographs until one of the entertainment show hosts poked a mic in his face and began interviewing him, even as more of the A-listers of Hollywood were arriving.

"What does it feel like to go from relative obscurity to becoming the latest Hollywood commodity?"

"Frankly, its surreal. I'm trying to roll with it."

"It can't be easy. I hear you've been living in France. Was that to get away from all of the attention?"

He flashed his irresistible grin for the camera. "You've got my number."

"Obviously this is your first film premier, are you prepared?"

"It was described to me that it's like an initiation. Everyone has put a ton of hard work behind and in front of the camera. It's a celebration and acknowledgement of that. We've achieved something. I think the public is going to love this film. Stewart Abrams is a genius. And Penelope and Noah turned in Oscar-worthy performances."

"Who is this handsome young man standing next to you?"

"This is my nephew Tyler. He's got a small part in the film."

"I'd say your gene pool is pretty blessed."

"Thank you."

"Where's your beautiful co-star?"

He feigned looking at his watch. "I'm sure she'll be here any minute."

"Well speaking of...here comes the queen herself, Penelope Winters."

Griffin felt his stomach lurch, and he turned to see Penelope being assisted out of the limo, by no other than Noah Davis. It hurt. He'd be lying if he said otherwise.

His eyes widened. Was that a baby bump? She looked pregnant! It was all belly, so he knew she hadn't just put on weight. He knew nothing about having babies, so he was no judge of how far along she was. She wasn't about to pop but she wasn't in the early stages either. *Shit!*

Even from a short distance, Penelope still took his breath away. Her metallic green sequined gown was sleeveless and high waisted to accommodate the swell of her belly. It had a low vee neck, revealing the swell of her breasts, now even more lush from her pregnancy. Her hair was swept up in a Chignon with tendrils already escaping, framing her delicate beauty. The gown was split all the way up the side, providing tantalizing glimpses of her shapely thigh.

Tyler's jaw dropped. Griffin narrowed his eyes and gave a slight shake of his head in warning. Dolly and Ben got out right behind Penny and Noah. Dolly saw them and waved, he waved back, then turned to the woman interviewing him when she asked another question.

"Oh my! This is quite the reveal! I'm sure it's old news to you that your co-star is pregnant. Is that why she's been avoiding the press?"

"No comment." He turned and walked toward the entrance, with the fans clamoring. "Come on Ty."

"Griffin, Griffin, over here."

"We love you Griffin!"

"Griffin will you sign my magazine?"

He smiled and saluted the crowd but kept walking. No more autographs, no more interviews. He wanted to get inside and away from public scrutiny as quickly as he could. He was in shock. Was it possible that it was his baby? He needed a stiff drink.

The three of them, along with Stewart, would be introducing the film. Maybe he'd get a chance to pull Penelope aside before then. There was an after party being held later; he could always corner her there if she'd talk to him.

45

Penelope thought she'd mentally prepared herself for seeing Griffin again, but she was mistaken. *Damn him.* She had seen his shocked expression the exact instant he'd realized she was pregnant. Her face had heated with embarrassment and guilt, but even more than that, she had felt a familiar heat and desire.

As she watched Griffin and Tyler disappear into the theatre she had wanted to run after him and beg his forgiveness. She felt horrible. It wasn't too late to make it right. Seeing him again had cleared the fog. It was his baby too. She had no right to keep it from him. He was a decent man. It would be different if he were an abusive awful person, but he wasn't. She loved him. That too, was suddenly crystal clear.

Noah kept his arm possessively around her waist. He had promised to shield her from as much chaos as he could. He was her linebacker for the evening.

"Penelope, when are you due?"

"Penelope is it a boy or a girl?"

"Penelope who is the father?"

The same woman who'd been interviewing Griffin from *Entertainment Tonight*, blocked Penelope's path and planted herself right in front of her. She thrust the microphone under Penelope's nose while her camera operator vied for a good angle.

"I see we have some baby news?"

"Yes."

"When are you due?"

"I have another three months to go," Penelope said, forcing a smile.

The host looked at Noah and said, "You must be thrilled."

Noah smiled, "I'm very happy for Penny. She's going to be an incredible mom."

"And you? Are you excited to be a father?'

Noah ignored the fishing expedition and looked down at Penelope and said, "Shall we go? We're going to be late if we don't get in there."

The TV host laughed, "Oh I'm quite sure they won't start without their two superstars."

Noah smiled and pushed his way around her, pulling Penelope along. It was madness. The fans were in a frenzy as the biggest names in Hollywood kept coming. They hurried away, avoiding any more interviews.

When they entered, she looked around and spotted Griffin standing in front of a white silk backdrop getting photographed. He was one gorgeous man. He would have his pick of films after this. Tyler as well.

She had no doubt that would appeal to Ty, but what about Griffin?

Stewart found her and corralled her over to a photo op booth to get some photographs taken. Stewart wanted her to get some with Noah and with Griffin, then all three together.

Griffin was now leaning against the wall next to the theatre entrance, talking to Tyler and another famous director. He straightened when he saw her looking at him. He'd been waiting for her. Her throat tightened.

His expression tugged at her heart. He looked wounded. She'd done that to him. She felt like crying. Any lingering doubts she'd had about telling him seemed to melt away. By the time he reached her his face was set in an unreadable expression. If she had not seen the pain moments before, she would have sworn he was immune.

Her voice wavered as she greeted him, "Hello, Griffin."

"Penelope, long time no see. Did you miss me?"

Dolly ran up and hugged him. "I missed you."

"Glad someone did," Griffin said, his smile not reaching his eyes. He turned back to Penelope and their eyes locked.

"Got a minute?"

"Stew wants us to have some photos taken together before we go into the theatre."

"We can take a minute after that."

"Okay."

There were at least twenty photographers snapping away as they posed and changed positions for a variety of shots. There were lots of stars and directors here as well as producers and crew.

"Let's cut out for a minute. Ty, I'll be right back. Wait for me here."

Tyler glanced at him briefly already in a discussion with an up-and-coming young actor.

Penelope's legs were so shaky she wasn't sure they'd hold her up.

Griffin crooked his elbow, and she slipped her hand through his arm. Even though there were hundreds of people milling around it could have just been the two of them. He pulled her into an alcove and turned his back to the room, effectively blocking her from anyone's view.

He put his hands against the wall on either side of her, then leaned in close, "Got something you'd like to share with me?"

Clearing her throat, she said, "Griffin...I...I tried calling you when I first found out I was pregnant..."

"So, it is mine?"

She looked up into his vivid blue eyes and nodded.

He blew out a long breath. "Wow."

"Yeah," she said, her lips turning up at the corners. She had tried to imagine this moment a thousand times, what she would say, what he'd say, now here it was, and she was speechless.

"Do we know what we're having yet?"

Her heart leapt in her chest as she absorbed that statement. "A girl."

He closed his eyes tightly. "A girl...I like that."

Penelope reached up and stroked his hair away

from his brow and he frowned. "Pen, when were you going to tell me? Or maybe you weren't."

"Griffin, I was scared to tell you. During our last fight, you told me you didn't want anyone to need you... I didn't want you pinned down...can you understand?"

"I'm not sure. I know I should have called you back, but I guess I was trying too hard to forget. You could have tried a little harder to reach me." There was so much emotion behind those simple words.

Memories came flooding back. Their lovemaking, their adventures, the intimacy, the friendship. Why had she been such a coward. What had she thought she was protecting?

"I'm sorry," she said.

"I know," he said gruffly. "I'm sorry too."

Dolly approached and said, "Hurry you guys. They're ready for you to introduce the film."

Griffin nodded, without breaking eye contact with Penelope, he said, "We'll be right there, Dolly. Thanks."

"I'll let them know you're on your way."

"Penny, will you ride with me to the after party? We can drive around for a while and talk. Ty can grab a ride with Stew."

"Yes, I'll come with you."

"What will Noah have to say about it?"

"Noah? Oh. Griffin we're not together, not like you're thinking. He's seeing someone else. We rode together and Noah volunteered to be my bodyguard for the night. This is my first public appearance since I started showing. I was able to hide it up until about a month ago."

"Are you sure about Noah? Look I remember the

day he got shot like it was yesterday. I've played it over and over in my head. That is one of the main reasons I didn't call you back. It was so obvious that you loved the guy. You didn't even spare me a glance."

"You weren't the one shot and bleeding out. God Griff. Do you have any idea how much I blamed myself? It was my fault. All of it. If you or Noah had died because of me, well I'd never have recovered."

"Stew is motioning to us; we'd better go in. You look amazing by the way," he said. She held on to his arm as they went to meet Stewart.

46

*A*fter navigating through traffic, Griffin asked his driver to keep going. He liked seeing the city lights at night. "Take us around the city before you drop us off at the party," he instructed.

"Will do sir."

He took off his tie and suit jacket and threw them across the seat facing them. He unbuttoned his top buttons. "That's much better."

"What do you think of our film?" she asked, curious for his response.

"I'm blown away. I can't believe I was a part of it all. Amazing special effects. The music is as good as your *Fifty Shades* soundtrack." He smiled as he remembered that day.

"It is going to be a big hit. Griffin, your life is about to change dramatically."

"I kind of had a taste of that when I walked the red carpet."

"What are you going to do? Is it a one and done or are you hooked?"

"One and done," he said, without hesitation.

They both sunk back into the luxe seats, exhausted from the intensity of the premier. "You have a place here?" he asked.

"Malibu."

"Is that where you stay most of the time?"

"It depends. As much as I'm able to, I like to be at my Montana ranch. But I love Malibu for different reasons. Are you into horses?"

"I rode some as a kid. Why?"

"Just wondering. I have horses at my ranch. I want to teach our little girl how to ride."

Griffin smiled.

"What's this party going to be like?" he asked.

"I may be the wrong one to ask. In my opinion, if you've been to one, you've been to them all."

"Spoken like a truly jaded movie star," he said.

"I heard you were on Jimmy's show last night."

"Yeah, didn't you watch?"

"No, I wanted to, but I couldn't. It would have been too much."

Head resting against the seat, he turned to look at her, "You mean that?"

"Yeah, after seeing you with the famous French model, I've been avoiding social media, entertainment shows, talk shows..."

He grasped her hand and brought it to his lips, "I'm sorry I didn't call you back. I was a fool. But I still don't get why you didn't try harder."

"There seems to be more than one foolish person

sitting here. I was planning on telling you soon, I swear. I promised Dolly I'd tell you in the second trimester. I lost my first baby at six months. I'll feel like I can breathe again after I get past that marker."

"When is that?"

"In a week, I'll have carried her longer than my first pregnancy."

"What does the doctor say?"

"Not to worry. Baby's healthy, I'm healthy, so far so good."

"What comes next...with you and me?"

"You tell me. You can be in the baby's life as much or as little as you want. I want her to know her daddy, so for us, the more the better." Penelope suddenly giggled. "She's got the hiccups, here feel." She took his hand and placed it on her belly.

He felt a rhythmic twitching and smiled, suddenly choking up. He felt a different sensation, almost like a bump.

His voice was thick with emotion when he said, "What was that?"

"That was her kicking. She does a lot of that. You know, she can hear us right now? At this stage she's beginning to focus on sounds on the outside."

He placed his lips against her belly and said, "Hello baby. I'm finally here." He felt Penelope's hands entangle in his hair and heard her sniffle. He looked up and saw her eyes flooded with tears. His throat tightened, "Pen."

"I'm okay. I don't know what all of this means but I'm so happy right now I could burst." She swiped the back of her hand across her eyes.

He sat up and slung his arm across her shoulders and leaned down and brushed his lips lightly across hers. She sighed and parted her lips, tempting him to deepen the kiss as she wrapped her hands behind his head and held him to her. He responded by drawing her bottom lip into his mouth and sucking. Her breath hitched.

"It feels so good to be with you again, I've missed you," he said.

"Oh Griff. We'll figure it all out. I'm relieved to have it out in the open now."

"I suppose we should head over to the party. They'll be wondering what happened to us."

"Yes."

Griffin knocked on the partition and the window slid open. "Let's head on over to the soirée."

"Yes sir."

"Thanks."

They were both quiet the rest of the way. Griffin was lost in his thoughts about possibilities and his future. He thought about the baby kicking his hand and felt a connection already. He wanted to teach her to play piano and teach her French. Read her bedtime stories and kiss her skinned knees. He hoped that whatever arrangements they came up with that he would have plenty of time with her. He wanted to be a positive influence in his daughter's life.

47

"Penelope! Man, this party is blowing me away! I saw Dakota Johnson and Robert Pattinson!"

"It's certainly the place to be," Penelope said, smiling affectionately at Tyler's enthusiasm. The energy of the room was electric. The party venue was elaborate, even by Hollywood standards. The premier had accomplished what it needed to, creating a buzz and excitement around the film.

"I hope it's okay for me to ask, but does Griffin have a horse in this race?" He said nodding at her belly.

She laughed out loud. "That's one way to put it. But the answer is yes."

"I guess I'm going to have another little cousin."

"Yes, a little girl."

"No shit?" he grinned.

"No shit."

"Does this mean Uncle Griffin's going to hang up his superhero cape?"

"I hope not!" she said.

"He's a wild-ass. He can't continue to risk his life when he's a dad. You two are OTP."

"OTP?"

"Google it," he said, grinning.

"You can't do that to me, what does it mean?"

"One true pairing."

"Tyler, I need a dictionary to keep up with you. Where do you come up with them?"

"That's what Faye says. Anyway, congratulations Penelope."

"By the way, I've had several directors asking me about you. Spielberg thought you had a certain star quality. He said you lit up the screen...even with only those few lines."

Ty's eyes widened, "You're kidding me, right? Spielberg?"

"I swear. You have a real shot at it."

"That's amazing," he said.

Penelope saw Constance, her manager, striding purposely toward her.

"Where have you been?"

"I took a slight detour on my way over here."

"Roz Dunlap is looking for you."

"Roz? She is?"

"Yes. She has a script you'll definitely be interested in. Who do we have here?" she asked looking Tyler up and down like he was an acquisition.

Griffin walked up just then holding a glass of amber

liquid. "Hey, sorry got caught up in a discussion with Stew."

"I think the father of the baby should have to abstain for nine months too," Tyler said. "It's hardly fair."

Griffin snorted, "Who's side are you on?"

"The one with the most connections in the biz," he said. Griffin and Penelope burst out laughing.

"That would be Constance here. Tyler, Griffin, meet Constance Monroe, my manager. Constance, this is Griffin and his nephew, Ty."

"You both were simply fabulous in the film!" Constance said.

A waiter in formal attire approached, carrying a tray of hors d'oeuvres. Tyler took a napkin from the tray and loaded it with a variety of appetizers.

"Thanks. Don't go too far," he said to the waiter, grinning as he bit into a shrimp puff.

Penelope rolled her eyes at Constance. "Can't take him anywhere."

"He can do anything he wants. I'd love to represent you Tyler. Pass your information on to Penny and I'll be in touch." She patted Tyler on the back.

"That's awesome. Thank you, ma'am."

"Puleeze! Don't call me ma'am. Makes me feel ancient."

"Sorry, Ms. Monroe."

"Just make it Constance. I'm going to make the rounds, darling," Constance said. "Griffin if you need me to represent you, just call."

"Thanks, but this is it for me."

"I'll be around if you change your mind."

"I can't believe this is happening," Tyler said, his eyes sparkling as he scanned the room. "I'm going to go mingle."

"Have fun," Penelope said, watching him saunter confidently away. "He has no fear."

Griffin chuckled, "Yeah, that's what I'm afraid of."

"He's a lot like you."

"Weird isn't it? Genetics are a funny thing. Nature verses nurture. He grew up with nothing. No father, no family that he knew of but his mom. We didn't even know he existed until last year. Now I can't remember what it was like without him. I love the kid."

"He obviously worships you. Don't get rid of your cape."

"What?"

"He mentioned you'd have to hang up your super-hero cape now that you're an expectant father."

"Aww, really?"

"Yes, he's definitely got you on a pedestal. I don't want you to change for this baby. I want her to get bit by the adventurer bug, just like her dad."

He slung his arm across her shoulders as he sipped his drink. "You really know how to get to a guy."

"Griffin, Penelope, I've got someone who wants to meet you," Stewart said, approaching with Roz Dunlap. With several successful blockbusters under her belt, she was one of the women who had climbed the near-impossible hurdle of directing in a male-dominated industry. She was paving the way. It was slowly changing but there was a long way to go.

"I'm a huge fan!" Penelope said in awe.

"Thank you. I have a script I'm reading right now

that you'd be perfect for. A complete one-eighty from what you've been starring in, but I think it would be a fabulous change of pace."

"I'm intrigued. It would be an honor to work with you. Obviously, I'll be tied up for a few months," she said, holding her belly.

"I see that. We're not even close to casting yet. Just keep it in mind. I'll send over the script."

"Can you give me a hint?"

"It's a biographical film about Nellie Bly."

"The writer?"

"Yes! You know of her. Not many do. Her christened name was Elizabeth Cochrane. She was brilliant. Lived a fascinating life."

"I'm extremely interested in getting my hands on that script. I'll look forward to hearing from you." Penelope's cheeks felt warm and her body tingled with excitement. What an opportunity...not only to work with a female director of her caliber, but to spread her wings and take on a different genre of film.

Roz held out her hand. "You were fabulous in this film. I'm so impressed with your nuanced performance. Stewart here is no dummy."

"Thank you for thinking of me. My manager Constance Monroe is floating around here somewhere. She'll be in touch."

Griffin smiled down at her. "This is exciting."

She whispered, "Pinch me."

Up until now, she'd mostly been cast in rom coms and romantic suspense, and she was grateful for the work, but this, well...it could open up possibilities for her. This type of film would rely less on her youth and beauty and more on her acting skills.

"It was so nice to finally meet you and I'll look forward to collaborating in the future," Roz said. Stew winked at Penelope before turning and walking away arm in arm with Roz.

Griffin gazed down, his eyes scorching her skin. Penelope felt a sudden tingling between her legs.

"You deserve this Penelope." He waved his arm wide, "All of this. I love seeing the light in your eyes."

"Thank you, Griff. But honestly, it all amounts to nothing if you've got no one to share it with. I'm glad you're here."

He traced her lips with his thumb, "I'm here as long as you'll have me."

She smiled up at him, "Good to know."

The End for Now...

A Note From The Author

I hope you loved Penelope and Griffin's story as much as I enjoyed writing it! If you want to catch up with how they are doing, check out the Christmas novella coming in December. Griffin and Penelope are hosting the Bennett family Christmas at their Montana ranch. Kyle and Ella along with Faye, Jesse and Ty will be there as well as James and Giselle. Oh, and lest I forget—Finn and the twins! Brothers, sisters, kids, babies, parents, dogs and friends...all come together to make this a holiday they're not likely to ever forget!

Here's the universal link to Book Four, *A Billionaire's Christmas*:

mybook.to/billinairexmas

Here's the universal link to Book One of this series, *Seduced by a Billionaire*:

mybook.to/SeducedbyaBillionaire

Here's the Link to Book Two, *Secret Billionaire*:

mybook.to/SecretBillionaire

If you haven't read *The Heartland Series* here's the link to the complete box set:

mybook.to/BoxSetHeartlandSeries

Please join my **Facebook readers group**, for give aways, teasers and pre-release excerpts:

https://www.facebook.com/groups/179183050062278/

BOOKS BY JILL DOWNEY

The Heartland Series:

More Than A Boss

More Than A Memory

More Than A Fling

The Carolina Series:

Seduced by a Billionaire

Secret Billionaire

Playboy Billionaire

Happy Reading!

Printed in Great Britain
by Amazon